In 1982, Iris Nolan won the Bank of New Zealand Historical Novel Competition for *Bells of Caroline*.

BELLS FOR CAROLINE

In the 1800s, Caroline — proud, strong-willed and independent — sets off from Norway for a new life in New Zealand. She was in love with William, an Englishman, but his father wouldn't accept her. However, William follows Caroline to her new country and the young couple marry. Life is very hard for the pioneers and they suffer years of hardship and deprivation as they bring up their four sons and three daughters. Eventually, at the request of William's ageing father, they go to England to run his public house and orchards in Kent, but there tragedy strikes . . .

IRIS NOLAN

◆

BELLS FOR CAROLINE

Complete and Unabridged

ULVERSCROFT
Leicester

First published in New Zealand in 1986

First Large Print Edition
published 1999

While events are historical fact, all characters are
fictional except for one much loved relative who
passed away nearly a decade ago.

British Library CIP Data

Nolan, Iris
    Bells for Caroline.—Large print ed.—
Ulverscroft large print series: general fiction
1. Large type books
I. Title
823.9′14 [F]

ISBN 0–7089–4162–1

Published by
F. A. Thorpe (Publishing) Ltd.
Anstey, Leicestershire
Set by Words & Graphics Ltd.
Anstey, Leicestershire
Printed and bound in Great Britain by
T. J. International Ltd., Padstow, Cornwall

This book is printed on acid-free paper

To our daughter Lynne for her introduction to the competition and her encouragement, and to my husband Maurie and our friends for their patience during the seven weeks when Caroline took charge of our Diamond Harbour home.

Grateful thanks are expressed to the Bank of New Zealand for its sponsorship of the first award for a New Zealand Historical Novel, and to the N.Z. Women Writers' Society whose fiftieth jubilee occasioned this sponsorship.

Thanks are also due to the Norwegian Consulate and the Alexander Turnbull Library for their prompt replies to urgent questions as the background of the novel took shape.

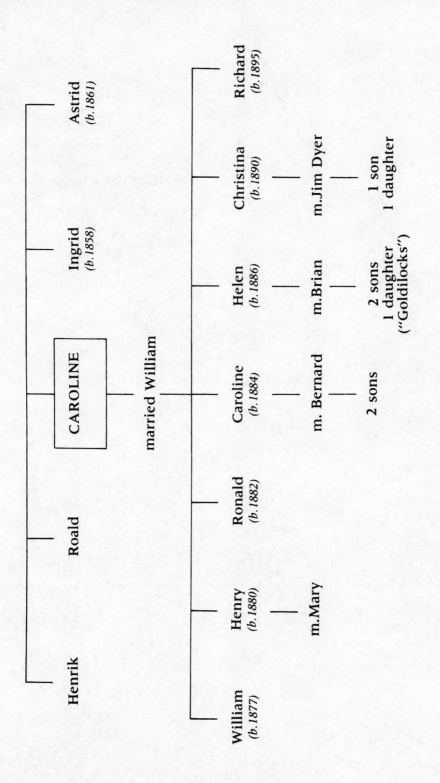

1

A warm February morning. Out of bed, washed in cold water, dressed not long after daybreak, when the birds, even on the outskirts of the city, were whistling clearly enough for the dulled hearing of nearly eighty years. Regardless of this new-fangled daylight saving that had nothing to do with God's time, Caroline had made her bed (airing it first), dusted, swept. No vacuum cleaner for her — a vigorous shake of the rugs every morning in the yard, so vigorous that the fringes had disintegrated long ago; and a straw broom for that larger carpet square which her son had persisted in buying for her.

In mid-winter mornings and evenings, a candle provided enough light. If she had been allowed to keep the old kerosene lamp that her family described as dangerous, the electric light switches would never have been touched. The gas stove was showroom clean. Only when Richard came home was one burner lighted; as for the oven, never! There was the Orion range which she had got to know so well in her early days in New

Zealand, with always enough kindling and split wood to boil her kettle in summer, make her porridge in winter, and keep her warm at the same time. At least the gas had a flame, so you could see it was alight. But electric ranges, jugs, irons, heaters — they were ridiculous, no sign of heat, or only a red glow like the embers of a dying fire.

Before the last of the cars had gone by, rushing men in collars and ties to those offices in town, she had finished her work. For someone living alone in a tiny cottage near a port used only by the little coastal steamers, how much of a summer's day did that take?

Yet it seemed an hour since the swish of cars on the metal road. The only reason for cars and drivers, Caroline had told her daughter, was just to run an old lady down. To the giggling school children, seeing her waiting for ten minutes until no car was in sight for a half mile in either direction, and then scuttling across a street where there might be no traffic for an hour or more, this was a joke to be told and imitated over and over. But Caroline was convinced that these machines were dangerous, designed expressly for her destruction.

She would travel on a train, reluctantly; but she would find a horse-drawn cab to take her to and from the railway station, if the one family she ever visited in the Wairarapa could not meet her, or she would walk. And it must be the son-in-law who drove, not her daughter. Women could not manage these machines. Caroline refused to believe that her daughter drove very competently over the winding Rimutakas to Wellington, and coped there with rushing traffic and narrow streets.

Once, indeed, she had climbed down from the train to be greeted only by her daughter and grand-daughter.

'Where's Jim?' Caroline asked.

'He's rather busy just now,' her daughter replied. 'He won't be long.'

Grandma walked beside her grand-daughter, while her daughter briskly opened doors for her passengers and the one battered suitcase. Before Caroline could think of getting out of the car, for she was a determined old lady, and would have walked the two miles rather than be driven by a woman, her daughter had put the car into gear and taken off. Just as determined as Caroline, she would see to it that her mother was brought home by car, even though Jim was forty miles away. Squally weather had held up the shearing, and he must have the sheep back in their paddocks before the kowhai blossom fell, and the usual floods came.

Once, earlier, when Caroline had allowed herself to be driven the two hundred mile journey from Wellington, a slip had blocked part of the road, carrying away the outer edge, unseen in the darkness and limited range of those weak Oakland and Chandler headlamps. Fortunately, the drop was slight and Jim alert to make the best of things. Even so, he had a long walk to the nearest homestead, where the owner cranked up an old truck to drag the car back onto the road.

But to Caroline it was just one of those events that happened with cars when she was around. She still had the utmost faith in Jim's driving; but she would travel with no-one else. Why had men bothered with four wheels and a motor, when their two legs — or the four legs of a horse — would have taken them anywhere they wished to go?

Schoolboys arrived with the swish of bicycles — noisy, those voices, no more the sound of birds. She had heard a lark this morning, but not the tui that sometimes dipped its beak into the flax flower across the road — not the eery flap of the wood pigeon's flight in the tops of tawa and totara in the Forty Mile Bush.

Hot, breathless, still.

The seas rolled sullenly onto that beach of grey pebbles that stretched from the river mouths of the Tutaekuri and Ngaruroro to the Bluff above the unsheltered piers. The seas — the still waters of the Port, Port Ahuriri — but her boys had called it the Iron Pot. Caroline had never asked them why.

Those still waters and that slight breeze had sent two of them tacking across the Inner Harbour to the Watchman, and brought only one back, twenty years ago.

William, the boys' father, had told her of the watchman that used to call the time in those London streets: 'Past ten o'clock and all's well!' She had heard the drawn-out emphasis on the word 'all' herself, lying in bed on the second floor of the Duchess of Edinburgh.

Now from the High School across the road the school bell rang out, and the yard, as she called it, was full of shouts as the young jostled for places on this first school day of 1931.

Caroline shuffled, bent now, dim-sighted, slightly deaf — only slightly, for she could hear a whisper in the next room if she wished — into the shabby basket-chair beside the coal range. Too warm, still, that range, though it had been kindled only to boil a kettle; but there was the favourite corner, in

5

the kitchen, and the favourite chair.

School bells . . . funeral peals and black crepe for Queen Victoria — and for William, too, that same year, after the bonfires and rejoicing at the relief of Ladysmith, Kimberley, Mafeking — stranger words than the English Caroline was still trying to understand.

Church bells . . . the Diamond Jubilee, with that other little old lady sitting so upright, almost unsmiling, on her way to the Abbey. The grimy streets of London — no trees, no birds. Her father-in-law taking them down to Kent to his apple orchard and cider press; English trees in that smiling Kentish countryside.

Rocking slowly in her chair — swaying? — she thought of the trees of the Forty Mile Bush. The great teams of Clydesdales snigged the huge rimu and totara logs down the bush tracks to the sawmill. The pine-trees of her Norway, and her old wooden home not much different in size from this weatherboard cottage. How different the snowfall in winter, the brilliant contrast of summer — twenty, forty, fifty, seventy years back.

Sleigh bells, and laughter in the snow . . .

2

Little sisters long forgotten, sliding down the crisp snow, the great gloomy pines above. Young Roald putting the sledge together from slats salvaged from fish boxes (and hidden from mother, who wanted kindling while father was away at sea). Those short days in winter, not so far from the great fiord, the rare trip to see the shops of Christiania, especially at Yuletide, to admire the glittering decorations in wealthier windows.

School for a few years, until the day when a fishing boat did not return from that cold Arctic Circle with its twenty-four hours of daylight or of darkness.

Born in 1853, Caroline recalled little of those early years. Her father owned one of the larger fishing vessels; all Norwegians were fishermen or foresters, it seemed — at least all the friends and the cousins, and Uncle Carl, and brother Henrik, too. So much older than Caroline, Henrik was away in the north most of the year in the forests and mills. If he could find time and money to travel before the depth of winter, when great pines split of their own accord and the forests were too dangerous to work, he would breeze into the cottage, greeting his favourite little sister with a great bear-hug. Then sleighing would be extra fun; so much further afield they could go if he was there to look after her. Mother could stay home with the toddling baby. Caroline would have her brother all to herself.

Always warm and comfortable, that life stretched uneventfully ahead. Father was at home more often, now he had shares in a second fishing boat. There was less need for him to go far to the north into the cold fiords under the Northern Lights. Often he told Caroline of the flaming brilliance and eery movement of the aurora borealis, little dreaming that she would one day glimpse in the other hemisphere the Southern Lights.

How old was she? Ten? Twelve? She did not remember the year her father did not come home — the days that turned into weeks, the weeks into months. The neighbours stopped talking when the little girls were in earshot. Firewood would overnight be stacked by the door, a friend would bring in some biscuits. Old family friends who lived a different, more glittering life would find their daughters had suddenly grown out of their frocks. Caroline and Ingrid, now about five, she thought, looking back, would find near new warm clothes in the cupboard. But Mother did not laugh now, ever.

Caroline could not remember, either, the year in which she knew that her father would never come home. Did someone tell her about the bleached wreck of a fishing boat found a season later in the rocky inlet of a northern fiord?

Neighbours helped, and there was a little money put in the old tea-caddy that had come from far across the water; but neither could keep the family of five forever. Henrik, tall and heavily built even at fourteen, had his work in the forests. He had no wish to follow in his father's footsteps. But Roald, at thirteen, was looking far beyond those cold northern waters to a country called America. His friend's uncle was there — somewhere. Summer days and winter days were not much different in length, he had written to the schoolmaster, a friend of his; and there was snow, but not much. The leaves turned red in the 'fall' of the year — the schoolmaster explained what that season was to the interested boys — and fluttered down, leaving the trees bare. He was not going further north to that other country, Canada, for he had seen enough of the great tall timber that, he had heard, was very like the pines of Norway. (To Henrik, learning of this from Roald, Canada was a magnet.)

With fierce independence and pride, traits that Caroline herself was to display in the future, the widow looked for ways to support her young family. Henrik must not be required to remain a bachelor so as to send the greater part of his small wage south; his mother knew, also, of his wish to cross the oceans to another forested country.

Roald would find work on one of the fishing boats — that was best.

But the little girls — the baby of two, and Ingrid and Caroline, what of them? Caroline must mind her two younger sisters, while mother turned her hand to whatever work she could find. Her own snow-white wash soon found her laundering for some of the wealthier homes in Christiania. Yet there was time for the sledge in winter — and the seashore not far away in summer.

Then a visitor came from the north, from Trondheim, their own uncle Carl who, like so many of his countrymen, was tired of the poverty and narrowness he saw about him; tired of a king who lived in Sweden, tired of being a second-rate citizen in the eyes of those other Scandinavian nations.

Perhaps Uncle Carl realised that he was

lagging behind. For thirty years or more a great stream of his compatriots had left Norway for good, mainly for America, where there was a chance for all to grow rich, and to be equal. Uncle Carl would talk for hours about democracy (which, thought his sister-in-law, would not feed and clothe the little family).

Caroline, too, as soon as her sisters were old enough to be left alone, must find some way of earning: a kitchen-maid, or a parlourmaid, setting the places around a massive dining table where once she would have been invited as a guest. Or a nursemaid, perhaps, for the father's death had come too early for her to reach any standard of learning that would fit her for the position of governess — or even companion. As for marriage — to another fisherman whose boat might be wrecked? Not for some years, at least.

So for a year or two — or more — the older Caroline could not count the seasons, seventy years later — still the sparkle of snow in winter and the sleigh bells jingling, still the summer sun.

3

Suddenly, changes.

Uncle Carl had a free ticket on the next passenger vessel. Perhaps he would meet Henrik, the young Caroline thought. It couldn't be a very big place, America. After all, Uncle Carl had come all the way from Trondheim to visit them in Christiania. (It was not until many years later, in a very distant land, that Caroline sometimes found a moment to wonder if Uncle Carl had really come to see his brother's family for a second time. Or had that ship on which he had been offered a free passage been sailing only from the port of Christiania for Norwegian passengers?)

From his fishing trips Roald came home occasionally. He sent them most of his poor wages, for, as little more than an apprentice in other trades, he worked for his keep.

In the meantime Ivor, a family friend, lost his wife, and was left with a young family. He had been a successful fisherman in his twenties, along with Caroline's father; he was, in his forties, a very successful businessman. He owned not one fishing boat, but three. His home showed his success: he was kind, he needed a mother for his little family. Caroline thought it had been very sensible of mother to remarry — no more laundry work; in contrast, some other widow would help mother, and there would be a maid.

Now Roald could keep his wages, could afford to come to see them more frequently. But he was growing restless; one or two letters from Henrik wrote of an easier, more adventurous life across the Atlantic: great lakes were mentioned, with kinder shores than many of the fiords. From the time Roald had gone to sea, he had looked for further oceans.

Pretty clothes, new boots, a real sledge for the little sisters and the other family. The battered one, built so long ago, it seemed, by Roald, had fallen to pieces. Caroline, at fifteen, was faced with a new life — what could she do with her time? She who had cared for her sisters, and cooked and cleaned to her mother's satisfaction — and mother's satisfaction was not easily achieved. She could read, and write, and sew, and manage a house. But none of that was needed now.

She had a share of her brothers' adventurous spirit, unusual in a young woman of that time; but there were fewer passages on steamers now. Caroline had some idea that she could easily find Uncle Carl or Henrik, if she could only cross the ocean. (Those ideas she kept to herself; neither her mother nor her new and very kindly stepfather would approve, let alone encourage her in those wild dreams.) Caroline had grown tired of poverty and minding the children, but she very quickly grew equally bored with the social occasions that began to come her way. Her stepfather had something to do with those invitations; and so did Uncle Carl, though she never realised that he had tried to keep the widow and her family in touch with wealthier friends. Proudly poor, mother had refused all invitations for her children; when she married again, the situation was different. Now, at last, Caroline's mother could see her in crystal white, dancing a stately minuet.

On one occasion a man who spent his life walking upside down was pointed out to Caroline and her partner: Francis Dillon Bell was visiting Norway, Sweden and Denmark, to select suitable immigrants for a little country far beyond Caroline's grasp of the distance to America. The only matter of importance to Caroline was that this man walked as any other Norwegian did — yet, when he was on the bottom of the world, his head must surely be the other way up;

14

unless the natives of that country, a kind of Holland, she thought, having a most muddled idea of history and centuries, got about on their heads. Two years later, the *Hovding* sailed for New Zealand, taking immigrants to Mauriceville and Manawatu.

Then her stepfather introduced her to a Norwegian friend who had lived for several years in New Zealand. Mr Friberg, finding the young woman interested in his task, told her about the forest blocks which Mr Weber was surveying, forty acres for each man who went out there. Forty acres? Unbelieveable!

Meanwhile Caroline grew more and more bored with the parochial and strait-laced society in which she was now expected to move. A letter from Henrik, or Uncle Carl, or from Roald — any of these would set off another mood of frustration. Her mother was contented, Ingrid and Astrid growing into pretty girls, happy to be in a situation where they could look forward to social functions.

Only amongst the foreign visitors did Caroline find some interest. An Englishman on the 'grand tour', William seemed to return her friendly concern. He was a welcome visitor to their home, apparently comfortably placed. For he stayed in Christiania much longer than any other foreigner; he even went to the length of doing a little genteel tuition — nothing so vulgar as working, he thought.

Had she only known, Caroline's mother would have been happier if he really had worked, instead of talking of his orchard in Kent, and the 'hotel' in London, and of the amount of the remittance sent over faithfully by his father. He had a hobby, he said: he was very good at cabinet-making, a true craftsman. But asked by Ivor if he would like to make some fine furniture for a special friend, William reacted angrily. He had no need to work like a common carpenter. Ivor did not tell him that the 'special friend' happened to be his adopted daughter, Caroline.

However, Caroline's mother, perhaps a little beguiled by the young man's perfect manners and apparent breeding, thought him a good match for her eldest daughter. Caroline was clearly dissatisfied with life; and there were, after all, five young women in the house, for Ivor had two daughters about the same age as Astrid and Ingrid. Marrying all of these girls off was going to be a problem — their only sound future was a really good marriage.

Besides, even if Caroline went to England with her new husband, the distance was not unthinkable. William's attitude certainly suggested that it was not very far away.

4

Soon the *Hovding* would sail again, and the *Ballarat*, the woolclipper famous for her sixty-nine day passage from Melbourne to Aberdeen nearly twenty years earlier. Nearly five hundred Norwegians would set out to make a corner of Norway somewhere underneath the world.

Among the 74 married couples, with their combined total of 280 children, were some close friends. Caroline's mother found it difficult to be enthusiastic and encouraging with them, while discouraging her daughter.

That little country across two or three great oceans seemed to attract Caroline's interest — that would never do! There were savages there, and earthquakes. The quietly anxious mother wished Ivor would not invite Mr Friberg so often to the house; he spoke in such glowing terms of forests and fields, free passages and land.

Thank goodness for William. If only his father would write with his approval, a date could be set for the wedding. Caroline would forget all about emigrant ships, then. She really could be quite tiresome on the

17

subject. On the other hand, Ivor would not agree to Caroline's marriage to a foreigner (especially one so dependent on his family for money) unless William's father also agreed to the plan.

When the letter did arrive, there was no question of a wedding.

William's father wrote that life had been far too easy for him. No Scandinavian, lady or not, was going to be mistress of those faithful retainers of his. Prejudiced in his outlook, father suggested that if William wanted to marry a foreigner, more welcome nationalities would be Danish or Swedish. At least, he continued, those countries had some culture. And to consider marrying the daughter of a former fisherman (thinking no doubt of Billingsgate market) and step-daughter of a present fisherman! The fact that Ivor owned a fleet of fishing vessels, and was now more of a businessman than an active deckhand on a trawler, was disregarded entirely. Until William proved that he could keep a wife, there would be no welcome for either of them in Kent; and possibly, if he still persisted in this nonsense about a Norwegian girl called Caroline, there would be little welcome even if he did set about earning his living.

Caroline's mother was tearful, Ivor was

not surprised, Caroline disappointed, but not broken-hearted. She recalled the years after her father's death: she was not anxious to take in laundry like her mother, especially if it was a matter of earning a living for a healthy husband. Norwegian women worked hard, but their husbands worked hard, too. However, William would soon make good, once he realised the position. If she did not love him very deeply, she had great faith in him.

However, work suitable for a foreigner whose knowledge of the language was very limited, and who considered detailed study of it unnecessary, was hard to find. William had acquired a smattering of Latin at his small school; he could recognise some of the Greek characters; a little French of the 'Stratford-atte-Bow' style, a grunt or two in German, the tourist's guide to essential Italian. For the rest, like many of his compatriots of that century and this, he believed that if one talked loudly enough one would be understood. Not enough Norwegians wanted to be taught in William's genteel way to speak English, not even enough to give William a livelihood once that remittance no longer came his way. And certainly there were not enough fees to keep a wife.

Little hard work was required of the

owner of that small estate in Kent. The orchard and its cider, of better than average quality, had kept a younger son in comfort over several generations. Cousins on the Broads might succeed to a title and larger estate, but the latter did not provide the income of this merchant with the apples. Father did not work in the orchards or at the cider-presses; nor would he have considered managing the London public-house which also had added to the family fortune. His son's education should reflect his position.

So William had been sent to less well-known private schools; no scholar, he was useful with his hands — when he felt like it. No tutor was able to interest him in anything other than carpentry. Cider barrels intrigued him; given any encouragement, he might have become a cooper. His father's horrified reaction to William's leaning towards a trade was greeted in an angry moment with the retort that 'Jesus was a carpenter'. The uproar over that remark was heard even by the coachman.

The net result had been this 'grand tour' — William could get those ideas out of his system. But the tour was somewhat restricted by wars and uncertainties in Europe. France was to be avoided at any cost, and Germany also. Sweden and Norway had learned to live with their difficulties. Possibly his father thought that meeting the members of the upper class of some European countries would teach William that carpentry was not a creditable calling.

Father, in one way, was sound in his judgment: William could put pieces of timber together, but he was no cabinet-maker. And he lacked incentive.

Ivor's friends were soon to sail; the young girl who was to have looked after their children on the voyage decided to stay in Christiania. Her future husband had found work in the forests of Norway; she could now be married without going to a new country. Would Caroline care to join them instead?

No future wedding had been mentioned, and Ivor saw no reason to encourage his stepdaughter to think about it. If she was unwelcome as a daughter-in-law, there would be no wedding as far as he was concerned. Any opportunity to keep her apart from William would do very well. Ivor's friends would look after her, and though she was minding the children she would not be treated as a poorly trained nanny.

Her mother was too grateful for her own changed circumstances, even if she would ever have thought of taking the opposite view to her husband's, to raise any argument.

So Caroline sailed on the *Hovding*; and William? Always dilatory, even when in love, he let the ship sail without him.

5

The basket-chair creaked as the old lady tried to relax her aching joints. The gnarled hands clenched for a moment, as the school bell emptied shouting boys from the class-rooms.

Bells . . . ship's bells.

That was one of her earliest memories, the strangeness of those bells, so different from the sleigh bells of home, calling the crew to go on watch. The cold waters of the North Sea and the Channel made little impact on a young woman whose family and friends were concerned mainly with fishing and the sea. But the weeks that elapsed before the tropics were reached, the often glassy seas with little movement in the lofty sails, even the warmth, reminded those on the *Hovding* that it was far from home. Caroline's two little charges rejoiced in the freedom and warmth, while their parents made it clear that she was the daughter of a friend, even although the place she had filled was that of a steerage passenger.

As the ship zigzagged down the South Atlantic, the more familiar cold and rain greeted them, each day wetter and colder than the last. No longer could the children run off their high spirits, even though the ship was almost becalmed. Where there had been plenty of good provisions at the start of the voyage, even in the saloon there were now some complaints. The pork was as salt as brine and as hard as leather, said one burly passenger who had not been unused to short commons. Water was limited to half a gallon per day for each adult; with the rain pelting onto the deck, that was hard to understand. Unfortunately, the cook was one of the most disagreeable people Caroline had ever come across; and the steerage passengers relied on his goodwill, as they had brought their own flour to make their bread, the cook charging them one penny for each loaf he baked. The allowance dwindled to one slice each at each meal. After only two months at sea, the ship was short of biscuits.

But it was the storms that frightened Caroline, the squeaking of the fittings through the strain put upon the ship by the wind and waves, the tin plates flying about the floor, the dreadful lurches, so that the passengers really thought they were going to the bottom. For four wretched days they were beaten about like a carrot and Caroline felt her only desire was to be on the unmoving

24

earth, upside down or not.

The basket-chair swayed slightly even as she recalled the voyage.

By now a small group of children had attached themselves to the two for whom Caroline was caring. One mother had been ill for weeks, but when the doctor ordered beef tea, the cook supplied arrowroot. The angry husband found out that the arrowroot was cheaper than beef tea; he grumbled angrily to Caroline about the way things were done on board ship. Yet he was from the northern forests, where he had lived very frugally with his wife and children.

His great rumbling laugh and expressions of thanks broke out, however, when one of the passengers made a present of a loaf of bread to the young family. The sailors, too, were good to the children, giving them raisins, and sometimes a piece of cake. A baked rice pudding appeared once by magic — probably the cook was very cross about its sudden disappearance from the galley. One day raspberry puffs arrived, one for each of Caroline's little group. Did it ever occur to her that her charges were favoured more than the others? As one of the few unattached young women on board, she attracted more attention than she realised. Her position was quite different from that

25

of others who were caring for the children of saloon passengers; her berth was steerage, but she had the freedom of the saloon deck when she was with the parents. Caroline did not understand how much her stepfather had smoothed the path for her. Even so, when the steward gave her a few white biscuits for the children, a middle-aged couple complained to the Captain.

Many years were to pass before a grand-child with a flair for geography traced the ship's course on the great oceans. Once into the Roaring Forties, it seemed to this young student that the storms that beset the vessel were always encountered about the limits of the ocean's ridges. To grandmother's amazement, he pointed out on the page of the atlas the Mid-Atlantic Ridge, then the Cape and Agulhas Basins. All Caroline could recollect was that the *Hovding* had rounded the Cape just after what had been at that stage of the voyage the worst storm. The vessel was shipping seas continually. One wave knocked the butcher down — he was a heavily built man — and carried him several yards along the deck. Indeed, Caroline had been so vague about the course that she had thought they would round Cape Horn. Mr and Mrs Greiner, explaining to their children, had enlightened her.

The grim business of a burial at sea made more impression, though she rarely spoke of it. Later her own children gathered that the mother of three of the children of her little group had died, the storms proving too much for her.

Now a grandson traced the route across the Indian Ocean, over the Amsterdam St. Paul Plateau — three feet of water in the saloon, the seas broaching over the side every few minutes. And the fire put out, too; no bread baked that day. This storm was worse than the earlier two, but it lasted only three days, not four.

Caroline remembered 'passing Australia' — Tasmania, actually — which of course intrigued her grandchildren. Vividly she always recalled the alarming storms, and the great excitement when a drum of tar caught fire. The vessel was fumigated at times by putting a hot poker in the tar; on this occasion the tar caught alight, defying all efforts to put the fire out. One of the seamen, Hans, picked up the drum, rushed to the deck and threw it overboard. Passengers were well aware that they had been saved that worst of all experiences, a fire at sea.

Then the very worst storm of all, somewhere off the notorious Auckland Islands.

The galley fires were put out twice in the seven days of gales and mountainous seas. One wave larger than the rest carried away one of the lifeboats, breaking the davits as if they were made of wood, smashing another of the boats like a matchbox, and tearing to pieces the sheep-pen. Two of the sheep had their legs broken. The saloon doors, nearly an inch thick, were knocked out; four feet of water swished about in the saloon itself. Thirty feet were ripped off the bulwarks. Below, wet berths, gear floating across the floor with each lurch of the vessel, children crying, wet and cold, no chance of hot food — seven days of it. One man, older than most, said quietly with complete faith, 'It's a good thing to be ready to go home when it seems the will of God for your time to come.'

Five days later land was sighted — Stewart Island. Like all vessels making for North Island ports, the *Hovding* must make a northing to pass the east coast of 'Middle Island'. After the storm not even those who understood the mysteries of latitude and longitude could trace a course, for the board had been swept away during the last day. At last they saw the entrance to Cook Strait, and after a stormy passage up the east coast of the North Island, graveyard of many sailing ships, the *Hovding* anchored off the beach at Napier.

All that mattered to Caroline was land — a strange land, but a shoreline — after nearly four months at sea.

At anchor was the *Ballarat*, the wool-clipper with the famous record. From London, she had arrived seven hours earlier, with English, Scots and Irish immigrants, and 71 Danes to join the thirteen pioneers who had arrived in October, bound for the Forty Mile Bush, stretching from the Ruataniwha plains to the upstream entrance to the Manawatu Gorge.

6

'Ach! the dreadful boat!' Caroline would say in later years to her own grown children, who had wallowed on the Talune — or the Paerata — or the Ruru — for days, after leaving Napier for what was supposed to be a short run to Waikokopu or Wairoa.

With others she clambered down into the rolling long-boat, to end this voyage across the oceans. Fortunately, the surf plunging onto this wide sweep of beach was not very heavy; there were no fears of stranding, as the *Star of the South* had done a few years earlier.

Englishmen on the *Ballarat* saw in the white cliffs of Cape Kidnappers, where the gannets nested then as they do now, a reminder of the Dover landscape. For the Norwegians, however, everything was strange, even the language. Since there had been so many of that hardy race on the *Hovding*, their smattering of English had fallen into disuse. It was no easy task for those agents on shore at the Immigration Barracks, built for the strangers' arrival, to understand and advise the 74 gaunt Norwegians, whose womenfolk and children were dressed, far too warmly, in their best. The children, pleased to be on land, yet fractious in the heat and restive under firm parental control (sometimes reinforced with fearful tales of taniwha and tohunga), were eager to run about and shout — strictly forbidden until all the formalities had been completed.

With the mothers now taking charge of their own families, Caroline stood aside on the fringes, neither fowl nor flesh nor good red herring. She was not one of the few servants, so no towering bushman approached her as a suitable helpmeet in the pioneer struggle ahead. Yet she had no man of her own, thus she was not one of the group waiting for their husband's decisions. After all, she had travelled steerage from Norway, in that vacancy left by the young woman who had first been engaged to care for the Greiner children.

Not that these parents had forgotten her. She was expected to travel and live with them for a year or two; that would give her the opportunity to marry one of her own race, Olav thought, and settle near her friends. With other wives, Maud Greiner imagined there would be dwellings ready for them. Her husband thought there would be good prospects in opening a store, which surely the two women could look after if he needed to fell any trees. He had started his working life as an axeman, but nothing warned him of the tree-felling that would be necessary before he could find space for more than a tent.

A few days in the bare building on the hill — or a few weeks, time telescoped in looking back; quiet walks up Tennyson Street, where the local newspaper office, Dr Spencer's house and St. John's Church were pointed out as being 'old'. To Caroline, after Christiania, those buildings were new and ugly. But they had been there for at least twelve years.

By now most of the Norwegians had some glimmering, either from interpreters or from those of their countrymen who could speak English, of what to expect. Thirteen Danes and six Norwegians had reached this northern stretch of the Seventy Mile Bush less than two years earlier, and what was to become a thriving township barely existed as a village.

The Danes from the *Ballarat* were not more than a day ahead of this larger group of Norwegians. Perhaps original racial disharmony embittered the latter, whose forty acres of unfelled bush — the word 'forest' would have painted a more accurate picture — neighboured the Danish blocks. Yet the name of Dannevirke commemorated the work of Danes (the great wall built across the peninsula of their homeland to keep the Saxons out), and it was always the Danish settlers who were praised for their pioneer struggles. The name of Norsewood, seventeen miles further north, hardly suggests equally demanding and harsh conditions.

The Cobb & Co. coach worked its way over the forty mile route to Abbotsford, later renamed Waipawa, from the name of the river beside which it was settled. At least, when Caroline and her companions travelled, a bridge had replaced the ferry (a punt) across the Ngaruroro river, near Clive, not very far from where the immigrants had first set foot on the beach. But tales of sudden floods and drowning tragedies sent a shiver up Caroline's spine.

A mile or two further on, the coach wove between sandhills that sometimes stopped the regular service, the passengers blinded with dust-storms, and the mails covered with grit.

Not far from Napier, thirteen or so miles, was the thriving settlement of Havelock — no dark forests here, but pastures and streets of a kind. Inland, tracks led across the rivers and swamps to the marshes and low-lying plains of Hicksville, frequently flooded before the Ngaruroro changed its course. The coach route skirted the swamps and shingle beds, through a wilderness of fern, 'a habitation for bittern and coney', one Englishman wrote. Wild pigs abounded on the bracken-covered hills.

The Norwegians had their minds set at rest about cannibals and savages. Relations between Maori and Pakeha had been reasonably good, despite the demands for 'grass money' in the vicinity of Paki Paki a decade or so earlier. The chiefs Karaitiana and Noa had kept their pact with McLean when they signed the land sales in 1865: 'You should prevent intruders on your side, and we on ours. Let it remain so.'

Indeed, on the completion of the *Hovding*'s next voyage, many Maoris were among the crowd on the Customhouse Wharf, waiting to greet the immigrants. The welcoming dance of Paora Rerepo, accompanied by the usual grimaces and his own singing of 'Rule Britannia', frightened some of the passengers so much that he was persuaded to go away for a time, while they disembarked from the *Fairy*, which was running a shuttle service to the *Hovding* in the Ahuriri roadstead. Unfortunately the Captain had tormented his passengers with horror stories about the Maoris; they were not out of Oslo fiord before he had told them that any passenger complaining would be put under arrest, and that when they went ashore they would be slaves driven with a lash. Once ashore, however, they found their complaints received seriously by the authorities. There was no mistaking, either, the kind intentions of Paora, who returned, accompanied by his friends Tareha and Paora Taki, to grasp in friendship the hands of all new arrivals.

Such had been the conditions under this Captain that the immigrants regarded the barracks as 'comparative luxury'. Poor food, short rations, insufficient water, unsuitable food and no extra water for sick children — Superintendent J. D. Ormond, the Minister for Immigration, the Commissioners, all took notice of the complaints, and regretted that action could not be taken, as the ship had sailed from a foreign port, and therefore the Captain was not under the jurisdiction of the Emigration Act.

The detailed complaint begins: 'The contract states that we should be allowed good and substantial food; this we have not got.' The Captain's comment, that the food was 'good enough for poorhouse people', may have been the final straw in advising their 'countrymen not to ship on board any vessel Captain Nordby commands.'

Small wonder that the immigrants expected cannibals and slavery.

Caroline had been told that she must not be fearful of these darker-skinned people — the flax skirt and the moko, that blue-black tracery of pattern chiselled on the face and outlined in the pigment of burned kauri resin, were only signs of a different civilisation. This thought influenced her throughout her life. She was interested in the raupo-thatched dwellings, and the intricate carvings that decorated meeting-houses and the storehouses on stilts which kept ground birds and animals from the food. The ancestral legends thus carved with blades of stone, often greenstone, fascinated her.

7

Those arrivals on the later sailing would be quickly offered employment all over the province. But the *Hovding* pioneers, after a few days, were sent off by wagon, leaving wives and young children to wait in the Immigration Barracks until shelter could be provided for them in the dark forests further south. The hardy Norwegians, with the older boys of the families, trudged beside the wagons, their first overnight stop at Te Aute — only fresh horses could drag loads up the steep hill just beyond. Even the passengers on Cobb & Co's coach walked while horses struggled up such inclines, the men often putting their shoulders to the mud-coated wheel-rims. Further south, the coach route was a strip forty feet wide, with trees up to two feet in diameter lying beside the undergrowth. Sometimes furze and branches carpeted a patch of bog; the river crossings, even with the wagon teams, were almost as alarming as the storms on the ship. The team would jib as they pulled the conveyance out of a newly-formed hole, quite close to the steep bank of rolling stones. The coach driver, used to these daily happenings, would crack his whip; and onto firm ground the coach would rumble once again.

Abbotsford, with its scattered cottages, was the last of the 'towns'. Across the river was the tall timber of primeval forest. Even from a distance, the difficulties of felling were apparent to the tired Norwegians.

Beyond the straggle of Waipukurau, another overnight stop for some, a trudge round the base of the hill, where the river ran swiftly, brought them to the last fifteen miles or so across the Ruataniwha plains.

A few miles further south, below the confluence of the Mahuranui and the Mahuraiti with the Manawatu, the loop of the river enclosed the Te Whiti clearing.

Here Mr Friberg, who had travelled with this party all the way from Christiania, conducted the ballot for the forty acre allotments, one for each settler, married or single. The holders had to pay £2 per acre for their land, as well as the passage money of £16 per head. Some who had assumed the passages were offered free of charge were now almost without money even for food, as they had waited, out of work, until the *Hovding* sailed. Many of them were disillusioned; these towering totara trees were of a size undreamed of in

Scandinavia. There, too, the forest floor could be seen; here was a luxuriant wilderness of vine and undergrowth, some of it with jagged thorns, like the bush lawyer that festooned trees, and the fortunately rare matagouri. The latter would be the curse of second growth, when despairing settlers were forced to leave their partly cleared allotments. The survey pegs, driven in by Weber and his surveyors two years earlier were concealed in the undergrowth; finding one at each corner of the forty acre lot took time.

The track to the area was a nine-foot bridle path. Pack horses replaced the wagons, and the men themselves were laden with as much as they could carry of the gear being left for a second packhorse trip.

For eight settlers the journey to the balloted allotment was even longer. Not enough forty acre lots had been surveyed round Norsewood to provide one for each settler; there were more towards Dannevirke, and those who had missed out on the Norsewood ballot were directed to allotments further south.

In spite of disillusionment, they set to work with their crosscut saws, mauls and wedges. Houses built of slabs from trees just felled, or from the boles of tree ferns, were soon completed. Others, rather more elaborate, were built of slabs, with squared beams; roofs were thatched with strips of totara bark. At first the windows were made of calico, but that soon changed where the settlers could afford glass. The essential furniture — beds, tables, stools — was at first constructed of slabs, too. Fern leaves were strewn on the earthen floors.

The women and children were then asked to leave the Immigration Barracks, most of them being anxious to rejoin their menfolk. A few, like Maud Greiner, her children, and Caroline, could afford to travel by coach; the transport provided for the majority was a convoy of drays, which took them close to the Te Whiti Clearing. The barracks there — whares or huts — were too small to hold them all, and quite a number, with older children, had to sleep outside, sheltered by the huge fallen tree-trunks.

When they finally reached their new homes, isolated in these forty acres, many were too tired and bewildered even to cry. At first life was as grim as it had been on the ship. Axes rang all day, the great logs were crosscut into wide, thin slabs, and somehow the cottages were completed. The women made the most of what they had: the earthen floors were swept, and fresh fronds laid, the camp ovens were wisely used. In these first months milk was never available, and commodities for Norsewood settlers were carried from Waipukurau. Considering the low wages, prices were high: 100lb. flour cost $3, 40lb of sugar $2, loose tea 40 cents per lb., candles 25 cents.

Worse still was the lack of a doctor. One lived at Abbotsford but he could not get through if the rivers were flooded.

Those who had little money left were in a serious position. They had a home and land; but there was as yet little demand for timber, and no logging trails or bullock teams to snig the huge tree-trunks to the newly set up mills nearer the township. Some of the men worked on the roads between Norsewood and the Te Whiti Clearing, being paid fifty cents a day. With their allotments to clear, they could work only four days a week, just enough to buy essential food supplies. Crops of cabbages and potatoes were grown from seed provided by the government. Some settlers, including Olav, bought a cow. Pigeons — the native wood-pigeon made a tasty pie — were plentiful, and wild pigs roamed almost too close to the settlements. As the clearings developed, settlers brought in a few sheep.

While railway construction pushed south, men were employed splitting totara sleepers at fifteen cents each, but they had to pay one-fifth of that as royalty on the timber. The women stood by their menfolk, making do in the most economical way, spinning and dyeing with native plants, wool for the needed warmth where the winds whistle bitterly down every gully in the Ruahines. It was a hard winter. Even in Napier snow fell thickly. Here, away from the coast, the foothills were inches deep in snow, the great totaras groaning with the unaccustomed burden.

In another land the snowfall would have delighted the children and Caroline; here there was no room for sled rides down sparkling slopes, and who had time to make a sled? Here the dark forest was filled with strange birdcalls, even at night, the kiwi and the weka, and sometimes the laughing owl. Then rain, and mud, and murky skies; the children were subdued, almost sullen.

Olav Greiner, with enough money saved so that he need not tramp the beginnings of roads in search of work, went ahead with his plan to buy a store. Bringing in goods from outside would be costly; some of his compatriots would be able to spend only very sparingly, solely on absolute necessities. It was almost impossible to produce anything for sale outside the settlements. More timber had been felled in the clearing than could be used locally. But once the railway was through, all that would change — and by then it would be too late to start a store, for outsiders would be quick to seize any chances.

The dampness of the bush, the isolation and loneliness, and above all the scarcity of food caused much illness and sometimes death. Accidents in the bush, often serious, were left untended — who could afford to call the doctor from thirty or forty miles away? Death and permanent disability were caused, too, by the lapse of time before skilled attention could be obtained.

Living was frugal, even when Olav had bought his store, but not as frugal as it had been just after Caroline's father had been lost at sea. Children often did not attend the newly opened school, for they were kept at home to work on the land, while fathers, with their tools and blankets in a swag on their backs, were away, tramping the roads for work. The teacher who understood the children's native language would often not bother to teach English; the lack of a suitable teacher closed one school for a full year.

The township was a rough place, with the pioneers busy on their allotments or out of the district. It was no place for a woman to walk alone, even in daylight. At

43

night, of course, no woman with a good reputation would be out-of-doors, even in an emergency. A Salvation Army Officer managed to last out ten weeks before he was almost run out of town.

When the rough and tumble bush-whackers, hanging over the many public bars, heard there was a replacement on the way, they turned out in force to meet the train, at their drunken worst. They would frighten this officer into staying on the train. Not even ten weeks would they put up with this next one.

However, two pairs of trim, black-stockinged ankles changed the onlookers' language, as two 'Sally Lassies' stepped down from the steam train. The nineteenth century form of the wolf whistle replaced the jeers. Not recorded is the number of years these Salvation Army officers stayed; but the Army stayed for good. Those men and women with little wish for hard work and less moral fibre drifted somewhere else, eventually leaving the district to the pioneers.

Not far from the store was Greiner's cabin, well-built and warm now, with the towering totara and graceful rimu still standing in the southern corner of the forty acre block. The fat native pigeon, with its noisy flight, feasted on the tawa berries in the treetops and the konini berries by the stream; the tuis and bellbirds imitated now the screech of saws, then let fall their liquid bell chimes.

Bells — the chime of countless bellbirds at dawn, the white flash of the blue-black parson-bird, the tui. The basket-chair creaked again, as Caroline dreamed on in the heat of the February morning.

8

Nearer the township the whistles of the sawmill were the dawn call, especially in the frosty winters. Patient bullock teams dragged the great logs from the bush allotments, now, to the nearest mill. Down by the Mangatera, a very early steam engine puffed along the rails from a larger section of native timber.

No longer must the coach from Napier terminate its journey at the Te Whiti Clearing. The road was through to Dannevirke, and further south, through the southern part of the Seventy Mile Bush that stretched from Takapau to Manawatu and on to the northern edge of the Wairarapa plain at Mauriceville.

Palmerston was growing, a thriving inland centre; but Saddle Hill, above the village near the head of the Manawatu Gorge, was a steep pull for the horses, as the coach road wound up and up, with snow often on the summit in winter. The gorge route was a difficult track, too, though not many years would pass before a train would snake its way through tunnels and across viaducts high above turbulent rapids, while wheeled traffic would make constant use of the other bank, tall cliffs often crumbling above and below what had been a track.

Occasionally letters came, perhaps once in three months, from across the seas, when Astrid or Ingrid would write. Less frequently Henrik, settled and content in the Canadian lumber world, would give Caroline news about his family.

Unlike his brother, Roald was not content. He was tired of fishing — a hint of the dangers and demands of fishing the Newfoundland Banks came through — but not of the sea. Soon he hoped to join a ship trading to New Zealand ports. Perhaps he would find one sailing to Napier, when he might be able to see his sister; after that, he might consider coastal trading.

As for William, a very formal letter after he had returned to the Kentish orchard told Caroline little. It certainly did not suggest undying love, or a determination to cross the seas to find her again. Her reply, months later, was equally formal. Both of them, of course, were bedevilled by the language difficulty. William had troubled himself little with learning the Norwegian written language, for a touch and a smile could convey much; Caroline's spoken English, now, was quite wide ranging, but her letters were borrowed from an even then old-fashioned book on etiquette and letter-writing, stilted and cold. Half the time she did not understand clearly what she copied; and the other half of the letter did not express her meaning or her feelings.

One day a stranger came off the coach as it pulled up in front of Greiner's store. Olav was mystified when the new arrival asked, not for stores, but for Miss Caroline.

Weighing goods in the back premises, Caroline heard the request.

'Roald!' she exclaimed, as she rushed through the curtained doorway, to fling her arms about him. 'How did you get here? What are you doing? Where have you been?' — all in Norwegian, the accented English completely forgotten in her excitement.

But the puzzled reply was in English, a compound of Norwegian accent overlaid with Canadian French. Roald had spent so many years away from his compatriots that his native language was stranger to him than English; he had a smattering of French, too, for some members of the fishing crews had come from Quebec to the Newfoundland port.

While Roald stayed for a few days, Greiners saw a new facet of Caroline's character. Upright, almost severe, kind to the children but showing little warmth or affection, she had been as matronly and restrained as the most struggling pioneer mother of five. Now there were glimpses of the young lady who had danced in the crystal white gown not so many years ago.

'Perhaps she was in love with that young Englishman after all,' suggested Maud Greiner, out of earshot of brother and sister.

'Nonsense, woman, you're a gossip. Caroline will marry one of her own race,' stated her husband firmly. Already he was considering a bachelor friend, a few years younger than himself, as a husband for Caroline; she would have a good, steady provider, older, of course, but that was as it should be.

Roald, as if to make up for months at sea and away from family, from whom he had heard nothing, could not stop talking and asking questions. On a voyage up the St. Lawrence beyond Montreal and into the Great Lakes, he had visited Henrik, now married with a family, as Caroline knew from letters.

The Greiners were as interested in his life as Caroline was; he told of narrow escapes on the fishing smacks, bitter cold and ice floes a constant threat as they fished the Banks. None of that was different from his father's experiences up in the North Sea, and in the fiords. Roald recalled that once at least their father had been to the Dogger Banks, imagining that the conditions there would have been similar. Seeing Caroline's still face, he went on quickly to talk about cargo ships sailing to South American ports, where mahogany timber would be loaded.

They were sitting at the meal table, after the perpetual cabbage and potatoes.

'We found a strange vegetable down there, Olav,' he said. 'I wonder if you could get asparagus in New Zealand?'

'What's that?' asked Maud.

'It's a fleshy stalk — very tasty. It grew wild on the banks of some of the tidal rivers where we loaded mahogany,' he continued. 'The cook wanted fresh greens — we'd been a long while at sea and scurvy had shown up. The mill foreman showed him where this stuff grew — we lived on it while we were there. — No more scurvy.'

'Is that the only place you've seen it?' Caroline asked.

'The only place I've seen it growing — and wild, at that,' replied Roald. 'But some of the big shops overseas sell it — I've seen it on display, and very dear it is, too.'

Caroline thought that her brother had sailed every sea. He had rounded the Horn,

50

a far worse voyage than rounding the Cape of Good Hope; he had sailed on a ship taking prospectors to Alaska for gold. Was there anywhere he had not voyaged?

However, his last trip had decided him to change to coastal shipping. He had been very fortunate, and a sailor could not rely on good luck too often. Violent storms, broken gear and finally fire in a cargo of grain had forced the captain to order his crew to abandon ship. As on the *Hovding*, lifeboats had been damaged; but fire at sea is one of the worst dangers, and no time was wasted in abandoning the ship, which might have blown up at any minute. The remaining lifeboats had drifted apart during the night, and Roald's group was becalmed for days, so that the sail flapped uselessly in the tropic sun. Damaged oars were little use, even if the crew had the strength to use them. Currents had carried them near the Sargasso Sea; they could not expect rescue so far off the normal routes, nor could they hope to make land in that direction. By now they were far from where they had abandoned ship.

A little of the despair they had felt crept into Roald's voice.

'You wrote to me that you were allowed only half a gallon of water a day on the *Hovding*,' he continued. 'We were down to half a cup each when we were picked up — what was left of us.'

'You were thousands of miles from here,' said Caroline. 'Why did you come out to Napier? You must have signed on to another ship specially to see me.'

'I never thought to see you again. We didn't care if we fetched up in China, and I think we'd have stayed there. But the steamer that rescued us was bound for Napier!'

Not all of that group had survived. They heard no word of the other life-boats. And their own troubles were not yet over — discharge certificates, tickets (Roald had his First Mate's ticket by now), clothing and gear had of course been lost. Then the donkey engine that distilled sea water into drinking water for crew and passengers broke down. Roald felt again the horror of those days drifting with little water and no prospect of any. But two young engineers came to the rescue, hand-turning the bearings of the donkey engine; the superstitious among the steamer's crew decided that they had not rescued a Jonah after all.

Roald was safe — and here, in the Forty Mile Bush. Caroline was delighted, even more so when he told her that he had signed on as First Mate of a coastal vessel trading out of Napier. That would be his

52

home port. Most of his voyages would take him only up the coast, although the owners, he had been told, had been considering the kauri trade, from Coromandel and Great Barrier Island. (Only names, these, to the inland Norwegians, but they liked to hear Roald's plans for the future.) Perhaps, if the chance came, the trader might go to the West Coast, shipping timber out of the Northern Wairoa.

'Why not use our timber, the totara?' Caroline wanted to know.

'Kauri is a much better timber,' Roald answered. 'It's slower growing. You think these trees are big — they tell me kauri will be eight feet and more in diameter.'

'You were not interested in timber, once,' Caroline reminded him.

'No — it's the sea for me, always. But I've had enough of fishing. And Henrik is getting on faster than I am — and Uncle Carl seems prosperous, too.'

Mrs Greiner bustled in, then. 'How long can you stay with us, Roald?'

'Only two more days,' he replied. 'My ship sails on Friday.'

'You're wise to leave yourself with a day to spare,' said Olav. 'With floods so frequent, the coach sometimes can't get through. I read in the *Hawkes Bay Herald* a while ago that the mail was delayed 'as usual'. Deliveries, even if the need is urgent, can't be guaranteed.'

The mail did get through the next day, bringing a letter edged in black, addressed by one of her sisters, and posted in Christiania.

Caroline's bright colour faded.

Who had died? Her mother? Her step-father? Not Astrid, surely? Henrik?

'Perhaps it's just a friend,' Roald tried to reassure her, while she fumbled with the letter.

He peered over her shoulder as she read the sad news in Norwegian, news telling her that her brother Roald had been lost at sea.

Brother and sister burst into gales of laughter.

The vessel which had been abandoned had not burnt out, nor had it sunk. The look-out on a passing steamer had reported his sighting, thinking that it was undamaged but in difficulty.

When they sent a life-boat alongside, there was no sign of life, but every sign of hasty abandonment. The ship had suffered severe storm damage, that was obvious from the remaining unseaworthy life-boats. There had been no storms for the last day or two, so either the crew had been already rescued, or vanished over the horizon, or drowned when leaving the ship. The steamer, bound for London River, reported the derelict and its missing crew to Lloyds. Caroline's mother, informed by the ship's owners of her son's death, requested a memorial service at the family's church.

Fluttering to the floor was a cutting from a Christiania newspaper, with an 'In Memoriam' notice and the report of the service.

Roald had to ask his sister to translate, so much had he forgotten his native tongue.

'I'll be one of the few to read his own death notice,' he roared, laughing as he shared the joke with Olav and his wife.

When he left, the following day, on the coach, in the mailbag was a letter from Caroline, to tell her mother that Roald was very much alive.

He would not often have days to spare for the journey to the Forty Mile Bush. As the coach rumbled down the hill to the Mangatera crossing, Caroline began to think about Napier, the beach and the sea rolling in. A bitterly cold wind blew down the gullies of the Ruahines; by day the saws screeched and great trees fell; by night the moreporks called, the night birds hunted their food in the forest still not far away.

Could she find a job — laundry work, housemaid, nanny — in Napier? Would Roald have enough put by for a cottage there? But it was time he married. He would need a home for a wife, not a sister.

Perhaps they could talk about her idea when he next came south on the coach. She hoped it would not be too long before he came again.

9

Meanwhile, as more and more of the allotments were cleared, some pasture appeared, studded with tree-stumps, it is true. While, earlier, the provident might have a dairy cow milked by the wife or the children, few would have the chance of providing their own meat, or expect to do so. A few sheep were brought in from homesteads towards the coast. Quickly the area was turning from the bush settlement of those early pioneer days to a town centre for local farmers.

Caroline began to watch the shipping news from the Port, and to plan a coach trip when Roald's ship was due. Even if he were ashore for only a day or two, with a light cargo to unload or load, there would be time to talk, away from any other influences.

She had no wish to offend those who had befriended her.

Gradually they began to understand. Caroline would discuss her wish to be more closely in touch with the only one of her family in the Southern Seas, as she liked to think of the area. She would not hint that she was tired of living in someone else's home. That would be unkind. Besides, Olav would then remind her that she could have a home of her own, among those of her own race. His bachelor friend Hans needed only the opportunity to declare himself; he had discussed this matter of marriage to Caroline with Olav, more than once.

Caroline dropped back into her former withdrawn ways, always kind but very quiet; the only animation they had seen was on the occasion of Roald's visit. They grew more concerned about her as the days went on. Comfortably settled now, and well content, all Olav and Maud wished for Caroline was a similar life, with Hans for a husband.

He was more frequently asked to join them for a meal (perhaps to prove that Caroline was an economical and excellent cook), but he made no headway. Far from encouraging Hans, Caroline thought increasingly of Napier, and escape from this somewhat rigid Norwegian world.

Was this all there was to life? Caroline asked herself, weighing out sultanas or salt, giving change to customers who would chat a little in English or Norwegian. (Few of Olav's customers were Danish — another store was run by a man of that race.) Anything from Wellingtons to hairpins might be required, but the variety of goods was no novelty to Caroline; she could have been interested in the invoice and order required for goods from Napier — the book-work, but this Olav handled himself. It was, in that day and certainly with that race, the man's job to control all ordering; the women would clean and unpack, and if Olav was busy, or away from the store, Caroline would be allowed to serve the customers. Otherwise her place was in the back premises.

Though they kept her occupied, she felt she was no longer essential — she led an easy but undemanding life, but Olav and Maud could manage without her. Caroline had already shown some of that independence which had been a quality of her mother's, and which, in the future, would change more lives than her own.

Where were the bright dreams of crossing the great oceans to a tropical paradise, always warm? Caroline drew her shawl more closely about her shoulders; another fall of snow, covering the foothills this time, and more to come, from the look of the ominous brownish-hued clouds piling up over the glistening peaks. There might be snow on the Takapau plains; it had happened before, such a fall that the coach could not get through for two days, delayed by drifts two feet deep. And after that, the thaw to fill the rivers with madly swirling waters, bank to bank.

There could be snow on the foothills that curled in a semi-circle about the Napier flats and the Ahuriri Lagoon, she knew. The salt winds could be cold, too. But Napier became a kind of magic word, her El Dorado.

What was wrong with Caroline, Olav asked his wife, that she would not marry Hans? He was a hard worker. Single-handed he had cleared his allotment, leaving only a fringe of shelter to the south, with a few trees to break the cutting wind of the gullies above Umutaoroa. He had bought two good cows, and several hardy sheep. He had built a very comfortable slab house, as large as the Greiners, and well-equipped with home-made furniture. It was clear that he was preparing a home not only for a wife, but for four or five children too.

Caroline's coolness Hans accepted as the reserve of a well-mannered young woman from Christiania. There was no hurry — he was busy, and she was a good worker, not yet too old to bear a large family. She was well looked after by Olav and his wife, gaining household and business experience. (If he had cared sufficiently to ask Caroline about her childhood, he would have learned

60

that she was an experienced housekeeper when she was fourteen years old.) Olav would make sure that Hans was the only man encouraged to think of Caroline as a future wife.

'Hans will be in to dinner tonight,' Olav said, one bleak morning.

'He works so hard,' replied Maud. 'He should have a good woman to cook for him, clean his house, and wash his clothes . . . '

'I don't know why he doesn't get a housekeeper,' interrupted Caroline, who was finding that so much more needed to be perfectly prepared if Hans was to be Greiner's guest.

Olav smiled. 'Surely, Caroline, you realise that Hans is looking for more than a housekeeper.'

'Why doesn't he marry her, then?'

'Oh, Caroline,' Mrs Greiner pleaded, 'wouldn't you like a home of your own?'

'It's time I got the children ready to go to school.'

How could she tell these people who had been so good to her that she wanted to escape from this exclusively Norwegian society? Roald's freedom was something to be envied. That was not within her grasp, as a woman, but surely her horizon need not be bounded by the peaks of the Ruahines

61

and the language of her childhood, not when she had come so far to escape from the northern winters and the narrow and parochial society in which she had moved. She missed her mother and her two sisters, but never Christiania itself.

When would Roald have time to travel south again?

Then an opportunity presented itself. Maud's friend wanted to send her two daughters to Napier, where they had been offered a holiday beside the beach. The mother, with twins eight months old, did not want to leave home herself. If Caroline's fare was paid, and her board, would she escort the two little girls? She need not stay more than a day or two; the friend with whom they were to stay would bring them back, as she wanted to visit the mother, and see the twins. The date of the trip could be arranged to suit Caroline — and Roald.

Caroline was delighted.

If Roald's ship Caroline hinted, was in port for some time, it could be a week or two before she returned.

10

Of the coach trip to Napier, the older Caroline recalled little. The two young girls, not as well-trained as the Greiner children, were restless and irritable. Uninterested in what was pointed out to them, they found the journey tedious. At coaching halts Caroline had to watch them closely.

But the dullness of the journey was nothing to the disappointing news that greeted her on her arrival.

Roald was at the coaching terminal. He was full of his own plans, for it seemed that he might have only one or two more trips on this rather dull Poverty Bay run before the owners would send the vessel to the Coromandel and the timber trade. While Roald was brimming over with excitement at getting back to the tall trees, each word drew the narrow Norwegian net closer about his sister.

The little girls were met by their mother's friend. Caroline and Roald walked along the dusty street to a boarding-house where Roald had stayed occasionally.

'I'm so glad you've come up,' he said.

'There's only two days before we sail, and there wasn't time to go down to tell you my news. We just made the tide last evening. I'm getting tired of this run, it's either wait for the tide, or the bar isn't open. We don't often get as far as Gisborne — that's quite an interesting place.'

'The *Herald* expected you to berth a day earlier,' Caroline explained. 'It was good that you could meet me — you must have got my letter.'

'It was waiting for me at the shipping agents. It had been there three or four days — we were held up by the Wairoa bar after we had loaded. I hope we don't get delayed by the Northern Wairoa bar as much — if we ever get there.'

This was no time to talk to Roald about a cottage in Napier. Just as he had grown tired of the sameness of fishing the Newfoundland Banks, so now he wanted to go further afield in New Zealand — a genuine adventurer, Roald, always looking for somewhere new. In their ancestry somewhere was obviously a voyager to foreign places.

It was a while before Roald noticed that his sister was very quiet. He had expected her to be excited about this trip to Napier; she had been delighted at the prospect when he first visited the Forty Mile Bush. Perhaps she had found the two children rather tiring. Tomorrow she might feel more energetic, and they could make the most of that one day; the chance was unlikely to come again.

As for Caroline, could she make her brother understand that she shared his wish to escape from the known into the unknown? Would he tell her to go back and marry Hans? It was most unlikely that he would encourage her to stay in Napier, now that it would never be his home port.

He talked about the monotonous difficulties of these voyages out of Napier, the short time at sea, the long waits for surf on the bars to moderate, the delight of first seeing Young Nick's Head, when they had a cargo for Gisborne. Because the Hau Hau leader, Kereopa, had been executed in Napier only the year before the *Hovding* arrived, for the murder of the missionary Carl Volkner and the surveyor Falloon in the Opotiki area, Caroline was now a little fearful of the darker-skinned people she met in the streets.

Roald, on the other hand, had worked with the Maoris, loaded and unloaded cargo with and for them; and he had been interested in finding out a little about this Hau Hau cult, which had originally stemmed from Te Ua's ideas of Pai Marire (goodness and grace). He had read about Te Kooti, a young Maori who had served with the combined white and Ngatiporou forces against Kereopa. The white settlers, understandably fearful of anything to do with Hau Hauism, had insisted that Te Kooti be shipped to the Chathams with other prisoners. From that time, Te Kooti, bitter about his treatment, was savagely antagonistic; as he had been imprisoned after a military trial had found him not proven guilty, with other prisoners he seized the schooner *Rifleman* at the Chathams. Four months after landing in the south of Poverty Bay, he led the massacre of seventy-two men, women and children, forty of them Maoris, at Matawhero, near Gisborne. Te Kooti escaped to the wild fastnesses of the Urewera Country, after Major Ropata and Colonel Whitmore attacked the Hau Hau force at Ngatapa. It was 1871 before the series of raids and battles ended, when Te Kooti broke through to the Maori King's territory in the Waikato, and the government of the day decided to leave him alone.

As the Maori saying goes, 'This was between you and me'; thanks to Ropata te Wahawaha, with colonial forces under Major Fraser and Captain Biggs, the Hau Haus were never closer to Napier than a few miles south. In the sunny morning, Caroline could understand Roald's point of view; what had happened was past history, and his broader outlook could put it aside, while the Forty Mile Bush people might wonder if such disasters might happen again.

But Roald's mention of strange places like Ngatapa and Matawhero reminded Caroline again of her restricted life.

There were other Scandinavian settlements in the Seventy Mile Bush: Mauriceville, probably at that time the largest, exclusively Scandinavian, with no intermingling of British settlers; Eketahuna, Matamau, Norsewood, Makaretu — all much closer than Gisborne was to Napier. But for Caroline, to whom the Greiners still acted as though they were her guardians, despite her age, these outer settlements might as well have been in the 'other island'.

Added to the difficulties of travel between the settlements — for instance, Dannevirke was regarded as being in the midst of the Seventy Mile Bush, while Mauriceville was at the southern extremity — were language difficulties, not only with English, but with varying dialects. The Norwegian form of Danish, called the national tongue, and the 'country language' of the isolated communities had many differences.

Half listening to Roald as he enthused about the northern harbours, and the warmer waters, mangrove-studded, and half recalling the narrowness of the communities which had followed the pattern of the old world, Caroline heard him break off to ask when she was returning to the Forty Mile Bush.

'I'm not!' said Caroline, surprising herself as well as her brother. Until this time she had not realised how much she disliked the life, disliked it enough to step out on her own.

Astonished, for Roald had not heard her complain before, he asked, 'Why ever not, for goodness sake? What have you done? Have you offended the Greiners?'

That would be the first question from an older brother with a traditional background, Caroline thought. A young woman would never leave home, except to marry, unless she had quarrelled most bitterly with her parents.

'I haven't offended them — yet,' she retorted, 'but they are expecting me to marry Hans. And I won't! He wants a good housekeeper and a good mother for his children — that isn't enough for me.'

'But, surely, if you explained this to Maud and Olav . . . '

'Olav can see no further than a good provider,' Caroline interrupted, 'affection is something that is expected to come after marriage.'

'Yes, I see. That wouldn't be enough for me, either.'

'Olav is already annoyed because I won't encourage Hans,' she said.

'Surely you don't need to stay away because you're refusing to marry the man Olav has selected for you? And, anyway, you might not meet a better man.'

'It's not only that; it's Norsewood and Dannevirke, and the bitter winds . . . '

'Newfoundland is colder,' he interrupted. 'You have no other prospects, you'll have to put up with the cold.'

'You wouldn't!'

'But I'm a man, hardship is nothing to me. You wouldn't know how to manage.' Then he realised that argument was no way to persuade his sister out of what he considered a disastrous plan. 'Later on, when I settle somewhere, you could spend some time with me . . . '

'Later on . . . how much later?' she asked. 'And I should like you to settle down with a wife, not your sister. You might want to go back to Canada — or over to Australia.'

'That's all for the future,' he said. 'Go back to Greiners, for a year or two, until we work something out.'

'A year or two? Not even a month or two, if I can avoid it. I'm away, now, without offending any of my friends. If I go back, it must be for good, or there would be an argument. There must be someone in Napier — or Havelock, I wouldn't mind going there — who wants a housekeeper — or a seamstress — or even a nanny of sorts, for I couldn't be a governess — or a housemaid — '

Roald was horrified. 'At your age, and with your background and experience, a housemaid? That's nonsense.' He had forgotten the trying times after their father's death, when only his small wage and his mother's laundering had kept the family together.

'I'm really only a housemaid now . . . '

'Don't be stupid. You're a friend of the family, you're treated like an older daughter.'

'Yes,' Caroline agreed, 'I know I'm treated like a daughter. But I am not Olav's daughter, and I don't see why I should marry the man he chooses for me.'

'Hans seems a decent sort — is there someone else you like better? Back in Christiania?'

'No, Roald, that's not the point. You want to move on, and the move has come your way. Can't you understand that I feel exactly the same? And I've stayed in the Forty Mile

70

longer than you've had Napier as your home port — '

'And I haven't been in Napier much. All right, I see your point. We'll just have to try to do something about it, won't we?'

Together they walked along the streets, looking at the shops; top hats, frock coats, even the somewhat outdated crinoline and the more modern bustle were part of the Napier scene. The other side of the picture was life at the port and the Inner Harbour — the excitement of arrivals, wrecks and disasters.

In the twenty years since Napier had been a Customs Port of Entry, eight vessels had been totally wrecked, driven ashore on the Petane Beach.

No wonder Roald preferred Caroline further inland. Understandably, she would take a personal interest in the shipping news; if she lived in Napier, she would be sure to make enquiries about Roald from the shipping agents. They, in this raw country with little communication, were apt to presume losses instead of delays. Years earlier Caroline had experienced those dragging months when her father was missing — it would be better if she did not hear too much of overdue ships, particularly if her brother should happen to be aboard.

His captain had a brother in Havelock; perhaps he would know of some temporary place for Caroline. It was clear that she wanted to find something without referring to the Greiners. That meant skivvying in a boardinghouse — or worse. But a discussion with the captain might lead to a personal recommendation, and work in a pleasant home. It was time, Roald thought, that fate helped his sister along — he had been very fortunate himself in finding exactly what he wanted, and she was as good a housekeeper as he was a mariner.

11

And so, before Roald left on the voyage to Coromandel, Caroline found herself housekeeping for an orchardist in the Havelock district, whence she could see the gargantuan bite taken out of the rocky summit of Kahuranake by the giant, Te Mata.

At first, the position offered had been temporary, while Mrs Brown was convalescing, and unable to help in the orchard. But both Mr and Mrs Brown found her hard-working and seemingly contented — happy to work outside, too, picking fruit for an increasing market or helping with the work concerning young trees.

In a very short time she found herself regarded and treated more as a friend than an employee. 'Living in', it needed to be so, in that six-roomed house. Here was no sheep station, like those on the sloping hills, with separate quarters for those working on the place; nor was there any landed gentry from England, as she had thought of William's father, looking down on their servants as past generations had done.

Remembering the reaction of William's father, she was surprised to be so quickly accepted by the Browns and their friends. She did not realise that her own determination to escape from the narrow confines of the Norwegian village life of the 'Bush' had brought her into a multi-racial New Zealand. Particularly in the Havelock village itself, origins did not seem to matter, for the surnames stemmed from every nation. The fact, too, that Cobb & Co. had driven their coaches through the township for so many years, on the Napier-Waipawa trip, had probably widened personal horizons. Later, Tatum's Waipawa Conveyance had travelled from Napier on Mondays and Thursdays, with the return journey on Tuesdays and Fridays.

Perhaps it was because the area had been settled earlier. Perhaps, although the forbidding peak of Te Mata towered over the rolling uplands, it was because the country was kinder. Whatever the reason, it was certainly a complete contrast to the rigors and restrictions of the 'Bush' further south.

Roald wrote more frequently. He knew, now, that Caroline would understand his letters, sharing not only the language but also the independent outlook and the wish

74

to learn about the adopted country. These letters might be two or three weeks on the way; but it would not be six months before one could expect a reply, as was the case with letters to the family in the northern land.

He would write of the kauri loaded onto the scow for the usually quiet trip across the Firth of Thames, with its almost continuous shelter of islands and extinct volcano.

'Auckland is nothing like our city of Christiania,' he wrote, 'but it is growing fast. They tell me that when Port Nicholson, as some of them still call Wellington, became the Capital of New Zealand, ten years or so ago, the commerce people feared that Auckland would go backwards. But in the main streets there is much building activity. Houses are quite close along the shore line, and people even seem happy to build homes on the slopes of the extinct volcanoes.

'You'll be wondering about these volcanoes. Most of them look like any other small hill, but they are shaped like a cone with a flat top, and there's an old crater hole in the centre.

'Rangitoto, an island with a rocky coastline to the east of the channel, is a landmark for sailors and landlubbers alike. But it is all volcanic rock, though some scrubby trees grow there. No real timber — that is on

75

another island almost joined to it — there's only a foot or so of water at low tide.

'Away to the northeast there's an island of kauri, not far from the tip of the Coromandel Peninsula. We might load there, some time.'

Replying, Caroline told him that she was enjoying her life. There was a wider range of interests: she had been taken to a concert at the Mechanics' Institute and in the winter there were penny readings. 'Capital entertainment, Mr Brown says, and there's always a good fire burning. But I don't know why they worry about good fires here. They wouldn't, if they had spent a winter or two in Norsewood or Dannevirke.

'Mrs Brown says that the women hoped the penny readings — and the good fires — would keep the men out of the hotels. There are only two, the Exchange and the Havelock, but one of the older men working in the orchard says there used to be five.

'The Annual Show used to be held here, too, but now we have to cross the river to Karamu. Sometimes it floods badly, though not as much as it did years ago, they say; the beasts had to be swum across flooded rivers to get to the show one time. It almost seems as though they might have got a prize for bringing their animals through this way.

'We can still go by coach to Napier, but

76

with a bridge over the Ngaruroro it will be easier to go to Hastings, which is much nearer but hardly any bigger than Havelock. There is a train going between Napier and Hastings.'

The Browns shared a common interest with other pioneer orchardists nearby. Goddards was mainly a nursery, but he was growing grapes under glass (a venture regarded as crazy by some local folk). Another orchardist, William Guthrie, was to end up with 26 acres of apples, plums, lemons, oranges and currants, black and red.

Caroline wrote of the pink and white of orchard blossom to Roald, who was by now writing of the Northern Wairoa — the kauri gum and the gumdiggers, many of them Dalmatians, and the rough township of Dargaville, where the river met the northern arm of the Kaipara Harbour. Bullock teams snigged the tall trees — 'sixty or eighty feet high in the forest, and some over one hundred feet' — to the mills. This Caroline could appreciate. But when Roald added that they had beached the scow at low tide up the river beside the sawmill, she was at a loss. He went on to describe the ship-building yards at Kaihu and Aratapu, the latter further down the Kaipara than Dargaville. They built hulls far longer than the fishing boats they had

77

both known a few years away in time and thousands of miles away in distance.

The letters to and from Roald had a two-fold effect: Caroline wrote less formally, but still only occasionally, to William in Kent; her letters 'home' became very stilted indeed, as she struggled with a language no longer heard. Soon she would find reading her mother's letters as difficult as Roald had done when the news of his 'death' had reached Caroline.

The temporary position became permanent. Mrs Brown was well again, but there were young children and there would be more. The orchard demanded time that she did not have to spare from household chores. Caroline, always willing and pleasant, was happy always to work there, picking fruit or packing it.

Two letters — one for Mr and Mrs Brown, one addressed to Caroline — both postmarked Maidstone changed the pattern of life yet again. Mrs Brown, noticing Caroline's faint blush, commented on the surprising coincidence of the postmarks. How could they both have relatives or friends in the same area? They knew Caroline's brother was still in New Zealand waters; only the previous evening she had been asking them about the legends of the district, for Roald's letters showed more and more interest in the Maori tales of North Auckland.

Indeed, Caroline had begun to wonder if Roald was interested also in someone of that race. Many of the young women were very attractive, warm-hearted, charming and gracious, with bright, outgoing personalities.

To her employers Caroline explained that she had a friend whose father had an apple orchard in Kent. That information was of particular interest to orchardists.

'What variety of apple does he grow?' asked Mr Brown. 'Those apples that von Sturm grows at Mangateretere are good keepers, but I'd like to find an earlier variety for the Christmas market.'

Ignorant of apples and, until now, of orchards, Caroline offered to ask when she next wrote to her friend.

But once she had read William's letter, she had to explain that she would not be writing again, as her friend by now was on board the *Helen Denny*. She did not explain why he was sailing. The Browns seemed to think that there had been a close understanding between the two young people, and that he was coming out to marry her.

That may have been William's idea. But his letter told only of a bitter argument with his father, ending in a threat on William's part to 'go to the colonies, since it seemed he wasn't wanted at home.'

Possibly — probably, since William rarely made real decisions, it had been an empty threat. Certainly he didn't expect his father to tell him to go, and offer to pay his passage. A small remittance, as he had a certain share in the income from the orchard and the public house according to his grandfather's will, would be paid to him every three months or so — once he could send a permanent address.

The Browns, knowing nothing, of course, of this, told Caroline to invite William to stay with them — his knowledge of orchards could be a great help. She could send the invitation in the care of the shipping agents. Or would she care to meet the ship? Mr Brown would escort her to Napier and the Port as soon as the ship was due.

It was always impossible for a younger generation to imagine the indomitable old lady as a shy and nervous young woman. She had undertaken that tremendous voyage in the *Hovding*, almost with strangers; she had travelled into the uncleared forest, slept in a tent, cooked with the camp oven, served in a store where customers were of all types and not always sober; she had made another break for independence in a way that could be envied by many women two generations later.

Would Roald be anywhere near Napier when William's ship docked? Not that he would know him, nor had Caroline ever mentioned him. Roald had been at sea when William took that 'grand tour'. Would Caroline's mother or stepfather have mentioned the possible marriage in their infrequent letters?

And was William thinking of marriage? Caroline did not know. How could she ask her brother to travel inconveniently to Napier to meet some foreigner whom she had known in Christiania? His letter suggested that he was coming to New Zealand permanently, so there was unlikely to be in England a woman he planned to marry. It was unlikely, also, that he was writing to someone else in this country — but how could she know? He had not been prepared, before, to give up his family to live in Christiania — why now, for New Zealand? Caroline admitted to herself that his inability to earn a living had made him less welcome in the eyes of her mother and stepfather. She had not shown herself a strong character then; she doubted if she had been really in love, or she would have been more determined. A show of determination on her part might have broken down her

81

parents' opposition.

Now Caroline had found out that she could cope with argument; and she had discovered, too, that what she wanted most out of life was a home of her own and a family of her own; but not so much that Hans would have been the answer. William — yes, thinking back, William was the husband she wanted, maybe not a good provider, perhaps even improvident, but together they could make a good life.

As for William's thoughts, she must wait for his arrival.

82

12

Dear William,

Mr and Mrs Brown, for whom, as you know, I work, have very kindly extended an invitation. They would like you to spend some days here, if you have no other plans.

They think you could advise them about apple trees

— No, he might know little about his father's orchard, and might be ashamed of his ignorance. In Christiania he had not seemed interested in apples or cider; perhaps he had not wanted to discuss his father's business undertakings. Now, however, Caroline thought he had known little about the trees or their care.

The letter was rewritten, in the careful copper-plate hand. Caroline had no wish to frighten William away; that was her only chance of getting in touch with him. When they met, she could tell him about the subject that interested Mr Brown, and the enquiries he would make. William set great store on tact; with forewarning, he would be able to conceal his ignorance. The Greiners would have judged him smooth-tongued, and they might have been right.

Yet he was not given to exaggeration; it was his father who regarded the Kentish orchard as an 'estate', somewhat of a misnomer, as Caroline was to find out much later. William was adept at avoiding awkward questions, but there was no guile about him.

Caroline was seeing and thinking very clearly. Nevertheless, she was quite sure that she wanted to marry him, even though he was so indecisive. She would provide the backbone in that partnership.

Only a few years had passed, and that quality of independence inherited from her mother had changed Caroline's outlook completely. Back in Norway she would eventually have married the man her parents chose. She would have proved an excellent wife for those days, completely subservient.

Subconsciously, her refusal to marry Hans had been due to this realisation. A completely subservient wife was what he would have expected; a woman able and willing to work hard, but with no mind of her own. Any signs of independence, any signs of decisive action would have had to be hidden with tact. There would have been no equal partnership in that marriage.

So Caroline's letter to William, rephrased several times, expressed in a guarded way her pleasure at seeing him again. Equally guarded was her letter to Roald, still sailing to and from the Kaipara harbour, the scow laden with kauri for southern ports.

Havelock

Dear Roald,
You wrote about the giant log, called Rangiriri, the taniwha of the yellow waters of the Northern Wairoa. My story includes a maiden as well as a giant. The legend tells the origin of the jagged skyline above the village. It is the body of a 'giant of a man', Te Mata, a chief of the Waimarama tribes. He fell in love with a beautiful maiden, who set him many tasks. (The Maori legends are like some of our own tales, aren't they?) The last task was to eat his way thru' the hill, and the first great bite, which you can see when you look up from Hastings, proved too much for him. The beautiful maiden was so sad that she threw herself over the cliff on the other side of the hills. The folds of her blue cloak float into the shadowy gullies at sunset.

85

The Englishman who often visited us in Christiania is coming out to New Zealand. He is a passenger on the *Helen Denny*, which is to berth at Napier. Mr and Mrs Brown have asked if he would like to stay with them for a few days. His father has an orchard in Kent.

Roald, reading the letter, wondered why there had been so few words about 'the Englishman', and so much about Maori legend. Yes, of course he was most interested in everything he could find out about this new country, and his sister shared that interest. But — 'a visitor who had known the family in Norway'? A few abrupt words, facts but no feelings.

Just as Caroline had wondered if there was a particular reason for Roald's stories about the past, he wondered now if she was writing in some detail about legends to hide her feelings. Letters from home had been rare when he was on the foreign fishing boats. Why, even so, had this 'Englishman who often visited us in Norway' not been mentioned? There had been little enough news. Why had Caroline sailed for New Zealand? Roald realised that he had never had a real answer to that question.

For a day or two he thought about joining

some other coastal vessel, trading out of Napier, perhaps the Richardson line — there was a rumour that Captain Campbell of the *Fairy* and Mr Richardson might go into partnership.

But his sister's marriage was her own concern, and surely she was old enough to make her own decisions.

Mature himself, he was considering marriage to Moana Hinauri, daughter of one of the chiefs of the northern tribes. Could Moana be happy as a seafarer's wife? She was used to community living, relatives and friends closely next door, a pattern of people. Yet Roald could see no future in trading only from the Northern Wairoa.

Certainly there would be kauri felled, sawn and floated down to the Aratapu sawmills for some years to come. One day when the scow had missed a tide with delayed loading, Roald had gone into the forest to watch the axemen at work. By the time he reached the scene, the scarf to determine the direction of the fall had been cut; from the opposite side the axemen began the crosscut, with a huge sharp-toothed saw, one man to each handle. The giant kauri fell with a booming thump, the smaller trees and undergrowth scarcely slowing the impact. Later the eighty feet of clear trunk would be sawn in three or four lengths before it was sent down to Aratapu.

Roald visualised the much needed buildings in Auckland and Wellington, and the coastal trade. The so-called 'free gifts' of forty acre farms to 'industrious men or women of good character and not through age, infirmity, or other cause unlikely to form a useful colonist' of twenty years earlier were no longer available. The passage money then, for Auckland settlers, ranged from $36 for open berths in steerage to $90 and upwards for cabin class; Shaw Savill & Co. were despatching from London 'every few days' one of their ten Clipper Ships — the *Kingston* and the *John Scott* of 1400 tons, the *Avalanche* and the *Mariner* (1200 tons), the *Gloucester*, the *Kinnaird* and the *Traveller* all 1000 tons, down to the *Lady Alice* (900 tons), and *Lochnager* (800 tons) and the little *Eclipse* of 600 tons. Those ships had sailed nearly two decades earlier for 'all the settlements in New Zealand, viz. Auckland, Nelson, Canterbury, Wellington, New Plymouth, Otago.'

However, those ships 'officered by gentlemen of proved experience' no longer sailed so frequently. Mostly, of course, they signed on crews in home ports; New Zealand seamen were paid $11 a month, English seamen $6.

If Roald took his bride down to Auckland, he could be home more frequently, especially on the Waitemata, where the trading vessels called at nearby places, such as Howick, across the Tamaki river. Or perhaps he could find a vacancy for an officer on the Thames traders. Gold was still coming out of there, and kauri, too, apart from the inward supplies needed by the settlers and miners.

He could build or buy a cottage somewhere — Newton Gully or College Hill — for about $400. As to this, he had made enquiries after he had decided that Moana Hinauri was the woman he intended to marry. On his trips up the Northern Wairoa he had met her father and her family, very fine people. They were not antagonistic to this man of another race. There was no inbuilt distrust of one man on account of the actions of early whalers on the other coast; wars belonged to the past and other tribes.

But Moana was contented some distance from the long beaches and menacing rocks, a little fearful of the great oceans, although, like most of her race, she could swim like a fish. The legends told by the tohunga might have had an insidious effect; she was named after Hinauri, who had thrown herself into the sea when her husband, for his cunning action, was turned into a dog by Maui.

It would be from this part of the legend, praising the faithful love of Hinauri, that her name would be derived.

When the story, with its incantations, went on to describe vividly the maiden's months of floating in the sea, her body overgrown with barnacles and seaweed, perhaps some fear of the sea might be instilled.

In much earlier years the daughter, even of a chief, might not hear the legends directly from the tohunga; a young boy, amused at horrifying his sister, would retell the story, enlarging on it as much as his imagination would allow. These legends in the 1870s had lost much of their former sacred tones, especially with tribes who had followed the missionaries' teachings for some years. Like the Norse sagas of Roald's race, they would be told most vividly, but not in a spirit of absolute belief.

For whatever reason, Moana preferred that part of her name. Perhaps she cared for him more than he imagined — perhaps she feared the sea would take him from her. Since it was so unusual in her race, this emotion must surely be personal.

Not too distant were 'the far sands of Haumu', the Ninety Mile Beach on the west coast north of Kaitaia. Cape Reinga, the rocky headland that juts into the foam-washed ocean above Spirits Bay, was the 'leaping-off place of departed spirits.' Who could criticise Moana for accepting a centuries old tradition? The annual northern migration of the kuaka, the godwit, from the cliffs above the Bay would lend substance to the legend.

Teasingly, Roald reminded Moana that the kuaka always returned.

Whatever her feelings regarding him, Roald was sure of her deep love for the forest and the birds — the wood pigeons that fly noisily to the tops of tawa, taller than the kauri of far greater girth, the tuis, the parrakeets, the chattering kakariki and the waddling kaka, and the tiny birds, the warbler, the rifleman wren, the bush canary and the fantail.

These little birds, with their merry cheerful note woke up the old woman who killed Maui. The legend states that this was the cause of the introduction of death into the world.

How could such a person as Moana be happy in bustling Auckland? or Port Nicholson, where the trees were bent by the winds of heaven? How could he ask her to live in a place where children of six and eight, starving and homeless, were sentenced to seven or fourteen days imprisonment and a private whipping?

One could send news by telegraph to Otago, but a fire could destroy 54 houses in Auckland, principally shops and places of business. The Newton Fire brigade was unable to find water; but a little girl carrying 'articles of trifling value' which, she said, her mother had given her to take home, would be sent to the Industrial School.

Roald had to admit to himself that even if he could rent a cottage in Panmure and find an officer's berth on one of the coastal ships, the pretty little township would not have much to offer Moana.

Onehunga, with its population of 2000, was a busy port, with good prospects for a merchant navy officer, but none for a young woman who delighted in the forest and the country.

Napier, then? There would be Caroline to keep Moana company. Or would she stay there? He would have to wait for her plans, especially regarding this 'Englishman'. It would be a fine thing if he took Moana so far from her family and her tribe, only to find Caroline setting off with her new husband for England.

As time went on, there were rumblings concerning the economy. The gold rush in Middle Island was over, and the cost of the wars in the North Island, financed by overseas borrowing, had to be met. To make matters worse, the price of wool was falling. More reason than ever for Roald to decide to entrench himself with a financially sound shipping company; more unemployed meant less demand for buildings, so less demand for timber. The kauri gum export trade might not last, either, but some overseas trade would continue, and some cargo and passenger traffic to small bays where the sea was the only road.

13

As for Caroline, in these two months or so, she veered from planning a wedding to finding a position in some distant area. She would look at linen in Newton & Co.'s shop — they had a better selection than any shop in Hastings. Or would she go on to Napier in Tatum's coach? Or travel by the train that ran from Hastings?

Of Roald's self-doubts she had no idea, any more than he suspected hers. The exchange of letters gave nothing away. Roald appeared to be settled on his scow, in and out of the Northern Wairoa. He wrote of a longer and stormy trip to New Plymouth, and a shorter voyage up the Waikato to Hamilton. The latter trip encouraged him to tell Caroline something about the Waikato Wars, now happily well over, and the transport of the militia up river to the stockade.

Some of the vessels reaching Napier earlier that year had sad news to tell. The *Clarence*, anchoring in January with 350 settlers had to report 21 deaths. Conditions on board had been extremely hard, with poor accommodation and ventilation. The

John Norman had taken 150 days on the voyage, becalmed in the tropics and beset by storms running down her easting. The ship's boat from the *Emily McLean* had capsized in heavy breakers on the bar; the five men on board were rescued, but the boat was wrecked against the pier.

Caroline would think about these troubles, wondering if William would really land safely. Mr and Mrs Brown were very helpful, for they would remind her of ships which had made good passages: the Shaw Savill barque *Hudson*, eighty-four days port to port, with 200 passengers, and a shipment of finches, sparrows, blackbirds and yellow-hammers, released later in Hawkes Bay, and the other Shaw Savill, *Countess of Kintere*, which brought another load of immigrants — two out of five, as Caroline was quick to point out.

When the orchards were in full bloom of pink and white, and some of the early plums formed, the *Helen Denny* was signalled. Caroline, despite Mr Brown's offer to escort her to the Port, had decided to wait until they heard from William. Just as the Greiners had seen a light-hearted facet of her character when Roald had arrived, now Browns found this new young woman a stranger to the somewhat remote and self-controlled housekeeper they had known. By this time they were quite sure that a romance had already blossomed. They were certain that they would lose their excellent housekeeper, and were quietly making plans for a wedding — in Havelock, they hoped.

When William arrived, a day after the ship berthed, time had stepped backwards. Both young people seemed the same as they had been over three years earlier. Caroline put off the black of her servant status; after a long sea voyage, William was no longer the too foppishly dressed young man of the 'Grand Tour'.

There was no doubt that romance was in the air; yet William was not seriously intent on a search for work.

Presently Caroline wrote to Roald, to tell him that a wedding ceremony would take place in two months' time, in Havelock. She wrote to the Greiners, too.

Napier might offer more opportunities for William than Havelock, they thought. There were cottages with two or three acres of land, out Meanee or Greenmeadows way; perhaps they could grow vegetables for the market, William thought, in blissful ignorance of soils and flooding. Put seeds in, the vegetables grew, they were gathered and he would take them to market in a dogcart. Two things

96

became clear to Caroline's friends: she would sow the seeds, keep the weeds down, collect the vegetables, and probably she would have dug the gound in the first place; secondly, William was not prepared for hard work.

They could hardly say so. They could, however, point to the Chinese, working daylight to dark all year round, sometimes cutting cabbages in the moonlight; living in one-room huts, thatched, some of them, like the original Maori dwellings, often walled with rusty flat iron, marked with its pre-salvage use. As well, the Chinese had an appreciation of land suitable for market garden use.

Roald was not surprised to learn of his sister's intended wedding. Could he make the journey? It would give him the chance, too, to find out if Napier would suit Moana, and if Caroline and her husband intended to settle there. He could also find out if any officers were required on coastal vessels based at Port Ahuriri. Fortunately, his ship was taking a mixed shipment of timber and gum to the Manukau harbour.

By now, having sailed with this ship for so long, he could take leave for one or two trips, if a replacement could be found. A coastal vessel in the Waitemata Harbour, across the isthmus, was sailing for Napier.

Given reasonable weather and not too many ports of call or coastal bars, he should make Havelock in time for the wedding. It would not be an expensive voyage, for he would be treated as a supernumery. He would have to sail for the north again the next day.

A week prior to the wedding, William noticed a cottage for sale — 'needing repair'. With their future still unsettled, it suited his pocket, so he paid the agent without inspecting the property. A journey to Greenmeadows seemed an unnecessary undertaking.

When the wedding day dawned, Caroline carried a gay little parasol loaned to her by Mrs Brown; her crinoline frock of white dimity might be outdated, but she looked charming. Her button boots were polished to a mirror finish with the mixture of treacle, lampblack, sugar, yeast and the grocer's oxgall. Roald, in his officer's uniform, was proud to escort her to the new church of St. Luke's. William, of course, wore the top-hat and tails that had so become him in Christiania: that was the correct garb for a wedding in Kent, and its unsuitability for a small village wedding and the couple's circumstances did not occur to him. The bells had pealed from the tower, even though they rang over fields — what more was needed?

After the ceremony, and a wedding-breakfast at Brown's home, there was the conveyance to take them to Hastings, and for Caroline her first trip by train. Years later Caroline would hear the shriek of the steam locomotive along the rails, the long wail of the whistle echoing across snowy hills. Again she would recall that first time the whistle shrilled, as the young couple, Norwegian and English, set off on their honeymoon; one night in a Napier boarding-house, then to the home William had bought, on the recommendation of an agent for the previous owner.

On a muddy back road the hired trap set them down. The orchard had spared fruit cases which held crockery and essential groceries. Portmanteaux and battered cabin chests held their clothing. Over a three foot ditch, a rickety bridge of two planks led to an overgrown frontage, grass two feet high behind a sagging fence. Outside, paint peeling to show sappy timber, second grade iron, unpainted and rusty, on the roof. Inside, the cheapest of paper peeling from damp walls, grease around the rusty stove that had never known blacking or elbow grease, floors not only unswept but an inch deep in mud tramped in over months. The corners were coved with dirt — Caroline had to dig those out with a four inch nail, uncovering new wood in the process. Mice and rats scuttled about the floor where boards were rotted through.

Horrified, William asked: 'Shall we go back to the boarding-house for a few days, Caroline?'

'No, the dirt won't go away unless we do the cleaning. This is our home — you'll be surprised how nice it will look. The dray will be bringing our bed and table soon, we must be here then.'

'There is nothing a man can do here. Shall I go for a stroll?' enquired the frock-coated bridegroom.

'Perhaps you would be kind enough to find the well, or the tank, before you go out, William.'

'That should be no trouble,' he replied, walking towards the creaking door.

His wife called him back. 'Your best clothes, my dear — the grass is very long, and we must take care of that frock coat.'

Caroline began to drag his cabin trunk towards the front room — that looked the least used and so the least grimy.

A little late, as he always would be, William began to help. Soon in slightly more suitable clothes, he went out to inspect his property. Looking after him, Caroline realised that she would have to suggest that he bought something more suitable for work, moleskins or bib overalls and wellingtons, she thought, if he really intended to paint houses rather than be a clerk in a shipping office at the Port, or at the stock and station agents. (She would never realise that, in spite of his copper plate handwriting, figures were somewhat of a mystery to him. When, bored, he had asked to help in his father's accounting concerning the cider and the public house, his inaccuracies had speedily been discovered. This failure contributed to the final argument which had sent William to the colonies.)

Caroline, in her dark skirt (no bustle frame to this) and flour bag apron was sweeping vigorously when he came back.

'I think I've found the well,' he said doubtfully, 'but there's no cord on the windlass, and no bucket. There's a tank, too, but the tap doesn't run very well.'

'It wouldn't,' sighed Caroline, 'it's probably choked with rust. We'll have to use the well — let's hope there's water in that. There's cord from our cabin trunks, and an extra bucket.'

William was useful with his hands. When

he returned with the first bucket of water, however, he found his wife, hair wrapped in a duster, flushed and sooty. Determined to scrub the bedroom first, she had tried to light the stove to heat water.

'I wanted hot water for these dreadful floors, once I've swept,' she explained, 'but I'll have to clean the stove before it will draw. I just hope there are no birds' nests in the chimney.'

'Would you like me to climb on the roof and look?' he asked, somewhat reluctantly. He did not really want to settle down to work that day — he felt like being a gentleman.

Caroline wanted him out of the way while she tackled what she described, to herself only, as a pigsty. The place could not have smelt much worse if it had housed four-legged animals.

As soon as William had strolled away down the road, swinging an elegant cane, Caroline set to work. A shower of soot fell onto the stove top as she opened the register plate — she would have set the place alight if she had remained determined to scrub that bedroom first. Then the grates and ashpans. Although the oven appeared to have been little used, it, too, was thick with grease and rust. After a vigorous dry scrub, to remove the worst flakes of rust and the grime of years, she set to work on the stove top and front with her concoction. The recipe she used to polish her boots did double duty in households where stove polish could not be afforded.

The shine on the stove did not please her; but a fire to heat water in the gleaming new iron kettle was needed quickly. Once the floors were scrubbed, ready for the minimum of bed, deal table and two rail-backed chairs, she would have time to make a really good job of the stove.

The walls could do with scrubbing, too, but that would have to wait. The broom brought down the worst of the dust from the grimy ceiling, disturbing spiders who might have been there since the cottage was built, possibly just for immediate shelter by an immigrant who intended to go further into 'the interior' when the Maori wars were over.

With the dust, the paper — some of it old newspapers to keep out the draughts that whistled through the cracks in poorly fitted and unplastered slabs.

William, as a carpenter, would fix that when he settled down, Caroline thought. It was only to be a few weeks before the penetrating wind that sent clouds of spray over Pania reef would goad him into filling the worst gaps with slivers of dunnage washed ashore; the smaller cracks he could plaster with a mixture of clay and water, as the pioneers had done in the Forty Mile Bush. He was more fortunate than some, for with Caroline's advice, he could use clay from the Port side of the Bluff.

The well water was brackish and salty in this low-lying area. As for the tank, the cover had blown away or been used for firewood. No wonder the tap there would not run; the sand blown across the lagoon and flats in those ship-wrecking gales had filled the roof gutters, then washed into the tank along with half-rotted leaves. The dead birds that Caroline, peering in, could see, had perhaps been attracted in the hot summers by the gleam of water or had fallen, injured.

Would she ask William to clean the tank? No, she had seen worse, and at least no dead rats added to the slime.

With the guttering and down-pipe uncleaned, little water was in the tank. Caroline was soon to find out that neither this nor the dry season were the sole causes of the low level.

Leaving the tap dripping into a bucket, she kilted her skirts, removed her boots and lisle stockings, and clambered in.

William, returning earlier than expected,

was attracted by the resounding clamour from the tank. Indeed, the last lump of debris nearly found a target. Then it was the scrubbing brush again, and push the downpipe aside until William would clean the gutterings. That would be a job for the following day; as a housepainter he was a reasonable tradesman, and he would clean the worst of the rust off the roof before he cleaned the guttering — he might even find some way of stopping the loss of rain water from sagging joints and small holes.

They would have to use the brackish water from the well for a day or two. That had one advantage — very little tea was needed to make a good black brew. As she poured from the brown china teapot, another bargain from the Havelock shops, the tea looked generously strong; the taste was strong, too, but not entirely the expected flavour. It was good to be able to stint a little on tea at 30 cents per pound.

Perhaps coffee, stronger in flavour, could be the subject of a similar economy. It was cheaper, too, at 17 cents a pound, though it did not go quite as far. Caroline preferred it; and if one kept adding water to the enamel coffee pot simmering on the hob, one good brew could be made to last a week. Sunday was the day for a fresh brew, rather weak, but by Saturday one could stand the spoon up in it.

The dray arrived with their poor pieces of furniture. The mattress was new, for Caroline would have nothing to do with second hand bedding. Later, for the children, she would fill washed sacking with straw; but her new husband made it clear that he could and would afford a proper mattress for the master and his wife. He would tighten the sagging wires, straighten the legs and recoat the chipped black paint. It would be Caroline's job to try to shine up the battered brass knobs — that they were still there was quite surprising. She would scrub the chairs, but first the table top, with sand she had collected from the Napier beach for this purpose. Mrs Brown had suggested she keep half the last batch of soap she had made there (from rendered down mutton fat, caustic soda, powdered borax and resin); just as well, for although the soap bars were well dried and hard, this first clean up had made inroads.

That soap, although with a slight excess of caustic, could be used as toilet soap, too. Who would pay for scented soap, or even laundry soap, when one could make it for a fraction of the price? There had always been a farmer or a butcher in both the Forty Mile

Bush and Havelock who would happily let a housewife use surplus mutton fat — and a tin of caustic soda went a long way.

Looking at the copper in the backyard, she thought a batch of soap might be the best way to clean it. In fifty years of soap-making, for as an old lady she still would not buy soap, nor appreciate the gift of any, she would only once come close to disaster. Making a double batch in a copper at Taihape, she had used fierce burning wood, some sort of maire, perhaps, and the brew had overflowed. Thank goodness the ingredients had already combined, for free fat would have burnt the house down; by that time Caroline had a wash-house, instead of a copper in the backyard. As it was, the fire in the grate was doused by the overflow — but the floor was an inch deep in almost cooked soft soap, a jelly-like substance, slimy and slithery. For once that recipe began to boil, it continued regardless of any heat under it.

Years later Caroline would tell her children and her grandchildren to make just a small batch of soap, leaving at least half of the container clear for the mixture to bubble up.

As for cupboards or drawers, they were a luxury that would have to wait a long time. William might nail the boxes together sideways; if she had any spare flour bags, she would use a lichen dye to colour them before they acted as cupboard curtains. Flour bags made table-cloths, teatowels and underclothes as well as aprons, although the material was rather scratchy on young skins. (Caroline's beautiful needlework would be kept until the linen was yellow with age.)

Within a week the cottage looked different — somebody cared. It smelled different, too — of harsh soap, perhaps, but sparkling clean.

Meanwhile, though the downpipe was in place, even heavy rain did not appreciably bring the level of the tank water up. One evening William found a stranger crossing the back of the section, bucket in hand.

When asked what he was doing, the shiftless character replied, 'Yer see, the water in the well don't taste so nice. That tank water's better 'n it used to be, too.'

It took some minutes to convince him that he would have to find water elsewhere. William thought this down-and-outer might have squatted in the cottage before the owner had caught him sleeping there.

Clean newspaper, pasted up with flour and water, covered the gaps and torn edges. William had bought glass at the Port, so there were no longer broken panes stuffed with cloth and newspaper. Some of the windows were jammed with swollen timber; he would attend to that, some time. Others would only be propped up with timber wedges, where the sash cords were broken. But Caroline, like many of her generation, had little faith in fresh air inside, especially at night.

'Best side to London' became a surprising and favourite remark; perhaps William had heard it from his mother. So he toiled on, not very efficiently, with a reap-hook until the tall grass in front of the cottage was cut and his hands blistered with the unaccustomed task.

The young couple would find someone to lend them a sheep to keep the grass down. William speedily discovered that market gardening would have held no attraction for him. As for his neighbour who dug the soil with a miner's shovel — William preferred not to dig at all, but a little working over with a light fork was agreeable for an hour or two.

Cabbages were sown first (no buying plants), and Caroline insisted on growing leeks. This William could not understand — she was not Welsh, and he had been brought up in a narrow English area which refused to acknowledge that the welsh national emblem might be a daffodil, not a leek. He had inherited more antagonism for the people of Wales than for any other race. Caroline was an expert at the best housekeeping ploys: one set of ingredients to do two jobs, like the blacking that worked on boots and wood burning stoves. Leeks had three or four points in their favour: they were more easily grown than onions, they made a tasty filler for a stew which contained the minimum of meat, they made an excellent soup and a fine vegetable — and the water in which they had been boiled was a good glass cleaner.

One morning, as he set off for another painting job, William asked 'Shall I buy a loaf of bread when I get paid?' These loaves that Caroline baked were not as light as those he had tasted at Browns. And the scones and buns there had been delicious.

Flushed from wrestling with a sulky fire — the damper had no effect on frosty mornings — Caroline replied, rather tartly, 'There's more we want than baker's bread'.

'I just thought — you work very hard — and you must have enjoyed Mrs Brown's bread, too.'

'That was my bread — and my scones and buns,' she retorted. 'I always baked for them, that was part of my job'.

'Some of the bread on board ship was

dreadful. But the cook said it was poor flour that was to blame'.

'So it can be, but we're getting good flour just now. My trouble is a hole in the oven,' Caroline explained. 'When you have time, would you bring me a little clay from the quarry?'

'Of course, but what could you do with that my dear?' he asked, not having intended to find fault. 'When my ship comes in, I shall buy you a new Orion range.' She was a good wife, of that he was well aware.

'We need good bread now,' she replied. 'I hate waste, and some of my batches should feed seagulls or pigs. And no, I won't have pigs. Fowls, yes, for eggs and meat when they are too old to lay. But I hate pigs.'

Did that dislike of pigs come from the winter days when the wild pigs would come down to the allotments in the bush?

'Very well, my dear, no pigs, But you haven't told me why you want the clay — there's some nearer than the quarry, I found, when I looked for it after I had plastered the cracks.'

'It is the quarry clay I want — and that was best for your job, too — they make bricks out of it. So if I fill the hole in the oven with it, it will bake there. Any other clay would dry and crumble.'

'Then today, if I finish that painting I'm doing before those yard gates close, I shall bring you a sack of clay,' he offered.

'Not a sack,' she exclaimed, horrified. 'That would fill the oven altogether. A little in a sugar bag will do nicely, and you won't be asked to pay for that.'

William's tired looking nag that scratched a living from the grass at the rear of the long section was already bridled and saddled. As soon as Caroline had the range lit and the porridge pot on — she soaked the coarse oatmeal overnight, winter and summer alike — she had caught the horse for him. It was an easy task, for the poor horse was too old and too lazy to move away, even from the bridle that meant work. Often, too, there would be a handful of oats or chaff if other horses were stabled where William was working; carrying his master might be rewarding sometimes.

The clay was brought home that night.

There were no more complaints about the bread or the buns, and while there was money for flour, cream of tartar and baking soda ('fancy' baking powder was expensive) a fresh batch of scones appeared frequently. William had told her flour would be dearer, for he had heard that the Canterbury wheat crop was poor this season. She would make potato scones, then; they were growing their own now, and saving every scrap of peel with an eye in it for replanting. But potato bread William would not like. Flour must be bought for baking bread, whatever the price. She kept her own yeast going, too, with a mother plant to which she added lukewarm water.

As William brought home odd sticks of timber, remnants of paint and even odd rolls of wallpaper from the high-studded walls of farmhouses, the cottage looked like a home of which they could be proud.

Caroline had dug a little front garden; with cuttings and pieces given to her by neighbours who admired the hard-working Norwegian girl, she created a bright patchwork of flowers before that much wanted first baby arrived.

14

Both young people had written to tell their families of their marriage. They had delayed their letters until they were well settled, and in spite of frequent sailings, now mostly by steamers, mail took a long time to cross the oceans.

Caroline's mother wished them well; by the same boat came a large parcel of household linen. Her stepfather, saddened by her marrying into a family who had wanted nothing to do with her, sent a kind word. In his mind, what was done was done; all he could do now was to help if possible, as generously as he could with the other four girls marrying in Christiania, and wanting a trousseau to match their chosen husbands' positions. Caroline too should have something for her 'bottom drawer.'

Caroline was rather glad that they lived so far away; no need for the family to know that there was not a drawer, literally, in the house. Chests made out of boxes saved the need for runners; William would get round to furniture sometime.

It was over a year before William's news

reached Kent, and a curt reply from his father really cut them off from England.

'Son William,

This is the last letter I shall ever write to you. Some years ago I ordered you not to attempt to bring a Scandy daughter-in-law to my home. You did not tell me when you set off for the colonies, having proved yourself useless here, that you were going to HER. I wish to have nothing further to do with you, unless she dies or you leave her. Send a cable if this happens, or take ship for England. Do not write. I will return your letters unopened.

Your FORMER father.'

William did not show her the letter, but he could not hide his anger at his wife's being treated so. She had seen the Maidstone postmark, but asked no questions; her husband would decide what he wished to share with her.

There was another cause for regret, as far as he was concerned. He had hoped — thought — there might be a few sovereigns or a banker's draft from his father, who could well have afforded a good sum that would set them on their feet. Now they must make do with the remittance — thank goodness father could not stop that bequest from grandfather — and what he could earn. The boom of the 'seventies was collapsing; those who worked at unnecessary jobs, such as painting and decorating, would be the first to suffer.

When, sometimes, he spoke gloomily to Caroline, she would remind him that there were still wealthy settlers. She was a good cook — but what about baby William? Most homesteads preferred a single cook, or a married couple without children. She was a good laundress — there were wealthy homes up on the hill above the town. She would go there by the hour, tucking William in the rickety fourth hand perambulator, walking four or six miles each day, but they would manage. Or, if the horse did not fall down dead before then, William could take the bag of linen in front of him on the saddle, and return it the same way. Somehow they kept their heads just above water.

Sometimes, with alarmingly high tides in the Inner Harbour, flooded rivers and overflowing drains, the floors would be covered with silt again and the babies up on the table while Caroline waited, agonised, for the turn of the tide. She learnt, in the hardest way, what Roald meant when he had written (so long ago, it seemed) of the scows going up river at high tide.

He no longer wrote of Maori legends. Instead, he had signed on with ships sailing from Auckland for San Francisco and other foreign ports. Later, on the one visit he paid, between ships, when he could travel by train from Wellington to Napier, thinking perhaps, in the middle of that long day, of the totara sleepers split by Olav and his compatriots, he told Caroline a little about the lovely Maori girl. Her father had decided that she would be happier with her own people. Roald was rejoining his ship at Gisborne; his sister was rather concerned about the way he would be transferred from the pilot boat there, swung in a basket from ship to ship.

The second boy was Henry, after the older brother of whom they had not heard for years. A quiet little boy, he was walking somewhat unsteadily when the third child was born, this time named Ronald, after the younger uncle. William, now five, was an imp of mischief, into everything, but adept at avoiding trouble. He would blame the younger boys if it was possible to put the blame on them; in this way they suffered several undeserved whippings. 'Spare the rod and spoil the child' was a firm belief in that household.

Father now wore dark glasses — no-one, not even his wife, ever knew why. As little William could not see Papa's eyes, he imagined that Papa could not see him. Sometimes Caroline rescued him, if her husband's outburst of temper seemed unmerited. If he deserved the rebuke, generally a clip over the ears, she was silent.

He was a hungry, not to say greedy, boy. It would have gone hard with the younger ones if Caroline had not kept an eye on swiftly snatching hands. And he was lazy: asked to go a message, he would whine 'Why can't Henry do that?' when Henry was not much more steady on his feet than Ronald now.

With three little ones, Caroline and William were in tight straits. All the vegetables they could grow went into meals, but the sour ground did not produce any bumper crops. The high water table saw to that. Sometimes there was a scrag end of mutton to add flavour to a stew stretched by leeks, carrots and turnips. Pumpkins grew easily, taking over the section; with the seeds of a water-melon Caroline grew a tasty sweetener for the children, and even made jam of a kind. The pie-melon made better jam, as it set more readily, but it was not as tasty eaten raw. If she planned to make jam, everyone but Father would be without any sugar at all for a week or two, so that no extra expense was caused by this addition to the larder. Once made, it was spooned out very sparingly; and the children had either dripping or jam, but not both.

Even a raw turnip was worth munching — by William, of course. He gave a piece to Ronald one day, then found an apple tree overhanging a fence on a quiet road. William could still find room for apples, green or not, but little Ronald sobbed, 'And me's full of turnip.'

William finally learned that Papa could see through those granny glasses. Father was rocking in his chair beside the range — there never had been a new one — while Caroline bent over a tiny eyelet-embroidered frock. The two younger ones were in bed; no nonsense about summer, they were sent to bed at half-past six, expected to stay there and go to sleep at once.

Hungry as always, young William quietly sneaked up to the bread bin — there had been one piece uneaten at lunch, and he would go without dripping. Just as he closed his hand on it, the wallop on the ear sent him flying against the wall.

Caroline pricked her finger with her needle, smearing blood on the carefully hoarded scrap of crepe-de-Chine. She had not noticed William's quiet approach to the

119

bread-bin, nor had she heard her husband leave his chair.

He was in a furious rage. 'Don't you speak up for him, mother,' he ordered. 'Our son was stealing.'

The effect of this episode was to cloud a lifetime. Young William longed to get away from home, or rather, perhaps, from his father. He was hungry, the bread was there, and who ever thought it was stealing to help yourself to food at home? Other boys were told by their mothers to help themselves to biscuits; here mother doled out one biscuit each day to each child. Hard biscuits, they were, and sometimes there were none; there might then be a potato scone, but who wanted that, without dripping or treacle?

The three little boys kept Caroline busy. William had to be the breadwinner. Though the shoe might pinch sometimes, the country generally was emerging from the depression, the 'boom and bust' of the late 'seventies and early 'eighties. Sometimes in the fruit season Caroline would be able to earn a little; she was a quick and careful picker, and on schooldays she was not distracted by William.

If only they lived on the Havelock side of Napier, she could have gone out to Browns for the fruit harvest. Once she had taken the boys out to stay two nights, but the business of getting the three sons and all their gear on the coach was too trying, especially with William getting under the horses' hoofs. It was also nearly as costly as the money she earned while she was there.

15

Then the first of the little girls came along — there were to be three of them, too, quite close together. William insisted on the first one being named Caroline, after her mother, but she inherited none of the latter's cheerful and equable temperament. If the younger boys tried to play with her, she would stamp and demand her own way, or retreat into a fit of the sulks. Ronald would be interested in helping his mother, but not little Caroline. To her father, so proud of this dainty little person, she would not respond with any show of affection. Unlike William, she was not mischievous or disobedient, but even at eighteen months she seemed withdrawn, not a part of that close-knit family at all — there was no sense of fun, only a coldness that, particularly in so young a child, worried her mother.

Caroline, too, was not particularly well during the fifth pregnancy. Large families were the norm of those late Victorian times; she had not expected any more bother with one than another. The heat of a very late summer, an 'Indian summer' some called it, had tired her more than she realised. However, June was not far off. When the new baby arrived, perhaps little Caroline would be interested in a playmate smaller than herself; she might be a little frightened of the boys, although they were so gentle with her.

One night in early June, William called in the motherly neighbour, and built up the fire in the stove to boil all the water she would require. (This was a standard way of keeping anxious fathers-to-be occupied, if they could not be sent out of the house.) He even wondered if he should walk into Napier for a doctor. But a doctor had not been needed for any of the other births; those women who had already borne children helped with their neighbours at this time. Sometimes there might be a midwife available, but rarely in poorer circumstances.

An hour or two after midnight, there came the sound of distant cannon fire. A great glow in the northerly sky beyond the Maungaruru range was shot with vivid flashes, breaking the darkness of the winter night. A light grey rain seemed to be falling, but there was no moisture in the air.

By daybreak the second little daughter had arrived safely. The weary mother was concerned about the cannons and the fire — had there been another massacre? Was another war party on the way, after all these years?

Rumours flew thick and fast — there had been an earthquake and forest fire at Tarawera, inland, almost in the centre of the wild hills.

No, said another, it was a volcanic eruption — look at the grey ash. All the tank water would be thick with it after rain, if the gutterings and roofs were not quickly cleaned. Ngauruhoe, the active volcanoe in the centre of the island, had erupted.

Another, nearer the mark, suggested the other Tarawera, the mountain near Rotorua.

William was painting a homestead near Greenmeadows, while the owner was away in Rotorua. Two years earlier he had sent his brother, still in England, a special correspondent's account published in the New Zealand Herald of the Pink and White Terraces. The writer was a traveller who had seen the Himalayas and the Alps, the Blue Mountains of Tartary, Fujiyama of Japan, and the Sierra Nevadas. 'For delicate, unique beauty, for chaste design and sublime detail of construction,' he wrote, 'never have I gazed upon so wonderful a sight as the White Terrace.'

When the brother came out to visit the Greenmeadows family, the two men arranged a trip of Rotorua and, twenty or so miles out, to Te Wairoa, the starting point for tourists who wished to see these famous silica terraces.

Presently a Special Edition carried the message telegraphed first to the Auckland paper by Rotorua's Mr Dansey, who had stayed at his post while others left the town.

'We have all passed a fearful night here. At 2.10 a.m. there was a heavy quake, then a fearful roar, which made everyone run out of their houses, and a grand, yet terrible sight for those so near as we were suddenly presented itself. Mount Tarawera suddenly became active, the volcano belching out fire and lava to a great height. A dense mass of ashes came pouring down here at 4 a.m., accompanied by a suffocating smell from the lower regions.' (A century later a New Caledonian boy would wrinkle up his nose at the smell of sulphur so prevalent there, and exclaim, in distaste, 'Oh! Rotorua!')

Mr Dansey went on to report that several families had left their homes 'in their night attire with whatever they could seize in a hurry 'and made for Tauranga. Others had horses and made for Oxford (now Tirau).

As William was to learn when the owner and his brother returned, they had joined the last party ever to see the magnificent Terraces. From Te Wairoa they had travelled by boat across the southern end of the lake, under the gloomy shadow of Tarawera to the isthmus and Lake Rotomahana on 9 June 1886.

Their Maori guide told them of the unaccountable rise and fall of the Lake in the past few days. The Green Lake, Rotokakahi, had surged in the same way, spilling into the Wairoa stream that plunges over a cliff into Lake Tarawera. He and his crew had seen, too, the phantom canoe on the lake — they had passengers, tourists who had pointed out the strange sight, one row of Maoris standing, the other kneeling to paddle, the huia and white heron feathers of death adorning their hair. The canoe was approaching them one minute, then it just vanished.

Old Tuhoto, the hundred year old prophet in the village, when told about the canoe, said the land would be overturned.

He was always calling down doom on the Tuhourangi, continued the guide, because they looked after the tourists — and sometimes, he added with a jolly laugh (the boat was out of the shadows of the mountain with its peaks of Wahanga and Ruawahia) he did spend money on waipiro

126

and other pakeha grog.

Mr Falloona, who owned the store at Te Wairoa, told the tourists some of the background to the story. The high priest from the Arawa canoe that had landed at Maketu centuries before had caused a huge chasm to form in the mountain top. He stamped Tamaohoi, the man-eating ogre, into the chasm. And old Tuhoto, the ariki to whom the tribe did not listen, had threatened to call Tamaohoi out of the mountain, to punish the Maori.

'Bad luck if the pakeha got caught, too,' said a tourist who heard the story at McCrea's hotel.

Tamaohoi did awaken that night in June. Wahanga and Ruawahia burst forth in hugh black clouds and fireballs, hurling red hot rock and ash into the skies. Then the rift where Tamaohoi had been imprisoned split down into Lake Rotomahana, blowing up the islets and the wonderful terraces and the lake bottom. Hour after hour hot mud, rock, ash and huge stones rained down on the nearer Maori villages of Morea (Moura in some records) on the peninsula and Te Ariki on the isthmus, and on Te Wairoa, nearly ten miles from the 4000 foot mountain.

Over 100 Maoris perished, along with seven white people.

McCrae's hotel did not collapse until six hours after the eruption, so guests and staff were able to escape. The searchers from Rotorua were surprised, at first, to find people alive, but they found tragedies, too. Although the schoolteacher's wife was dug out alive, three of her children had died beside her in the suffocating debris. The village was buried in rock and ash to a depth of five or six feet, and the slimy grey mud from the bottom of Lake Rotomahana added to the desolation.

No wonder people had left Rotorua with its geysers and bubbling mud pools near the foreshore. Further away, the faint-hearted felt New Zealand was no place for them 'when Tamaohoi awoke', there were other volcanoes, supposedly extinct — and earthquakes — and floods.

In Australia, rumour had it that the whole of the North Island had blown up — grey ash falling thickly on the decks of steamers in mid-Tasman lent colour to this story. By the time cables reached England, it was rumoured that New Zealand had disappeared altogether.

Old Tuhoto, who had prophesied the eruption (indeed, some Maoris said he had caused it), was dug out of his hut four days after that dreadful night, still alive.

The Maoris wondered why the pakeha did not leave him there, instead of taking him to the Sanatorium. They were not unhappy when the old man died a few days later, 'because,' they said, 'the nursing people cut off the ariki's long white hair.'

16

William would have left these unkind shores, as had several families, particularly those living in and around Rotorua. Others, even from Te Wairoa itself, had made another start: Falloona's had moved into the town, opening there the guest-house, Waiwera House, where a grandchild of Caroline's would stay thirty years later. Caroline was made of the same stern mettle; they would remain in Napier. Besides, how could one go to another country without any settled job, with three sons and a baby daughter? Certainly the fare to Sydney was only $1 — the competition between Huddart Parker and Union Steamship had resulted in cut price fares — but from all that they could hear, Australia was no better off than New Zealand. There was, too, that old slur of convict settlements. Caroline might be more tolerant than many of her generation, disregarding the almost recent Maori troubles; but she was just as narrow as many others concerning the original settlement of what she thought of as 'Australia.' She had no idea of the vastness of that country compared with the tiny seaboard penal colonies begun a century earlier.

Prices for wool and grain were improving. That first shipment of frozen meat from Port Chalmers in the ship Dunedin had opened up new prospects for farmers, and so for the economy of the country. If William had been interested in working on the land — but he was not. His wife had only to think of the vegetable garden to realise that his idea of market gardening had followed the pattern of the Kentish orchard. He would never work as the pioneers had done, labouring with their own hands to make a home out of the tall timber.

Possibly thinking of the irascible old gentleman in England, William quietly vetoed any idea of naming the second little girl after Caroline's sisters. 'Astrid' and 'Ingrid' were really too Norwegian to link to an English surname. He did not mind 'Henry' for 'Henrick', and 'Ronald' for 'Roald', but how could one translate these foreign-sounding girls' names? Why not call the chuckling baby 'Helen', after the ship he had travelled on? In this matter, her husband's word was law for Caroline.

Even over the question of leaving New Zealand, Caroline had not needed to argue; William lacked the drive and energy to make such a move, and Caroline had quietly let the matter lapse. It was she who would have needed to make the decision and the arrangements, though she would have kept in the background to make them appear William's doing, as was right and proper.

The Tarawera eruption had one good result for the family. William's father broke the silence of years, writing to ask if 'William and his wife had been safely rescued from the volcanic eruption.' To the old gentleman any part of New Zealand, let alone the North Island, was a neighbouring village. He was as ignorant of the great stretches of mountain, plain and bush as any of the first bewildered immigrants. Having determined to forget that he had a son, he certainly never bothered to find out about that primitive colony from where he last heard of him. Indeed, his earlier expressed preference for Danes rather than Norwegians was based on complete ignorance. As for the query about being rescued from the eruption; unspoken though the thought was, both Caroline and William wondered if his father would not have been altogether broken-hearted if only the husband had escaped. It was difficult to forget the unkindness in the English letter written so many years earlier. Caroline could forgive, but she found it hard to forget. William rarely explained his thoughts, possibly because he did not clearly understand them himself.

Anxious about her little namesake, Caroline watched the first longed-for daugher becoming more sullen, more withdrawn; she acted almost as a stranger in this close-knit family group. In some ways she resembled her oldest brother, always apart from the others and away on some ploy of his own. There the similarity in temperaments ended: he was mischievous, dodging any tasks that he could. Little Caroline had no vivacity, she did as she was asked, but sullenly, bored with everything, including play with other children.

As Helen grew, a happy child, developing early, as if to catch up on this remote older sister, she would try, in her toddler's way to please her. Little Caroline would take no notice; it was Ronald who would wheel the baby for a walk, Ronald and Henry who would play with her, although Henry was away at school, and already finding odd jobs to help the household budget.

If William was late home from school, he had some tale of being kept in, catching the schoolmaster's horse for him (as if William would ever have bothered!) or returning a stray cow. Henry never gave him away. But more than once something appeared in

William's hands that suggested he could find well-paid jobs after school, if he wished.

Henry would like to help his father when he could, particularly if there was coach work to be done. Sometimes he would find a delivery job, but the elderly might be there first.

The oldest brother would wander down to the Port when he could get away. If he helped, the men might sometimes give him the leftovers from their lunch, or perhaps a few cents that usually went on food in the nearest store — two or three biscuits, if there was nothing else. No more raw turnips — young William knew more about ripening plums or apples than any boy at school.

As for school, he hated it. What use was it? Not all his father's insistence would keep him there longer than he could help. He wouldn't like work either, but he wanted wages. His father seemed free to choose what jobs he wanted. (Young William had no idea of his father's background; parents never discussed either past or present — or future — in front of the children. 'Little pitchers should be seen and not heard' was the maxim.)

The weary horse was no longer pulling sadly at the grass at the rear of the section. It had collapsed under William when he was riding to a job at Greenmeadows. At his request, a local farmer had dragged the body away with his bullock-team, to use it for 'dog tucker'. The saddle William left with the farmer — one of the boys could carry it back home one day, and perhaps take it into town to sell it. The long walk and the heavy load for a young boy did not enter the father's head; if he thought about that at all, he decided that William was old enough to carry the burden, not realising that William would dodge the task, which would end up on Henry's shoulders.

Urged on by Caroline, who could visualize her husband without work if he did not have some form of transport, he bought a penny-farthing, paying for it little by little. It took him some time to manage the odd contraption, which he felt to be a little beneath his dignity. A hack, or his father's dog-cart — they were suitable for a gentleman; but this bicycle idea really suited a sportsman of sorts, or perhaps a clerk — or even a labourer. He left the 'tradesman', as he was himself, out of his reckoning.

Young William found the penny-farthing a real delight — and that was the cause of another argument with his father. It was also an opportunity for the son to threaten to 'run away to sea' — that probably reminded Papa of a threat he had made, when he had been much older than this boy of twelve. With what William termed 'disrespectful behaviour' from his oldest son, and the sulky moroseness of his elder daughter, the family group was falling apart. Just as well Henry, Ronald and Helen always seemed biddable, and happy, too, together or apart, while Christine, a joyful little toddler, tagged along behind these older children.

The third little girl had to be Christine — William's choice again, with its suggestion of his wife's birth-place. Caroline suddenly found herself with more freedom than she had ever expected, with such a large family, for Helen liked to do everything for the baby — she was the complete mother.

17

The report of the Royal Commission on Sweating kept young William at school a little longer. Factory work had been available for a young boy; generally he was not indentured, though referred to as an apprentice. After a year or two on a low wage, he would be discharged with little knowledge of his craft, to make way for another youngster on low wages.

The recommendation that only those over fourteen, who had passed the Fourth Standard, should be allowed to work in factories blocked William's hopes of leaving school. He could not earn much, anyway — until he turned eighteen he would not be allowed to work more than forty-eight hours a week.

At least the recommendation cut down on his undiscovered truancy. He had to pass the fourth standard, he realised, in case some interfering inspector spoilt his chances.

Among other boring subjects, the school teacher tried to explain the new voting system at the General Election: 'One man, one vote'. William could not or would not understand the difference. Henry, three years younger, but in the same large classroom, could explain it to Father; William senior thought it was absolutely wrong that the down-and-outer, who still helped himself to their tank-water when there was no-one about, should have a say in the government of the country.

Caroline rejoiced that son William, three years later, was living in a bach in Onepoto Gully when women's suffrage was announced. He would have gone on arguing, if only to annoy his father. The latter, stern keeper of the Victorian tradition when it suited him, stated that it was not proper for women to vote. They had not a man's intelligence, therefore they could not make sound decisions.

As for mixed bathing (in neck to ankle costumes, rather than neck to knee), bicycle riding, and, horror of horrors, bloomers! — none of these became any womanhood but those referred to euphemistically as 'on the street'.

Nothing was right with the world, according to Caroline's husband. Occasionally he would say they should live in England, instead of in this brash young colony where 'Jack was as good as his master.' Despite the tradesman's work that kept the family in food, William somehow regarded himself as a gentleman decorator. If he could have chosen, he would have worked in only the 'best' homes.

Caroline set cleanliness above all other considerations; work properly done was the highest compliment. Her husband, on the other hand, regarded status as the symbol of perfection. Neither voiced these thoughts, so argument never arose. In some respects they were an ill-assorted couple, the woman hard-working beyond all else, the man really a dilettante in an environment little suited to his character.

Once or twice a year the Kentish orchardist would write to his son. Somewhat ungraciously worded, the letter generally contained a banker's draft 'for the grandchildren'. That amount swelled the inherited remittance a little, but until, if ever, William allowed his wife to take in laundry, he would have to continue with painting and papering. By now, with experience, he had become a reasonable tradesman; Henry, watching carefully, would sometimes help, doing a better job than his father.

Getting along very well, young William was cadging meals from family and friends, without subscribing to the household budget. Work at the Port (provided it did not demand too much energy), light jobs wherever he could find them, spending on no-one but himself — he was leading an enjoyable life.

Father and Henry had helped him knock up the bach, mostly out of dunnage or off-cuts round buildings. William would wander around construction sites, helping for the odd day when he could see something he could put to use.

As the family had grown, Father had put up a shed for the boys to sleep in, at the rear of the Greenmeadows house. When Henry, too, left school — at a younger age than William, for he had set his sights on Standard Six and passed that examination — the shed was dismantled, carried piece by piece on a borrowed hand-cart to the Gully, to make a lean-to on the bach. It was nearer Henry's work than the family home; both boys lived there, and it was clear that Ronald, too, would join them when he left school.

Despite longer hours and constant work, Henry was the cook. William could not — or would not — boil an egg. Henry was indentured properly to a coach painter; fine work with the brush was his delight. In later years his only task on the passenger coaches would be the fine lines and the heraldic coats of arms on the doors.

Young Caroline was as lazy at school as her oldest brother had been. In the home, too, she would do as little as possible. Care of the younger ones, baking, needlework — if she was asked to do anything at all, it was done with a grudge. Papa had tried commands, then the strap. It had not worked with William, and it was no help with Caroline.

Her mother began to long for the day when this daughter could go out to work. Living in would be the answer; young Caroline was capable, but unwilling at home. Perhaps it would be a different story with strangers, especially with people who paid her wages. To themselves, daughter and mother both wished the first job would be several days' coach ride away from Napier.

With trains taking less than a day to Wellington, that was hardly possible. Somewhere far down the east coast, towards Blackhead or Pongaroa, would be best. For young Caroline had the undoubted ability to upset Helen and Christine very easily. Perhaps jealousy was the root cause — yet why? Caroline had been asked to do no more than other members of the family; less, really, for Ronald was looked after by Henry. These fits of sulks had shown up long before Helen was born.

18

Occasionally a letter with the postmark of a foreign port came from Roald. He had been sailing out of Tauranga 'when Tamaohoi awoke', so he had known his sister and her family were safe. To him the eruption was just such a storm on shore as he weathered so frequently at sea. The early experience of being adrift near the Sargasso Sea was not the only wreck he had lived through.

He arrived on the doorstep unexpectedly one day. Just as well Caroline had not known he was on the *Wairarapa*, he thought. The story of that disaster had appeared in the local newspaper a week or two earlier, mentioning only the names of the Captain and a few crew. They had been drowned when a freak wave swept them off the bridge. At first 113 were reported missing, the total later rising by twenty or more.

Caroline was delighted to see her brother, and the girls clustered round him, happy to see this uncle who had visited so many foreign places. Only young Caroline stayed apart; he was just any visitor, to her.

His sister overlooked asking him where his ship was berthed. Soon Helen and Ronald were asking enthusiastic questions about ships and ports. Was his ship in Port Ahuriri? Or had he come from Port Nicholson? By the train?

Ronald remembered all his life that first train trip with Mother to Havelock. He was sent off to the Gully to tell his brothers that their uncle had arrived. When Father returned from work, with the older boys, one of their early queries was about their Uncle's present ship.

'I've no ship just now,' Roald replied.

'Oh, are you going to settle somewhere?' asked Caroline, 'somewhere near?'

'No, I'll be going back to sea, that's my life.'

'Why haven't you got a ship, uncle?' asked his namesake.

'Give your uncle a chance to tell us,' interjected Father.

'You mustn't think about it, Caroline, but I was on the *Wairarapa*.'

'Oh no! Oh Roald, thank goodness you are safe!' Caroline exclaimed.

'Did you swim ashore?' asked Helen. She was thinking of their quiet games in the sea when the bay was quiet.

'No, my dear girl, no-one could have

lasted in that sea. Two brave men took a line ashore — '

'What fun!' said Henry.

'Not fun, children,' interrupted Father. 'I read the newspaper report. It was very rough.'

'So rough that the lifeboats were swamped. Even the bridge was swept overboard, with the Captain and most of the officers.'

'Was it a desert island?' enquired Christine. Brother Ronald had been telling her the story of Robinson Crusoe.

'In good weather it's a beautiful place, forest and birds, and sweeping beaches.'

'Did you land on one of those beaches?' William asked. The less he could bother with reading, the better.

'Don't you look at a newspaper, William?' demanded his father. 'Your mother knows more than you do about the news of the day.'

'We got ashore on the rocks at the foot of those 600 foot high cliffs of Miners Head,' Roald explained. 'It was a shocking night — very dense fog — I've seldom seen such a heavy backwash. That's what stopped the first two volunteers from getting the rope across. They might have been able to save more lives if they hadn't had to let the line go, to get ashore.'

'Tell us more about the storm — how did the passengers die?' demanded young Caroline ghoulishly, with her first sign of interest.

'No,' said her mother, watching Christine's saucer eyes, 'perhaps later.'

'You won't even let uncle talk!' Caroline interjected very rudely.

The old behaviour — in front of her uncle, too.

'Go to your room, Caroline!' commanded Father.

'Perhaps I could tell you about the island, now,' Roald said, 'and then when my little nieces are in bed — '

'Don't bother,' snarled Caroline. 'No-one ever does what I want.' Walking away, she slammed the door.

In the silence that followed, Roald asked what had upset her.

'She's always the same,' his sister answered, sadly. 'I don't know where I've made mistakes with her. The others have all responded to our discipline.'

'Never mind, mother,' said her husband. 'We'll deal with her later. You said, Roald, that the island — Great Barrier, wasn't it? — was a beautiful place.'

'Or was that for little pitchers?' asked young William, considering himself one of

145

the adults. In fact, despite his being three years older than Henry, the latter was much more mature.

'It's true,' Roald said. 'Anywhere but on those rocky headlands, below cliffs that can't be scaled, there are safe harbours — Port Fitzroy and Whangaparapara, though that's rather shallow, and Tryphena. On the ocean side — the east — the surf rolls in from the Pacific, but there's little backwash.'

'Didn't you take a load of kauri from there some years ago?' Caroline reminded him.

'Yes. You've a good memory for place names, sister. It was from Whangaparapara — we used to run the scow onto the beach.'

'Were the trees felled on the shore-line?' asked Ronald.

'No, there were huge kauris up in the valley, some miles away.'

'Did they drag them out with bullock-teams, as they did in the Bush?' Caroline enquired.

'Not up there. Few tracks wide enough for a team, and very steep. No, it was more like what Henrik first wrote to us about the American lumber — the logs were sent down to the shore by water.'

'There must be some big rivers on the island, then,' commented Ronald.

'No — on Great Barrier they are only streams, though there's a fair amount of water in flood-time. But the bushmen built a big dam first, with rocks and pit-sawn kauri. Then they rolled felled logs into the dam, and let the water go when they had enough logs for a shipment. You could hear the thundering roar as they shot down, where you waited on the beach at Whangaparapara — there was a whaling-station there, too, not so long ago.'

'How did you load those big logs onto the scow?' asked Henry.

'When I was there, we towed rafts of logs across to the mainland — we needed to avoid storms, though.'

'Where did they use that kauri?' his brother-in-law asked.

'Mainly in Auckland, William,' Roald replied. 'Any kauri for the west coast was usually cargo from the Northern Wairoa.'

'Did you often go down to Port Nicholson, uncle?'

'I wasn't in that port as much as in others. The ship I was on before the *Wairarapa* berthed there — Wellington was its only New Zealand port of call.'

'Is it like Napier?' Caroline asked, ' — or Christiania?' (the only two ports she had seen.)

147

'It's a magnificent deep water port,' replied Roald. 'But the entrance, seven or eight miles from the town, can be tricky. There's Pencarrow Head to starboard and Barrett's Reef to port.'

'They're doing great things with deepening harbours and building breakwaters — Napier's will make a great difference to the size of vessel that can be handled,' commented William.

'I don't think they could shift that reef in a thousand years,' said Roald. 'Of course the uplift all along that coast-line in 1855 probably shallowed the entrance. It would be interesting to look at old charts.'

'Are they building piers and wharves in Port Nicholson?' Henry asked.

'It's changing all the time,' replied Roald. 'About ten years ago we took the kauri for the Gear Meat Company's building on the main street right onto the beach. We ran the scow up at low tide, and the timber only had to be dragged across the road to the building site.'

'What's the greatest change?' William enquired.

'Parliament, maybe, now the Provinces have gone. But from my point of view,' continued Roald, 'the reclamations and the wharves. The days of the scow are numbered, except around Hauraki Gulf and Banks Peninsula.'

By now Caroline was bustling about, preparing a meal. Young Caroline came to help, for once without being asked, a little ashamed that she had behaved so badly in front of her uncle. Could he open the door for her to escape from home? She could not leave school yet, but always she kept an eye on any opportunity.

'It took three or four days before the news of the wreck of the *Wairarapa* reached Auckland,' commented William. 'The island isn't far from the mainland, is it?'

'No — only about twelve miles from Tryphena to the nearest land — but that's Cape Colville, so you're just as cut off there as if you were still on an island,' Roald explained. 'It's about fifty miles into Auckland itself, but you could land on the east coast beaches, north of the town, or at the Sandspit, inshore from the old Governor's place on Kawau Island.'

'Why did the news take so long, then?' his brother-in-law asked.

'There can be fairly stormy seas in the Hauraki Gulf. If there's nothing bigger than a whaler, you wouldn't want to risk the crossing. There are days when you'd be silly to row from one harbour to another — depends on the wind, of course.'

'How were you rescued from that headland, then?' asked Henry. 'Did you go overland?' The younger ones were having their meal.

'The centre of that island is all up and down — the highest point over 2000 feet, but it's the jumble of mountains and valleys that makes the tracks so long and steep. Maui's cunning brothers cut up the fish before the sacrifice could be made to the gods.'

'Who's this Maui?' asked his newphew William.

Ronald broke in. 'Don't you remember the story about the fisherman who caught the North Island?'

'Oh, yes, mother told us,' said Henry. 'Maui's enchanted fishhook is Cape Kidnappers.'

'Anyway,' their uncle continued, 'if you go over the Rimutakas by train to Wellington, you'll see what I mean. However, there you're looking at one mountain and one valley, by Crosscreek, but on the island I suppose there's hundreds.'

'It must be very difficult in emergencies,' Caroline interjected.

'That's right,' Roald agreed. 'They're going to start a telegraph service.'

'They couldn't put wires across that stretch of water, could they?' asked young William.

150

'It would be under-sea cables, anyway,' Henry corrected him. 'Like those under Cook Strait that linked the South Island with the North.'

'Not cables, either,' laughed their uncle. 'They're going to use pigeons.'

The young folk found this very amusing. When they had finished laughing, their uncle returned to the serious side of the subject.

'You wouldn't understand how much of a help that would be, boys. But your mother would — she remembers forest accidents when the doctor was twenty-two miles away. It took too long to get a message through and the doctor to come — the injured bushman died in the meantime.'

'Yes, I remember that very well,' said Caroline, stirring an iron saucepan on the stove. 'But island people would be worse off — more than twenty miles of stormy seas. At least we had a horse trail at first, then a coach route.'

'That's the difficulty on Great Barrier — if you're not in the bays or the harbours, it takes a long time to find help — it took ages to find a house, and we still had to get through to Fitzroy, where the *Argyle* could pick us up.'

'There've been other wrecks there, too, haven't there? asked Henry.

151

'Several, I think,' he answered. 'I know the *Lalla Rookh* was wrecked on the same headland seven years ago. Let's not talk about wrecks any more — I think your mother has heard enough. What are you doing with yourself, William?'

The talk became general.

Their mother was remembering the story of the phantom canoe on Tarawera before Tamaohoi awoke; she did not remind the children of it. That was another terrifying time to recall — this little country seemed to have more than its share of troubles. Still, there were wrecks in England, her husband had told her. And what about her father? But not her brother, too, please God (and thank You for saving him).

Roald was very interested in the family; William and Henry had shown him the nearly completed breakwater off the Bluff, as the most important sight for a seafarer. Almost he decided to look for a ship with Napier as its home port. There was very little sail left — he would have to move into steamers, though he did not like them much. The breakwater and the wharf would be more convenient than anchoring in the roadstead and sending ship's boats across the bar into Port Ahuriri. (Roald was not to know that the breakwater would not be a complete success, and the coastal shipping might again have to anchor in the roadstead, or return to the open sea.)

A week later they saw Uncle Roald off on the train for Wellington.

Did his sister think again about the phantom canoe? Or, as the train pulled out of Napier station for its daylong journey south did she recall the news of the disaster on the Rimutaka incline, when wind gusts blew two carriages off the tracks into a gully seventy feet deep? Her smile was what Roald remembered — she hid the tears and fears from him and from her children. Somewhere in her background, despite her very real and formal Christianity, were the suspicions of the old Norse sagas.

19

The house was very quiet when Roald had gone. Even young William seemed settled in a job; he and Henry were managing very well in the bach at Onepoto Gully. Henry was not far from the end of his apprenticeship; his mastercraftsman employer had told his father that the work was excellent — a little slow, but his signwriting was perfect.

Ronald was doing well at school; as Henry had done, he wanted to leave as soon as he passed Standard Six, and get on with his chosen work. He would be another coach painter, like his brother. He was not going to mark time until he was fourteen, like his oldest brother. Twelve now, he had the bigger Norwegian frame, like his mother and his uncle. Another year would see him achieve his ambition at school, and he was sure Papa would let him join the boys in the Gully.

Christine at five was always begging to be allowed to cook a meal for her brothers, as Helen did sometimes in the summer. At nine, Helen was a capable cook.

Sometimes, of course, her failures were fantastic, but Henry would quickly bury them for her, and replace the disaster with some of his own cooking. He never grumbled, although his wages would replace the wasted ingredients. One thing Helen should learn to make perfectly was an apple pie, a 'proper' pie, none of this stewed apples and throw a piece of cooked pastry on top. After the meal, failure or success, Henry would walk back to Greenmeadows with her; they were always home before the stars came out.

Caroline had only a cheerful little Christine at home — five was too young to walk the three miles to school and back. Perhaps at six — the schoolteacher wanted to keep roll numbers up, so he would not suggest that Christine should wait until she was seven. Her oldest sister had suffered from some kind of low fever — the doctor could not put a name to it — for months in her seventh year, thus she had started school only a year earlier than Helen.

It was just as well Caroline had the children off her hands. Now nearly in her mid-forties, she had lost energy and always felt tired; a disappointment to a woman who, at least from the time she had landed in the *Hovding* on the Napier beach, had worked happily from dawn to dark — and beyond, if candles could be afforded for sewing flour bags or materials.

Her husband, a little older, was slowing down, too, she noticed. He had a corporation on which to display his watch chain and keeper. His father, mellowing with every letter, had sent that out as a gift. She appeared to be thickening up, too, she who had always been gaunt and bony except when the babies were on the way.

When Christine pattered off to school one morning, with Helen holding her hand, Caroline felt very poorly. Young Caroline of course stalked on ahead — she wasn't waiting for babies. That was the last child gone from home — what was there to do all day? Moving slowly, she dealt with the usual chores; there was time, now, to sit in her husband's rocking chair, with idle hands. That worried her, too — 'the devil finds some mischief still for idle hands to do'. She rested till, guiltily, she saw by the imitation marble clock on the mantelshelf that young Caroline would be home soon.

The stew was already simmering on the stove — that was the only way to cook stringy ewe mutton. Although the boys were keeping themselves, her husband's wages never stretched any further; there were still four children to be fed and clothed. And Papa did not go short — she did not expect that of him. The carefully darned clothes were hers; when his reached that stage, she cut them down for the children: a skirt for Christine could be made out of Papa's trousers, now that Ronald was earning a little as an errand boy after school, and he was too well-grown for his father's hand-me-downs, anyway.

Sometimes she would find ends of material in the draper's shop. Christine and Helen could be clothed in this way. Caroline loved to see them looking pretty; her oldest daughter preferred to look ugly and untidy, but the little ones took pleasure in being neat.

Their mother used the goffering iron for all the ruffles round the legs of the white pantaloons. Although she found it so tiring in the heat of the summer, the frocks would be ironed with Mrs Potts irons standing on the hob of the stove, starched first to make that crisp rustle as the girls started off for school.

Daughter Caroline was quite capable of washing and ironing for herself; but she would wear her clothes until her mother felt she was a 'dirty' child. Asked to iron, she would fail to clip the wooden handle properly into the hot iron, and drop the latter on the hearth bricks. Every chip — and there were a good few — would have been made by this eldest daughter dropping the iron. Or she burnt herself when she checked the sole of the iron with a moistened finger, to test the heat. Worse still, she would forget to rub the iron on the waxed cloth, in order to clean it — result, a scorch mark that no amount of salts of lemon would shift, usually on the front breadth of a Sunday School frock.

Helen was not always perfectly behaved (for which her mother was quite grateful); as she grew older she found it trying to lag behind with Christine while other girls in her class ran and skipped ahead.

A plaintive little voice would call 'Wait for me, Helen, wait for me.' Christine realised quickly that asking her other sister to wait was a waste of breath. If there was an answer, it was an unkind sneer about short, fat legs — or 'Mother's girl — is she frightened?'

Helen did not mean to leave her little sister behind. She would forget her sometimes, as she chattered away to classmates and kept in a group away from some of the bigger boys who liked to pull hair and steal hair-ribbons. (Woe betide the girl when she reached home! Hair ribbons were costly for those on low wages.)

Home at almost the same time as sister Caroline one day, Helen was asked where Christine was.

'Oh, she's — just coming, mother,' stammered Helen, who could not remember where she had last seen Christine.

Mother, busy at the ironing, let a little time pass.

'She's dawdling along, Helen — that road is too busy for her to be dreaming along, or picking wild flowers on one side or another.'

Young Caroline sneered. 'She's probably run away.'

'Don't be stupid, Caroline,' said her mother. 'Helen, would she have gone to play with someone?'

'She knows she mustn't do that, mother. I don't think she would.'

'Helen, you go along the road to look for her. It will get dark early tonight, the clouds are so heavy.'

'You peel the potatoes, Caroline — don't waste, peel them thinly. I think I might sit down till Christine comes.' Mother stumbled a little — what was the matter? To do daughter Caroline justice, it had never occurred to her that mother might fall ill — mothers were indestructible — but she looked ill now.

No sign of Christine down the long straight road. No sign of anyone. Mother was right, it was getting dark early. There was a flash of lightning on the hills above Rissington, and a rattle of thunder. Helen hated lightning — too many stories of narrow escapes, at school — but right back she would have to go. She had forgotten Christine, and she must, must find her.

Half a mile of the three gone, and she heard a weary little voice calling 'Help! Please, help. Help, please,' in hiccoughing sobs.

That voice came from the three foot drain. There was, Helen had time to think, only a foot or so of water in it — thank goodness there had not yet been any rain, or floods in the back country.

Helen peered over the lip of the ditch — there was a slimy grey little mouse-like creature.

'Christine, what do you think you are doing there?' she demanded in angry relief. The child looked unhurt.

'Oh Helen! Helen, help me!'

'Come on, Christine, what happened?'

'There was a bull — and my pretty red frock, it's all mud. And I ran and ran — but the bull was pawing the ground right behind me — and — '

'Did the bull toss you in?' asked Helen.

'No — I jumped in. And it snorted and looked at me, and tossed its horns for ages.'

'Well, I didn't see any bull. Why didn't you get out when it had gone?' Helen demanded. 'Mother is waiting for you — I had to come back to look for you, she was so worried.'

'I — I can't get out,' Christine began to cry. 'I slip down all the time.'

'Don't cry, Christine. Look — walk along that way, towards home. I could help you there.'

'It's all sticky and slimy, and it smells. And there's an eel!' she shrieked.

'The silly old eel won't hurt you. Come on.'

'I might sink in.'

'No, you won't,' said Helen, firmly. 'I'll hold your hand.' Clambering along the top of the ditch, Helen did so.

Presently she could lean down to grasp the two muddy little hands. Tugging one foot after the other out of the muddy bottom, Christine half crawled, was half dragged up onto the road.

Watercress clung round her ankles, green slime on the white pantaloons, mud all over the pretty dress where she had tried to climb out and slipped down again. There was even cress in her hair, where she had tumbled into the water to escape from the menace of the bull.

161

Helen was liberally coated with mud, too, where she had leaned over to help her little sister.

The only solution, back at home, was a warm bath in the iron tub in front of the stove. By then the little girls were both shivering, and a little fearful of what mother would do to them for getting their clothes so dirty.

But it wasn't like that at all. For a few minutes she cuddled her two warm, clean-smelling girls. The mud certainly smelled horrible, the sooner those garments could be washed the better.

A meal for Helen and Christine, and into bed.

As her husband reached home — he was working some distance away — she lifted the iron tub of water. Pain shot through her. Suddenly Caroline realised why she had felt so tired, why her body had thickened up.

A doctor was more readily available now. William did not wait to ask his wife, this time; he had decided. He sent his oldest daughter to bring the neighbour over, and in the storm that had hung off for the little girls he set out to get the doctor.

Next morning there was a tiny baby brother for the sisters to admire.

20

After William had written about the arrival of a new grandson to his father, a surprising reply came by return mail:

'Dear William,

I was glad to know you had another little son now the older boys are working, and your Ronald about to leave school. You say your wife is not recovering quickly, and you yourself are not very well.

'I am not able to see clearly, and the doctor says it may get worse. So I enclose steamer tickets for you and your wife to come to England and bring the little ones. No one lives in the 'Duchess of Edinburgh', the publican comes in every day. So you could all live there, and stay in Kent sometimes with me. Perhaps the two little girls would be quite happy to spend a holiday here without you for a few weeks.

'I don't know if your oldest girl would like to come. The ticket for her could be cashed, if not. But I would like you to make your home in London or Kent, now.'

Go to England? With a family? And leave the boys behind? That was more difficult for Caroline than it had been to leave her home in Christiania.

William was delighted. He wanted them to be on the next boat — in ten days' time. It was Caroline who pointed out that they should let or sell the house; the boys were managing very well, it was better for them to stay there than take charge of the house, so much further from work. And one did not want to travel too soon with baby Richard. Caroline, unfortunately, had heard a great deal about the babies that had died on the early immigrant ships. She did not realise how different a steamer would be from a sailing ship.

As for their oldest daughter: she was old enough to go into service as a 'tweeny', if they could find a good place for her. She must make up her own mind.

Daughter Caroline speedily did that. Go out to work, when she could go 'Home' for a trip? And do nothing? Perhaps her grandfather would find a nice young man she could marry; and she could live on an apple orchard, too. Although reluctantly, she even began to help with the sorting and packing.

The battered cabin trunks that had come

so far from different origins were dragged out. Father's frock coat was there, carefully shaken out by his wife every few months; in the other trunk, a small pile of embroidery, handworked in those days in the Bush and at Havelock, had grown discoloured with age. The baby clothes had been packed away there, too, those that had replaced others outworn by the first four or five of the family.

Fortunately the little white frocks suited baby boys just as well as they suited girls — Richard would be well dressed.

He was a placid, contented child, but baby care of any sort was anathema to his sister Caroline. Indeed when she had first seen the bundle in her mother's arms, the morning after Christine's rescue from the ditch, she had said, 'I didn't want that!' Young Caroline did not show any interest in or affection for the baby brother. Later, when he would be toddling about the upper floor of the 'Duchess of Edinburgh', he would soon learn to keep away from her — the roughest smacks on tiny hands that wanted to touch even the chairs left bruises lasting for days.

Helen, as with Christine, could have taken complete charge, had it been necessary. Christine loved Richard dearly, too — the

165

three young ones made a most affectionate family.

The change in Papa's attitude made life easier for them all. He seemed to be training himself to become the English gentleman again — not often now the surly grunts, the outbursts of temper over minor matters. In an oblique way his father had been right in forbidding the marriage, not because the wife he had chosen was Norwegian, but because William had not sufficient gumption to be a constant breadwinner and wise father. Of the type to avoid responsibility, once he had taken it on he was faithful and constant. But the effort showed, with little happiness or real affection for the family.

While Caroline tried to organise a trip 'Home', William swithered, at one stage agreeing that it was just a trip, the next stating that they would remain in England. Even about the Greenmeadows property he would not decide. He had been told that he could not expect caring tenants; there were much better houses vacant, where the requirements were a good reference and low rent.

Caroline and William had done their best for twenty years with what had been intended as a temporary home. A reasonable offer for purchase was rejected by William, who wanted enough to buy 'a good home in England'. Caroline, hearing this, thought she might not see her older sons again. Never mind, her husband was much brighter. It was doubtful if he had enjoyed life as a New Zealander.

The foreign stamps on letters from Uncle Roald were quickly scooped up by Helen. She saved them for the two brothers who had been encouraged to build up a stamp collection. Stamps were just rubbish to her oldest brother, but Ronald was particularly interested, Henry helping him along with neat lettering in an exercise book. The price of stamp albums put them out of the boys' reach.

Foreign stamps, foreign places, even the names of the ships were foreign. That was a peculiarly personal judgment for a family whose forebears were equally Norwegian and English. Maori names — the Waiwera, for instance — were not 'foreign', but Norwegian names were. Indeed, as far as Napier schoolchildren were concerned, all were Scandinavian, former disputes notwithstanding — Danish, Swedish, Norwegian — all Scandinavian, and more often the butt of racist jokes than the Maori.

While William made the decision to return

to England — the steamer tickets were there — sailings departed without the family. The Kentish orchardist wrote again: the children would enjoy the Diamond Jubilee celebrations; they could watch the procession from an upper floor.

Yes, they would arrive in time for the Jubilee. William acted as promptly as if he had received an invitation to Buckingham Palace.

The boys could keep an eye on the house, or move into it, if they wished. William had no sentimental attachment to his New Zealand home.

They sailed in April. The cabin trunks and heavy luggage were on board before the weather broke — no gales or rough seas to delay sailing. The ships could not remain moored to that new pier that ran out into Hawke Bay to the protective breakwater in heavy northerlies, but must move to anchor in the roadstead. Calm, almost oily seas, constant rain — inches of it, in the back country and in Napier itself. The drainage ditches along the roadsides filled rapidly, extra high tides adding to the level of the Inner Harbour.

William uneasily watched the water in the ditches rise. The cab was to come for them in an hour or so; would they be able to reach it? The boys came in, rain pouring from their sou'westers.

'We think you'd better leave early,' said the oldest son. 'It doesn't matter how soon you're on board — and you'd have to paddle out to the cab, if you wait too long.'

'They say the Ngaruroro's a banker, and Clive is already under water — the Tukituki is over its banks, too,' added Ronald.

'The Tutaekuri still has a few inches to spare, but you know how it spreads out down here,' Henry said.

'So we've asked your cab to come early. We knew Mother would be ready an hour before.'

Helen and Christine had been peering out the window ever since they were dressed. In vain for Mother to tell them the cab would not be there for hours! They saw the brothers arrive, left off window gazing to greet them, then were both back at the front window again.

'Here it is, Mother!'

'Here it is, Papa!'

This duet by the girls put the boys' minds at rest. It was still possible for mother to walk out to the road — soon, Henry thought, anyone would have to be carried out. None of them imagined what they would see when the younger members of the family and their

169

parents were well out in the ocean.

The Tukituki broke over Clive with a roar like thunder, the Ngaruroro broke its banks in six places, the Tutaekuri surged into Napier to a depth of four feet. Every ditch merged with every other, until there was little difference between the Inner Harbour and all the lowlying areas around its edge. The house that had served as 'home' for over twenty years found the floodwaters too much for it; by the end of that disastrous Easter, after fourteen inches of rain in four days, it had collapsed — quietly, like the old horse. Built originally as a makeshift and temporary shelter about forty years earlier, it had served its purpose; the damp area and light floodings had made the piles and purlins soft and rotten — not heart timber in the first place, of course. Soggy ground and debris piling up completed the demolition.

Did William know the condition of the house? Caroline sometimes wondered.

Nodding in her chair, she would hear those ship's bells again, on a voyage quite unlike the one she had made on the *Hovding*.

The chuckles and squeals of the little girls — steerage class now was a contrast to conditions prevailing earlier, and this ship was not full. Perth — or was it Fremantle? — the Indian Ocean, 'crossing the Line' with

170

Father Neptune and his trident, and fun for the little ones, too — the Red Sea and the flying fish — who had ever believed that fairy story? But it was true, and some flying fish would land on deck to prove it.

The Red Sea was rather a disappointment to Helen; she had expected more than the reflected glow of reddish sandstone or tropical sunset. The Suez Canal was of particular interest to William; to Helen and Christine it was a narrow stretch of sea with towns at each end, but Uncle Roald had written from here. At least the Mediterranean was blue; and they were butting up the Channel, the journey nearly over.

Ship's bells — and the mournful toll of a lightship somewhere as they entered the Straits of Dover, bound for Gravesend and Tilbury. They had made a good passage — they were in time for the Jubilee.

21

First there was grandfather, formally dressed and very formal in manner. If he was pleased to see them, the pleasure was not apparent. Nor was there any hint of displeasure or criticism; he greeted his son's wife just as he greeted his son.

The family had the run of the upper storey of the 'Duchess of Edinburgh' and of the big gloomy kitchen downstairs. It might be gloomy — and Caroline was finding a scrubbing brush smartly — but at least the range heated the water. No more boiling up kettles and saucepans for the weekly tub — it was a tub, of course, to be carried where it suited.

Within a day or two the children saw the short, dumpy figure of Queen Victoria driving in the State carriage to Westminster Abbey, flags flying from every building, bunting, souvenirs, children with miniature Union Jacks, cheers from thousands as the royal coach approached.

What days those were! The crowned heads of Europe were story book figures come to life. What interested them more were the mounted colonial troops, the New Zealand contingent commanded by Colonel Albert Pitt, and the newspaper pictures of the Maori haka at the banquet given in London to honour the Queen's Jubilee.

Nothing dampened the younger girls' enthusiasm; aged eight and eleven, they did not notice Mother's sad face. She had written to her two sisters in Norway that she was coming to England — their mother had died some years earlier. Now she must write again; this time it was Caroline who must send that formal card bordered in black. As they had been crossing the Tasman, some news had filtered through of a wreck on the rocky coastline west of Black Rocks and Cape Palliser. Possibly the ship had set too far into a lee shore in a southerly buster, and had no sea-room to come about. Or perhaps Te Humenga Point had been mistaken for Cape Palliser itself; then the vessel would have been away on a course that would have carried her up the east coast, if she had already weathered the Cape.

No-one William had met on board had paid much attention to the name of the ship or its port of registration.

★ ★ ★

173

Not long after the Jubilee celebrations, the owners of the *Zuleika* informed the next-of-kin that the vessel had run aground in Palliser Bay, with the loss of thirteen of the crew.

Caroline was never to see that sad mass grave on the rock-fringed coast; a grandchild, one day many years ahead, would read the memorial stone with its date of 13 April 1897. A few survivors struggled to the nearest homestead, and the news went through on horseback to Te Kopi and Lake Ferry. Roald did not survive this third major wreck.

Before the schools opened in September, William and Caroline took the family down by train to Kent. Grandfather's groom met them at the station, packing them all somehow into the dog-cart that held three adults comfortably.

There was not far to drive — the children would walk, on their next visit. They tried to be quiet and well-behaved. Grandfather admired their good manners, but he also enjoyed, surprisingly enough, their high spirits in the orchard. The commercial apples were picked, but he had made sure that there was still some late fruit to be gathered and eaten by these little kinspeople from over the seas. He had expected them to be savages, he had met them as strangers; now he really was

'Grandfather', enjoying the relaxing emotions with some amazement at his former thoughts. Obviously, in spite of their mother's being a 'Scandy', she was an excellent wife and maternal parent. Grand-daughter Caroline, however, would not unbend at all.

As the English summer, a jubilee summer, turned into autumn, the leaves filled the gutters and the fogs began to drift in. Napier might have cold winds, but this damp chill was worse. When winter came, the children enjoyed going to school, especially when it snowed. It would be spring before Mother would feel like taking them to the orchard, to see the pink and white blossom that reminded her of 'home'. Little Richard kept his mother busy, while daughter Caroline made every effort, it seemed, to upset her father.

She wanted him to turn her away, it appeared, as his father had treated him, with less reason, twenty-five years earlier. She was a big, gaunt girl, plain of feature, as ugly and untidy as she could manage to be under mother's watchful eyes. In that area, on the fringes of poverty, she was one of the oldest pupils, yet not much ahead of Helen in school work.

But where was one of those New Zealand women, regarded as uncivilised by the

London houses that might employ them, to find a position where the family reputation was unchallenged? Mother had very strict views on society's behaviour; much of what she heard she did not like. The phrase 'The Naughty Nineties' might not have been current, but the behaviour of the more strident would invent it. When her daughter lamented the fact that she was too young to be a barmaid, she was bundled off to Kent.

For once Mother put her foot down.

Speaking to William, she said, 'Your father is not impressed with Caroline's behaviour. Nor am I. But if you hadn't brought us all to England, she would be in service in a home I could have made enquiries about.'

That was true. William, as an Englishman, could have checked out some of the circumstances in London. But he drifted on — their lodging was free, the quarterly remittance came in, he painted a little, he enjoyed being behind the bar; not as the barman — never — but as the owner's son. What difference that made to the job of filling pewter mugs with beer Caroline could not fathom.

The troops went away to the second Boer War with the usual cheers and tears. News came through that the New Zealand contingent was the first of the Australasian forces to land in South Africa. For a while it seemed that sacrifices would be in vain.

Then came the bonfires of rejoicing with the Relief of Kimberley, Ladysmith and Mafeking, the day that Helen remembered most clearly of the three. The troops should be home soon. It was the bonfires and the flags that took little Richard's eye; the reason for them did not matter to a five-year-old. Mother knew the older boys were at home in Napier; she would like to see them, but William was firmly settled here in London. She had accepted her brother's death; ties with her sisters, never very strong, had been reduced to a silk card at Yuletide. With young cousins the family had no contact at all. Small wonder that Richard was such a joy to her, the remaining company, until he, too, attended a London school.

Grandfather asked the children to stay for short periods. He had sent Caroline, his grand-daughter, to local friends, who tried to regard her as family as well as a domestic. She would have none of that. She did her work well, so well that her employers could think up no excuse to send this sulky young woman back to her grandfather, a close friend of their father. They had wished she would leave of her own accord. Not she; the wages were good, the position was concerned with light duties only. Nowhere else would she find such advantages; she would never overstep the mark, giving her mistress a reason to send her back to the family. There were no young children — she would not suffer children, especially young ones.

If she went up to London on a 'free' week-end, she loathed it. Let her go up during the week when the children would be at school. Her employers accepted her excuse, that 'she would see more of her mother when her brother and sisters were at school' — but that was nonsense, as everyone knew, though the knowledge was never aired.

Still the watchman would pass with his lantern: 'Ten o'clock of a fine night, and all's well,' he would shout, as he rang his bell.

The turn of the century emphasised to Caroline the fact that the younger family was now growing up as English, while the older boys were New Zealanders 12,000 miles away, making lives of their own. Papa had settled down in a world he knew; he preferred the home in Kent, of course, but meanwhile he would put up with the 'Duchess of Edinburgh'.

What was all this rejoicing? It was just

one more year in an alien country. Caroline had not been homesick for Christiania, or for Dannevirke (Hans's imminent proposal was the difficulty there). But how she longed for Napier — floods, storms, wrecks in the Bay, even bulls chasing her little daughter — she would prefer it all to these little velvet suits with Lord Fauntleroy collars which Richard wore, and to the girls growing out of schooldays but not into a working future.

In January the bells tolled again; 82 bells to mark the passing of that Queen whose Jubilee had brought them to London. In far away Auckland all the fire bells were tolled, with an interval of a minute between each peal. The colony had joined in the Jubilee celebrations, sent soldiers to the Boer War and welcomed over one thousand British troops to New Zealand; Queen Victoria had sent them on from the Australian Federation Celebrations, to exemplify the unity of Empire — Life Guards, Royal Artillery, Highlanders.

Certainly William would have come home some time — if only the children had been a little older, if the girls could have gone into service in New Zealand, so that their mother would have had a reason for leaving this still unfriendly world. She was not an English-woman, not a barman's wife, not a publican's wife; and not an owner's wife, despite William's pretensions, for his father still kept a firm hand on apple orchard, cider presses and his outlet at the 'Duchess'.

The drays would arrive, and the barrels of beer as well as the cider from the home orchard would be rolled from the footpath down into the cellar — peals of thunder she always hated.

Sometimes from the windows she would watch William standing by the horses, or helping to roll the barrels across the muddy path to the cellar trap-door. Caroline never knew why one day he stayed in the cellar after he had unlatched the door for the delivery; or why a barrel should suddenly roll in a different direction. Was he trying to shift something? She would never know.

For some days, while he lay crushed and broken on the upper floor, the clip-clop of the hansom cabs was muted by the straw laid in front of the public-house. The doctor would not suggest bleeding or leeches; the skull, fractured when he had first been knocked down between hogshead and cellar wall, would respond to no known treatment.

Funeral bells again.

William's father came up from Kent for the funeral, trying to show his affection

for the fatherless children. Black clothes
and hats for all of them, widow's weeds
for Caroline — widow's weeds for always.
Daughter Caroline was, as usual, remotely
withdrawn; nothing seemed to touch her.
She had not mourned her uncle's death;
now she behaved with Victorian funereal
decorum, but there was no emotion behind
that neat attire of mourning.

If Richard or Christine cried for Papa, their
oldest sister would say harshly: 'It's no use
crying, your father's dead.' Did she resent
leaving her position? For her employers had
told her that they must spare her to be with
her mother, a widow with all those young
children. They had praised her work, but
they had not asked her to return when her
mother was settled. A cheerful personality
who was less reliable as a domestic would
suit them better, though this of course they
did not say.

And what was Mother to do?

Grandfather offered to pay for the children's
education; after that he would keep the girls
with him in Kent until they married. Richard
was a bright boy, he should be sent to a
good preparatory school and after that to a
public school — he could come home to
Kent in his holidays. It would be better
for Helen and Christine to live there now,

a London public-house was no place to bring up fatherless children.

No reference to the mother's future was made by Grandfather. He employed a married couple, housekeeper and orchard manager who had been with him for years. He had a good cook, too, the groom's wife. No changes were envisaged or required.

Was his daughter-in-law to find a position with strangers as a housekeeper? She did not know. All Caroline realised was that the young family was being removed, and the older ones were far across the seas.

She sold little pieces of jewellery and china — no use pawning them, they would never be redeemed. She had a small hoard of gold sovereigns, enough for two full fares (daughter Caroline was too tall and bony to pass as a child) and three half-fares.

22

When Grandfather came up from Kent to take the girls and Richard back, to make their home with him, the pilot was dropping off the steamer at Gravesend — they were returning to the bottom of the world.

Young Caroline was furious: she did not want to go back to domestic service. Why should she? However, even at seventeen years of age she had not the gumption to stand on her own feet in a strange country. No young men were attracted to her — she never wondered why. It was a case of everyone being out of step but herself; whatever went wrong, it was always someone else's fault. (Richard's preferably, or Christine's or Helen's — rarely did she dare to blame her mother, yet after all it was her mother who had made the decision to return to New Zealand.)

The girls were older now, no longer allowed a free rein on the ship, as they had been coming over. Richard, however, could wheedle his way round most people without realising it. Young Caroline sat primly in a corner, lips firmly pursed, disapproving of all and sundry. Her mother was at her wits end. She would not get this gawky stranger off her hands. To make matters worse, young Caroline — how she resented that reference, yet she would not respond to a nickname or an abbreviation — had acquired an accent that was neither truly English nor was it the speech of the New Zealander.

Cheerful Helen would be offered the first place for which she applied. She was better educated than was needed for domestic service — rather a pity, thought her mother — but the only other opening would be in a factory. Those wages would perhaps feed her; they would not provide housing. Mother had used all her carefully guarded savings to bring the family back to New Zealand.

Christine, nearly thirteen years old, would have to go into domestic service, too.

The next question was where Richard and his mother would — could? — live. In the bach at Onepoto Gully — until she found a position as housekeeper or cook where her employers would accept a seven-year-old boy? She would have to move quickly; she did not want the boys to buy the food for them for too long.

They didn't even know the rest of the family was on the water. One could send a cable, Caroline knew; but not even from

184

Fremantle would she consider it. Every penny — she would have been disgusted with American terms like 'cent' and 'dollar' — was counted, as it would help to pay bread and dripping. No lollies were bought from the purser this voyage. Caroline hoped there would be no duty to pay on the clothes the children had worn for the funeral. No others were new; from the day William had died, nothing but food was bought, and the cheapest of that. It was back to the first days of the house near Greenmeadows.

Among those who shared the twenty berth steerage cabin was Mrs Smith, from a London street near the 'Duchess of Edinburgh'. The day they were to land, Bobby Smith suddenly put on weight. He could hardly move.

Caroline was horrified.

'Dear, oh dear, Mrs Smith!' she exclaimed. 'What disease has Bobby got? They'll put us into quarantine. Or has he got at some poison? He looks dreadful! — Richard, you keep away!'

'He's quite all right, it isn't catching,' his mother replied. 'Those customs officers aren't going to take any money off me.'

'But what's that got to do with Bobby's illness?'

'Everything.'

'They won't ignore you because your son

is ill, Mrs Smith — I do think the ship's doctor should see him,' advised Caroline.

'He'll be all right when we leave the wharf,' Mrs Smith explained. 'I made sure I bought enough suits to last Bobby the next five years. — They told me you could only buy flax skirts, kilts, really, in New Zealand — So he's got to wear them all till we're out of the Customs House.'

Poor Bobby — a hot Napier day, three full suits and four jerseys! Four pairs of sox and the largest pair of shoes — he could not wear more than one pair of shoes, but the others were grubby and apparently scratched.

They landed directly on the wharf, no longer needing to transfer to ship's boats to land on the beach, as Caroline had when she sailed in the *Hovding*, or to cross the bar from the roadstead into Port Ahuriri. No queries were raised regarding the children's clothes; Caroline watched with a smile as Bobby staggered along on his mother's supporting arm.

The cabin trunks came off — they could not carry those to the Gully. It would be a long hot walk anyway, especially tiring for Richard. Would her oldest daughter sit by the luggage until one of the boys could get a hand-cart?

Before Caroline could refuse, her mother

186

offered an alternative. 'Or will you take the children to the bach, and wait there till one of your brothers gets home?'

'I'm too busy,' she snapped. 'I'm going straight to the registry office — there's bound to be a job in the country, and I'm not staying one night in that horrible bach.'

Her mother wished this daughter were younger — perhaps her husband's ruling maxim of a 'clip over the ear' would have helped. It would have helped the tired and anxious mother, anyway.

Quietly, Helen asked, 'What would you yourself like to do, Mother?'

'Would you mind waiting here — near the pier, Helen. Perhaps Christine wouldn't mind waiting with you, while Richard and I walk along under the Bluff to town?'

'We wouldn't mind at all, Mother,' Christine broke in, 'and we're big girls now, you don't need to worry. Do let Caroline do what she wants!'

'You needn't try to soft-soap me, Christine,' interrupted Caroline. 'Don't think you'll get any of my wages!'

'I'd rather starve!' retorted Christine.

'Be quiet, girls, that will do! Caroline, you go up to the registry office. Don't take any job without finding out first if there's a decent woman in the house — and that it's a decent house.'

'You've told me before,' she grumbled. 'But I won't work where there's children. They drive me silly — always falling over, or shouting, or breaking things.'

Young Caroline started off. Although the road below the hill led to the shopping area, she was not going to walk with those chattering magpies, Christine or Helen — or with Mother and Richard, who would skip along so happily. His very freedom of movement annoyed her. Back at the wharf, they would spend the next hour discussing who should stay and who should walk to the Gully in this heat. Her sisters, the fools, would try to insist that their mother have the more pleasant task.

Mother looked sadly after Caroline. 'Papa's death has made life very difficult,' was all she said. 'Now, girls, it might be better if you walk up — ' Mother had begun to worry about two pleasant looking girls lingering round the wharves. Papa would not have considered it for a moment; but Richard would be certain to get restless, staying in one place for hours. Unless William was not working just now — the last letter had been one of sympathy after their father's death, and had told her nothing. Ronald had been the writer, expressing sorrow and sending good wishes to mother from these three sons.

When the news of their father's death had reached them, it was William who had wondered what their mother would do.

'She'll probably want to come back to Napier,' Henry replied.

'We could build on another lean-to for Richard,' said Ronald, adding, 'There'd be room here for mother.'

William would have none of it. 'If Mother comes here, I go!' he threatened. 'I'm leading my own life — it's bad enough with you two about.'

'How would Mother manage?'

'She can stay in England with the children,' stated William. 'Grandfather can keep them, he sounds as though he has plenty of money — the dog-cart and the groom, the orchard and the pub.'

'We were talking about if Mother comes back — ' Henry reminded him.

'Mother will write to tell us what she plans, I'm sure,' said Ronald.

'She can write,' agreed William. 'But she's not coming here with the brats — or without them, for that matter.'

Henry and Ronald looked at each other. Often this three-way arrangement irked them. Usually, particularly peaceable Henry, they did not argue; William took charge and his younger brothers did the work. He put less into the kitty, too — he took a casual job when money was getting short and he could feel that his brothers were about to refuse loans. (They were rarely repaid.)

Caroline had a fair idea of the tenor of this conversation. William would not lift a hand to help, Ronald and Henry would do more than they should. And she was not going to follow the pattern of her childhood, she thought then, when her brother had given most of his wages to their mother. If Roald had not helped to support them those first few years, would he have gone to sea? Would he be still alive?

No, none of the boys was to go short for Richard and her. She had decided to leave England — grandfather would have provided for the girls and Richard if she had stayed.

But he would have sent the youngest son to boarding school. Besides, since her husband's death, Caroline was bitterly recalling that first refusal from William's father. William had been forced to explain why his father refused to welcome Caroline. There was that other letter, too, not long after the wedding in Havelock. Caroline had not seen it, of course.

However, William's anger at the time

suggested that there had been some sneering remark. At the London school, too, the children were sometimes upset by fellow pupils jeering at their origin. Grandfather had tried, in his gentlemanly way — and you had to admit that he was a gentleman, although with the narrow outlook of a particular age — to cover up his dislike of most foreigners. But that antagonism showed through the veneer of manners occasionally, especially if the Scandinavian countries happened to be under discussion.

In her widow's weeds of heavy black serge, Caroline sat on one of the cabin trunks, thinking, planning. Now cargo was clunking onto the wharf. A curious glance or two had come her way; one or two of the labourers had asked if she needed any help. Could they call a cab for her?

She was glad that she had sent the girls on — they would, without thinking, have accepted the offer to put the heavy luggage on the wagons, and then the cartage would have to be paid. The boys — well, Henry and Ronald — would spare the few coppers needed, she knew, but she would accept as little as possible. Shelter and food until they could all find jobs, and may it be soon!

Meanwhile Helen and Christine were walking towards the town, up a road busy with laden wagons going to the business area, empty wagons returning to the wharf for another load. The draft horses, most of them well cared for, reminded Christine of the horses that drew the brewers' drays in the streets of London. Helen, more observant, noticed the tired old hacks of some teams, and the wagoner's whip.

'That horse,' she remarked, pointing to a drooping head, where a dray was standing in front of a public-house, 'reminds me of Father's.'

'Did he have a horse?' asked Christine. 'You mean Grandfather's?'

'Oh no, Christine. Grandfather would be quite cross if you thought this tired old nag was the same as his spanking Cleo with the dog-cart.'

'I didn't see Papa's horse,' Richard piped up.

'That was before you were born, Dick.'

Away from Mother, who had no liking for nicknames, Richard preferred 'Dick'. There was no doubt that in this colonial setting he would soon have his own way.

When the little party turned into Emerson Street, Helen remarked on the differences between London and Napier. One storey shops mainly, built of wood, rusty iron roofs — few of the brick buildings so common in London, no tiled roofs. Very few private carriages were moving along the roads. At a cab stand there were one or two tired looking pairs, each horse munching quietly from a nose-bag, the cabs less shiny than those in London. Saddle horses were tied to hitching rails, tossing heads and jingling bridles indicating breeding or impatience. Their riders were men in from the country — not here the smart jodhpurs and jackets of those who rode for exercise and status in Rotten Row. Riding here was a necessity, not a luxury or a pleasure.

Helen wondered if she could go to the registry office, while the younger ones waited. Just to give them her name in case something came up in the next day or two would not take long.

It was Christine who reminded her that Caroline would still be there.

'You know what she is. She'll be sure you're following her,' Christine added, 'or trying to beat her to the best offer.'

'You're quite right — and a ding-dong row in there,' pointing to the 'Domestics Wanted' placard that was more noticeable than the 'Registry' sign over the paint-peeled door, 'would stop both of us from getting a place. The lady might look sideways at members of the same family coming in one after another for jobs.'

Richard was lagging a little. His London school had not been as far from the 'Duchess of Edinburgh' as the Greenmeadows school from the girls' home. At his age, they had walked longer distances on rougher roads.

Back at the Breakwater, as it was still known, to distinguish it from 'the Port' (Port Ahuriri), Caroline dragged a trunk further into the shelter of a wharf office.

Presently one of the young officers who had been a shipmate of Roald's years before strolled past. He was off watch now — it was time to look at this town he had not berthed at before.

Steerage passengers were beneath the officers' dignity usually. Some regarded the lower berths as cargo holds; there were still cruel stories of suffering at the hands of men like Captain Nordby of the *Hovding* on its second sailing to Napier. Mostly in these days of steam, steerage class was ignored by officers, while saloon class was paid every attention.

This Third Officer, however, had noticed at the Company's office the surname of the shipmate with whom he had lost touch. Len Jones had long thought that some day in a distant port he would come across

194

Roald again. Although the latter was much older, he had been a good friend, and a help on a strange and not very comfortably run ship.

During the voyage Len had been shocked to learn, when he talked to Caroline, that he never would meet Roald again. The wreck of the *Zuleika* had ended that valued friendship. He was sorry for the sister, too; wrecks and drownings were part of a sailor's life, but Caroline had lost her husband through a freak accident on land.

There was little he could do to help in those difficult days, but he took Richard under his wing; if the oldest daughter had been at all welcoming, he might have seen marriage with her as a solution for one member of that large family.

Young Caroline ignored him. Let that Third Officer talk to that saloon passenger, not come making up to steerage women. What did he think she was? It was in vain for Mother to explain that Uncle Roald had written about his friend Len Jones. Caroline did not believe her, and made it clear that Len could look elsewhere. Helen was a little too young, Len thought, and a great help to her mother. Perhaps when his ship next tied up at Napier?

He stopped to chat to the solitary widow.

Could he be of assistance? Call a cab? She was not to proud to explain that one of the boys, probably Ronald, would come down for the luggage.

'Ronald?' Len asked. 'Or Roald?'

'Ronald,' Caroline answered. 'My husband wanted our children to have English names, so I did not suggest my brother's Christian name. I thought 'Ronald' would do very well.'

'I'd like to meet this son of yours. Does he take after his uncle, with a liking for the sea?' asked Len.

'No, he's a coach painter. But the boys wrote that they sometimes go out in a small boat on the Inner Harbour.'

'Well, I must be off to the town, if you are waiting for your sons. We had quite a good voyage, didn't we? Just as well we missed the fog.'

'What fog was that?'

'We've just heard about the *Elingamite* — she ran aground on the Three Kings in dense fog,' Len replied.

'That was what caused the wreck of Roald's ship, the *Wairarapa*. She ran aground on Great Barrier,' said Caroline. 'They lost so many lives that time. What about the passengers and crew of this wreck you mentioned?'

196

'Forty-five off the *Elingamite* are missing, presumed drowned, we've heard,' he answered. 'The *Penguin*, a warship, picked up eight survivors on a raft five days after the vessel went aground.'

'Five days on a raft!' she exclaimed. 'Still, they were lucky to survive.'

'There were sixteen at first,' explained Len, sadly. 'No water and no food — half of them died from exposure, or drinking seawater in sheer desperation.'

'Thank goodness none of the boys wanted to go to sea,' Caroline said. 'You take care, Len — Roald was lucky twice, but not the third time.'

'I don't know what I'm doing, talking of shipwrecks to you — ' Len was ashamed of his tactlessness.

'They happen all the time — we just have to go on,' replied Caroline, expressing her life-long principle in a few words. 'You must go on to town — come up the Onepoto Gully Road to the bach tomorrow evening, and meet my sons.'

'I'd enjoy that,' he said. 'Our ship's here for a few days, there's wool to be loaded.'

'We shan't be there for long, the girls and Richard and I, but my older sons are well settled.'

'They'd have Helen's address, anyway,

wouldn't they, if I'm ever back in Napier?' asked Len.

Mother was pleased. Not delighted, because she really did not want the family to have anything more to do with the sea. Two generations, now, had lost a loved one to the oceans . . .

In the flurry of surprised greetings and enquiries, when Henry and Ronald arrived together with a hand-cart, Caroline forgot all about Len.

Young Caroline had rushed into the bach, fuming because the luggage had not arrived. She was leaving for Hastings immediately, and going on in the morning to Waipukurau, with her new employer, who had been staying in Napier for a few days. The buggy would meet them in Waipukurau, to drive into the back country, to the homestead. Caroline wanted her clothes that minute, they were leaving for Hastings now!

Ronald and Henry found her behaviour amusing. Five years since they had met, and she could behave as if it was a week ago.

'Our oldest sister doesn't change, Mother,' said Henry.

'No. Well, I'm glad she's found a place to suit her. That's one less — William not home yet?' she enquired.

'Er — no, Mother,' Henry replied.

'In fact,' Ronald butted in, 'we don't know just where he is. He went off to a country job somewhere up Gisborne way, last week.'

Caroline was not disappointed. Like her oldest daughter, William had always been difficult to please. She was indeed very surprised that the three brothers had lived together for so long. Clearly, Henry and Ronald had either very equable temperaments, or goodly quantities of tact.

Young Caroline had no intention of being questioned by her mother. If she couldn't get clothes from the trunks without seeing Mother, then she'd send for them when they were needed. No farewells or thanks — what had she to thank Mother for?

With William away, there was just enough room in the bach — the girls doubled up, and Richard slept on a kitchen couch. But that was one wage the less; the boys, willing as they were, could not feed four extra on their pay. Times were better than they had been in that bad year or two last century; but Caroline was horrified at the higher prices. Not only had she been away for five years, she had been shopping in a depressed area of London. There, if the groceries were expensive, no-one bought them; so the shopkeeper subsisted on a bare margin of profit — but he did not go bankrupt.

Ten days later, when William drifted in, unheralded from his job 'in the country', it was to find, as he expected, that his brothers were alone.

'Any news from England?' William asked.

Before Ronald could give the story away, Henry replied, quickly, 'Yes, Mother's going to settle in New Zealand.'

'I've made it quite clear,' shouted William, 'that I won't stay here if they plan to sponge on us.'

'They won't be sponging, as you put it, on us,' said Ronald, furious.

'Well — tell me, then! Where are they going to stay?' William, sensing the warm co-operation between these two, was as angry as Ronald.

'No — er — ' Ronald, to annoy his oldest brother, was hesitating on purpose. 'They're settling here.'

'They are not settling here,' ordered William. 'If I find another job for a day or two in the country then, they can stay here for a night or two — otherwise the whole lot can go to a doss-house, for all I care!'

'They've settled — ' Henry decided he had better break up the argument.

'Where are they? Where's their clothes?' asked William.

'They've been — and gone,' Henry said.

'Now are you satisfied, you selfish oaf?' Ronald demanded.

William put his fists up. 'Don't you talk to me like that, you little whipper-snapper. Get out before I throw you out!'

Ronald laughed. 'Catch me if you can!' he called, as he shot out the door. He would come back later. William would simmer down — he always did. He only needed to remember that the bach and section belonged to all three; perhaps the only business-like thing Papa had done was to put the property — it had little value then — in all three names before he left for England. And William realised very clearly that the constant income came from Henry and Ronald; they also did the cooking and cleaning.

Henry did not need to remind his older brother that he would leave, too if Ronald found somewhere else to live.

23

Young Caroline was 'somewhere' on the East Coast, towards Pourere or Blackhead. She had directed her mother to put her clothing on the train, addressed care of Waipukurau railway station. Her employer attended every stock sale — he would pick up the parcel and take it out to the homestead; there was no hurry, she wrote.

On a big back-country station towards Taupo, near the coach route, Christine was 'in service' as a kitchen-maid. Although in desolate country on the Blowhard, the homestead was busy; constantly visitors were driven in from the route where the wagons brought the wool down to Napier through Omahaki, Konini and Puketapu through the Tutaekuri river valley. Wagons drawn into the interior took supplies and materials for the Main Trunk line, then being constructed. Christine's father had known her mistress's father in the old days — it was his homestead that William had been painting 'when Tamaohoi awoke'.

The contact had also led to a far-away place for Helen. The family had been known as hard-working — William and young Caroline were disregarded in this generalisation. Their sulky laziness was not apparent in any other member. The father might have been slow, but he did a good job. And it was better to have a man stay on a station a little longer, but once only, rather than board him twice over (with two return trips to pay) because the first effort was too slapdash.

Their Member of Parliament had taken his family down to Wellington; his wife did not think much of the domestic service offering there.

'These townies don't know what 'clean' means — and they waste water — and they don't dust the moulding . . . ' she wrote, 'and as for the backs of mirrors . . . ' The mistress of the property out on the Blowhard had the task of finding a reliable girl for her friend in Wellington when she was enquiring in Napier about a kitchen-maid for her homestead.

Helen suited very well — she had lived in London, so the city would not be a strange and bothersome area. Her mother was not at all worried about those Wellington complaints — it was evident that she had trained her daughters well. The big house in Marjoribanks Street should be a good home for Helen. She was a good girl, and wise for her age.

Sometimes she would be wanted at the Bay, her mother was told. Whatever the 'Bay' was, that would be all right, too. They had to go by water, she was informed. She could cope with that, also — had she not sailed to London and back? (None of them visualised the difference between the steamers on the high seas and the little launches that tossed about in sudden sou'westerly gales, near the rocky headlands of Wellington Harbour.)

Within a few days, the girls were settled.

For an older woman with a son of seven, the difficulties were greater than Caroline had expected. Jobs aplenty out in the country — housekeepers, cooks, dairymaids sometimes — but 'No children', or no schools.

She realised then that the young family would have been much better off with Grandfather to look after them. Richard would have had a good education, though it would not have fitted him for a return to their position in life in New Zealand. But he would have had a good schooling, on which her husband had set great store; now she must see to it that he attended school at least until Standard Six. That had been as much as could be expected. Her husband had done very well to keep all the others at school as long as that.

By now Caroline had forgotten the furore aroused in the early 'nineties by the Commission on Sweated Labour, and the subsequent minimum age of fourteen or a pass in Standard Six, for employment in factories.

No suitable positions were available in Napier: the wages were too low to allow her to pay her share and Richard's, if she stayed with the boys. It was fairly clear, whatever Henry and Ronald felt, that William would not want his mother, let alone Richard, to stay at the bach. Caroline had encouraged her husband to sign the property over to the three boys — that was before the Greenmeadows house collapsed in the floods the day they left for England. But what would happen if William wanted his share of the property in the Gully?

Grimly determined, she packed a gladstone bag, and with Richard caught the train to Dannevirke.

Perhaps she was tired of towns. So many years before she had disliked the forest and its hardships. However, people had led good and successful lives there. Henrik came into her mind, Henrik who had loved the forests. Milling could provide an opening for

Richard — one of her sons must work in the open. Caroline admired the expertise Henry and Ronald had achieved; but, underneath, she was a pioneer herself, with the pioneer woman's admiration for brawn — success achieved by muscle rather than artistry or scholarship. It was an outlook that was to pervade generations.

At the Napier registry there had been an enquiry for a laundress in Dannevirke, accommodation provided. She would arrive — perhaps do a day's work before they realised that Richard would stay with her for more than a week or two.

In the years in London she had lost touch with Olav and Maud Greiner — they might be dead, now, but there might be a tumbledown cottage somewhere.

Perhaps she would have to contemplate marriage with Hans, if he was still a bachelor (or a widower?) as a meal-ticket. She would cope with that, too, if it was necessary. William was dead. All that remained was to keep going, and support Richard at school until he could fend for himself.

Independent as ever, indomitable — Fate's nasty blows left her bruised but upright, sterner and harder than ever. Affection was not going to break through her crustiness again. It was probably the only way she could carry on, with Roald and William gone, and only one child out of the seven really needing her. In a confused way she resented the decision she had made, and the cause of it. There was no life for her in England; but she would not leave a seven-year-old fatherless and with a far distant mother. Besides, who knew what the future might bring? Supposing Grandfather, after educating Richard as a gentleman, suddenly turned against him, just as he had turned against his own son?

Richard had to be with his mother. Fortunately, she never asked herself if the mother should have stayed with Richard. It was only her pride that refused to accept what the children's grandfather had planned for her — a cottage on the estate, food provided, her only task to care for herself and her little son. It would be years before this offer would become clear to the next generation. Pride and independence had distorted two lives, probably three — there had been a family for Grandfather, and now he was alone again.

From the railway station to the hotel was not far. But it did not look a suitable corner for a young boy.

The sleazy proprietor took one look at her. 'Young women only. No married women — or are you married? Is that your son?'

Statement and question followed one another very curtly, with obvious implications.

In desperate need of a job Caroline might be, but she would not be spoken to in that manner.

'I am a widow, this is my son, and I am capable of a better day's work than any young woman,' she said. It was so long since she had worked for an outsider — and none had acted like this.

After grumbling, the proprietor said she could work for a week, and he would 'see'. He supposed Richard could sleep somewhere — in the top attic or over the stable. No wages, but they could both have their meals, that was fair, wasn't it? And there wasn't a clean towel in the house, she could start work now.

Mountains of laundry — when did they last have a laundress? The two other women, the cook and a housemaid-waitress, told her over a reasonable meal (the cooking was good, although the ingredients were the cheapest the proprietor could find) that the linen had been sent out. Customers were even leaving the bar with this skinflint who had not been the proprietor for very long; there was not enough money coming in to pay the laundry account.

There must be a better opening than

this, Caroline thought. Her own dwelling, and take in laundry — that would be a wise idea.

It was six days before the pile of washing was reduced to normal. Meanwhile Richard was off to Dannevirke South school; at night he was wrapped in rugs in a corner of the landing. Both the top attic and 'over the stable' were over-run with rats, and dirt too, piling up since the buildings were thrown together.

Greiners had died a year or two earlier, as Caroline had expected. The oldest daughter was living in town, as her husband had taken over the store, of which the living accommodation was now part. Somewhere on the outskirts, near the railway line and the main road, was a cottage which had belonged to her husband's family — if it was habitable, they would be glad to have someone living there.

She would make it habitable — she had done that before. Before she left the position in the hotel, she had arranged to wash and iron the smaller articles — the frilled pillowslips, the fine ironing. Olav Greiner's daughter was delighted to be able to send the little girls' befrilled and furbelowed frocks. Soon Caroline had more work than she could comfortably handle, dawn to dark and later, if the price offered would pay for candles.

Richard — 'Dick' now to all his school-mates, and to his mother, too, when she forgot — was in and out of mischief. If there was a ploy on, he would be in it, either as leader or the boy who had dreamed it up. Orchards were quietly raided — not destructively, just enough to eat. The only time they were caught was by a friend of Caroline's. She lined the little group up by her back door, and pushed a spoonful — a large spoon — of castor oil down each unwilling throat. Her orchard remained free of depredation thereafter.

Next to the cottage was a tumble-down shack inhabited by a very old Chinese. Round about he grew vegetables for which he found a ready market, especially in the hotel kitchens. He did not worry too much about what he grew; he worked, like others of his race, from daylight till dark.

At first Dick was a little frightened of him; his mother told him to keep away from that boundary. Other schoolboys had teased the old man, and his anger had kept them out of his way.

Presently the market gardener appeared at Caroline's door with an armload of cauliflower. When she would have found money to pay him, he refused.

'No, no, you keep that for the boy,' he said firmly, 'a good boy, eh?'

'Very good — sometimes,' Caroline replied. Had Richard been into the man's garden, she wondered.

'Very good boy — now say 'Good morning' to me?' the old man asked. 'My family far away, very far. In China.'

'I'm sure Richard will say good morning,' she answered, resolved to alter the rule about not speaking to the neighbour that very night.

'You work hard for him — I see your candle when I smoke the pipe — just one for sleep. Some day he work for you, eh?'

And he shuffled off, saying as he went, 'You not grow vegetables — no need. Grow pretty flowers.'

From that day on more vegetables appeared by the cottage door than Caroline and Richard could eat. They were not restricted to those freely available; new potatoes, peas, whatever was fresh and young came by stealth to the door.

It was months before the Chinese knocked on her door again, some strange stalks in his hand.

'I tell you how to cook, eh?' he asked.

'What is that?' wondered Caroline.

'They call it 'A sparrow grass',' he replied.

'Very special — cut so (leaving only the tender green stalk and the purple tip) — boil — a little.'

She thanked him again.

'No, no thanks. Your boy tell me if you like — more, plenty more.'

At meal-time Mother told Richard how his uncle had first seen this strange vegetable — by then she had forgotten the name of the river, but she knew it was in South America. When Richard spoke to the old Chinese, he could tell him the story.

From her two younger daughters Caroline received letters quite often. Christine had stuck manfully to her job near the Kaweka Range, between the sources of the Ngaruroro and Tutaekuri rivers. Helen was enjoying her Wellington stay; she found herself more of a Nanny than a housemaid, to her delight and that of the family of four.

When school holidays started, the necessities for four weeks were taken down to the jetty at Oriental Bay. Children and parents packed into the steam launch, which quietly chugged down to Worser Bay, on the Port Nicholson side of the harbour. Once everything was landed on the jetty there, the last means of communication puttered away into the evening. It would be two weeks before the launch called again, to take the husband back to town, and perhaps he would go on to his constituents beyond Napier. The little cottage was neat and comfortable; it was holiday time for Helen as well as for the family.

Ever since she had been with the family, her mistakes had been treated as jokes. She did not make many, but she felt, to the end of her life, that she would never go into a strange church again.

That Sunday she had escorted the children to St. Mary's in Boulcott Street, in the heart of Wellington. The first disaster overtook her when she reached the vessel of Holy Water; the older children dipped their fingers in, but she did not see them sign themselves. Instead, she thought they sucked their fingers because they were not tall enough to drink from the vessel — Helen had been used to Anglican Communion. However, few churchgoers noticed.

The next mistake was really obvious. The children genuflected as they walked down the aisle. Poor Helen tripped over them, causing a mighty clatter beside the pews. Then the little girls got the giggles, to complete the disastrous picture. Whether the parents ever heard the story Helen did not know; she was still asked to escort the children to church.

Within a year, when their parlourmaid left

to be married, her employers suggested that perhaps Christine would like to come south to join her sister. The two girls could share the domestic work between them, as they wished. Their mistress knew that everything would be done properly.

Of the oldest sister the girls heard nothing. Nor did their mother hear word of her. William, too, had quietly vanished.

Henry and Ronald were succeeding in their chosen work, gaining a reputation for excellence. But coach work was on the decline; that horrible monster, one of the noisiest and most objectionable machines that had ever been invented, the motor car, was taking over from the dog-cart and the hack. The days of the horse bus were numbered; presently, for long trips, the eight seater Packards would replace the coaches.

It was all in the air. But Henry and Ronald were making sure that they could turn to other work, house painting and papering as their father had done, signs for shops and hotels.

Before school, sometimes before breakfast, Richard would collect the soiled linen from Caroline's customers; after school he would return the snowy baskets of laundry. Then he would fit in a paper run — as far and as fast as he could go.

Throughout his schooldays he had gone down to the Livery Stables, mucking out, harnessing. Sometimes on a Saturday he would have the delightful task of riding a hack a few miles, to someone who wanted to hire. Horses Richard could handle. He was not fond of cows, or he could have milked for a dairy farmer at Umutaoroa. When there was a house cow that needed milking, however, he could make a good job of that, too.

As soon as he turned twelve, the Post Office would accept him as an extra delivery boy — the mail at holiday times, telegrams on Saturdays or after school. It was a proud moment when he became a full-fledged telegraph boy. Wages were poor, but prospects were excellent.

Caroline had always assured her sons that she was managing very well, and needed no financial help. She did not admit that the heavy baskets of wet linen were nearly beyond her. She was tired of the unending struggle — as a young woman she had met it, but now, old before her time with work and child bearing, she felt she would have to give in. But how?

Which customers could she refuse? When she turned someone down, that woman would find other help, perhaps even someone who would ride one of those bicycle contraptions to the home and do the work there.

If it rained for days, there would be complaints about late deliveries.

Richard made time before his seven o'clock start to collect laundry; but he could not take it back until after 5.30 p.m. All through winter that meant collections and deliveries in the dark — and the ladies did not like it.

Caroline thought of the old Chinese gardener. He had died, no-one to mourn him except his next-door neighbours, a year or so back. That was another blow — vegetables were necessary, and not easy for an older woman to grow on the exposed section, with icy winds from the Ruahines blowing into springtime. The owners of the cottage had it on the market. At first she had paid no rent, then a fairly low rental; but it was clear that any buyer would either want the place for himself, or would want a good return on his investment.

What had the old Chinese benefactor said? 'You work hard for him — some day he work for you.'

Wearily she put the last Mrs Potts iron on the stove. That was what she had come to — Richard would have to work for her. And he would have to bring home more wages than he was now. Caroline could not wait for yearly advancements and future prospects.

They made good money in the sawmills. There was one at the north end of the town that had begun nearly thirty years ago. In fact, Hans was the manager — she would ask him about a job for her son. They had met as old friends; Hans had forgotten — why shouldn't he? — that he had ever wanted to marry her.

He had a large family scattered round the district, in the mill, with the teams, managing shops, running dairy farms and the factory. If it was not a son, it was a son-in-law. There was no room for an old friend's son, a thirteen-year-old telegraph boy.

Up in the King Country, Hans advised Caroline, there were mills and the railway line construction; the Main Trunk route, with its crossing at Taihape, was almost completed, after twenty-three years. There should be plenty of work for Dick there. He was good with horses, too, Hans had heard — there was no likelihood of any other form of transport in that country for many years to come.

The indomitable old lady packed their bags again. The cottage had been sold, as she had expected, and they had to leave that dwelling, anyway.

The station bell clanged as they set off, signalling the end of her last sojourn in the area she was always to recall as the 'Forty Mile Bush'. Dannevirke she never mentioned by name.

Seventeen miles south to Woodville, with halts at all the wayside stations; the rhythmic clatter as the bogey wheels clicked over each joint of the railway irons kept her anxious thoughts company. Richard put his boyhood friends and his ambition to become a postmaster behind him. Mother had decided on the move to the tall timber about which Uncle Henrik wrote. For a boy of that age, then, there was no querying the decision.

After a lengthy wait at the Junction, the train wound through the Manawatu Gorge, beside the turbulent rapids, cliffs above and below, through the tunnels and across high-level bridges, to Palmerston. The railway line there ran across the open square, with the shops set around it, and the station within three minutes' walk. Three hours they waited, while the train from Wellington steamed up the west coast line, completed over twenty-five years earlier as a private railway system.

They found seats in the carriage now to be hauled towards the upheaved hills and deep gullies of the centre of the island. Through the darkness the locomotive puffed and grunted, through tunnels, over bridges and viaducts, two of the latter completed only a few years earlier. The sound there was different from that in the tunnels; it was hollow and penetrating, a reminder of the great heights spanned by the Makohine and Mangaweka viaducts, hundreds of feet long. Dick was not too adult to be thoroughly excited, his face pressed against the window-pane, to shut out the reflected light from the flickering gas mantle. Occasionally he would catch glimpses of wild country in the fitful moonlight, or the homely glow of a kerosene lamp in some remote farmhouse.

In the middle of the snowy night, mother and son were set down on the windswept platform at Taihape. Those were the days of blazing fires in station waiting-rooms. They kept warm there till daybreak.

24

Helen and Christine, during their mother's final years in Dannevirke, had spread their wings. Country girls at heart, they had grown tired of the same easy round of town life. They appreciated their pleasant positions; but soon there would be no need for two domestics as well as the cook in this Marjoribank Street house. One by one the children had disappeared for terms at a time to boarding schools such as St Patrick's, or St Bride's.

Their employer had cut his ties with that area in Hawkes Bay that first sent him to Parliament. He had other interests which would keep him in the city. Until that change of direction became apparent, the girls had thought there was a chance of being taken back to the Bay once again, when the peach trees bloomed.

Aided by their mistress, they obtained places in the Wairarapa, far up the coast. Helen and Christine travelled first by train, a long slow journey, with the steam locomotive chugging up the Mangaroa and Kaitoke inclines, and then the dragging haul, winding up beside the headwaters of the Hutt river, where pioneers first blazed an inland trail to the plains beyond. In the bleakness of the Summit, the locomotives were changed over, the little Fell with its third rail being shunted on to the carriages. The mighty gusts of wind, causing the first disaster back in the 'seventies, and the steep gradients, combined to make the Fell locomotive a necessity and this part of the journey unique.

Down at Cross Creek, the little railway settlement which the sun never seemed to reach, there was more delay. The Fell, replaced by a conventional locomotive for the trip across the plains, was ready to haul the southbound train up the incline beyond 'Siberia' to the curved tunnel with its rise and fall gradient, where the bell tolled as each carriage rolled over the highest point on the line.

At Masterton the girls took a cab from the station a mile out of the township. This time they need not walk, for, though wages were low, they had spent as little as possible. One of the men on the 20,000 acre station would meet them on the morrow; meanwhile the stock and station agents had arranged their accommodation and the coach fare for the next part of their journey.

That took another day, with horses changed

at Blairlogie, somewhere near the Devil's Elbow in the steep gorge where a team, out of hand for some reason, had plunged over the cliff edge, dragging the coach and its screaming occupants with it.

For Christine, with her rare coach trips down the winding Kuripa-pango route to Napier, it was nothing new. Helen, with longer years in town and little of this backblocks experience, found it rather alarming. Older than Christine, she was very glad to have her younger sister with her, taking the trip and all its demands so quietly and calmly.

At Tinui they were met by the gig which would take them the further ten miles or so to the homestead. Now the countryside reminded Christine more than ever of the Taupo road, as it was called — manuka and tauwhinu, few tall trees of the original bush, gullies and hills, elbow bends and steep grades. By the time they reached the black cliffs of the Maungamaungataipos, they began to wonder if they would ever reach their destination.

Helen had taken on the cooking, receiving somewhat curt advice from the agency that she would be cooking for six men and the manager, as well as the housekeeper and the domestic (Christine). Owners were not mentioned. Perhaps they lived in town — or was this another Member of Parliament who had moved from his electorate to the capital?

Gates to be opened — Springhill, Ruru — on what was little more than a cart-track.

At last there was the long one-storey homestead. Waiting to show them their duties was the housekeeper — horror of horrors — sister Caroline, grim and forbidding in her long black frock, the bunch of keys as her authority dangling from her waist.

Who was more taken aback it is difficult to say. For a long minute Caroline thought she would treat these two sisters as any other domestics, strangers, very much beneath the housekeeper's dignity.

Helen and Christine, glad to see any member of the family, ruined that plan. They rushed to hug her, her usual off-hand mannerisms forgotten for the moment. Her response was frigid.

'What brought you here?' she asked. 'Did you think you could come here for a holiday with me while the mistress is away?'

'The agency sent us,' said Helen. 'Why should we come for a holiday? We had no idea where you were — the last we heard you were up the east coast somewhere.'

'Well, you're here, so I suppose I shall have to put up with you. But remember, I am in charge — any incompetence, and out you will go!'

Helen was getting angry. 'We have very good references, Caroline, and I think the stock and station agents engaged us.'

'I've no doubt you think you are good workers, but you will need more training, and I'll see that you get it,' retorted Caroline.

'Are you playing some kind of game with us?' asked Christine, bewildered.

'No, I'm not! I don't want anyone to find out that my sisters are not up to the job,' stated Caroline. 'Dinner is at six; it has been prepared, as you have taken so long to get here — '

Helen broke in. 'We could hardly help that — the driver met the coach, and the gig did not stop on the way.'

'Never mind why — you are late. You'll change now and take up your duties or you'll go — tomorrow.'

Leave tomorrow? And a night's lodging owing? Not they. If this sister of theirs wanted to play ladie they knew how to act as domestic and cook — she should have no fault to find with their work.

'I don't think she could fire us,' whispered Helen.

'I'm sure she couldn't. But look,' said Christine, 'if she wants to treat us as strangers, why should we worry? Let her enjoy playing the slave-driver for a month or two — but I wonder why?'

At dinner they discovered the reason for Caroline's absurd reactions. She was married to the somewhat taciturn manager. When the owners returned, Caroline and her husband would move to the manager's house at the southern end of the station. It became clear to the two younger girls that their sister was wondering if her husband would suspect that she had engineered the arrival of part of her family. They were introduced as 'my sisters — the registry did not say who was coming, just a cook and a housemaid.' (And, thought Helen later, the registry did not say you enjoyed your authority so much that the last two left as soon as they had seen their month out — two of the men told the girls this, after they had been there a few days.)

Caroline's husband, welcoming them, said what a pleasant surprise it was for Caroline to see her sisters. 'Of course,' he continued, 'when we are settled in our own home, we should be expecting you to spend a holiday with us.'

'Helen and Christine will be too busy with

their work here to have time for a holiday,' Caroline replied.

'The boss and his wife are pretty good, you know. I'm sure they'd spare one or other of your sisters for a few days to keep you company.'

'I don't need — ' she began in a sarcastic tone. As she noticed her husband's surprised look, she changed the end of her sentence and her tone. 'I won't need any company, my dear, I shall be so busy.'

The sudden change of attitude almost reduced the younger sisters to laughter. This was apparently a different person from the one they had known in Napier and London, and different from the woman who had greeted them two hours earlier. Her husband, Bernard, had not come in from the station then — he had ridden out to the back-country, to find out how the scrub-cutters were progressing.

At first Caroline had bitterly resented her sisters' arrival, jealous of their own close companionship and of their ability to make friends. If she had introduced herself as married on their arrival, perhaps life would have been more pleasant. But for three months it was not too bad — the biggest drawback for Helen in the hot summer months was the range, which consumed quantities of willow wood. She was never short of it; the cowman-gardener saw to that, with a boy to help him. But it was a constant battle to keep the oven hot enough for baking.

The river that was the boundary line was not far down the hill. On hot afternoons the girls would bathe there, despite mud and eels. Once shearing was over, and the bales of wool away, the wool-shed dances would provide fun and friends. Decorated with trails of greenery from second-growth bush — it had been felled and cleared in the 'eighties, but where land had been abandoned later in the century it had reverted — the shed was well-disguised. Lycopodium was preferred, for then there was no drooping greenery to be replaced on the night. The natural grease from the wool made the smooth timber floor as fast as any ball-room; the sorting bins and the press were turned by fern fronds into alcoves for sitting out dances. The long wool-sorting table was scrubbed down; in spite of its ribbed surface, covered with linen sheets it did duty as the supper table.

What a supper! 'Ladies a plate' was the rule, and they vied with one another to produce the best or the most, from roast wild pork to cream sponges. Glad to retain good household help, station owners would see that there was time for all the extra cooking; station meat would be given to the cook 'for the woolshed dance'. Younger owners or the sons of older 'bosses' would share the buggy with their servants, or all the hacks would set off together. Some — owner or cowboy, manager or scrubcutter — would provide music with accordions, or whistles, or violins, or an orchestra of all three.

In winter, if the creeks were not too high or the banks too eroded, there might be a round of dances — Manawa, Annedale, Riverside, Ruru, Springhill — any of the stations, providing there were a few young staff or young people among the owners. One or two balls were held in the village hall, about twelve miles away. Helen and Christine would set off about 4 p.m. in riding skirts, with their 'ball gowns' in wicker baskets firmly strapped to the saddle. House cows would be milked early, so that the men could get away. By the time they rode home again, dawn would be breaking — time to start milking, go round the sheep or bring cattle into the yards.

The girls would stoke up the range to cook the massive breakfast of chops and eggs before the men went out. Most took a few sandwiches for lunch, which might be eaten on horseback, if the fencing or mustering was seven or eight miles out. The bigger properties had a contract fencer; but a good all-round farm worker would help anywhere, do anything. Sharp divisions of labour were unknown.

In winter on the roads the horses might be mired up to their hocks, rivers unfordable, and great slips in the papa country greasily slopping over the hill tracks.

Then in the staff sitting-room or in the men's quarters the well-thumbed books would come out — sometimes Dickens, more often Steele Rudd, Rider Haggard or Rudyard Kipling — or the accordion, and they would sing — 'Down at the old Bull and Bush', 'When Father papered the Parlour', 'Home Sweet Home', 'Galway Bay' — comic or serious. Not on Sunday nights, if the boss's wife was around, but on other nights a greasy pack of cards might appear, when they would play poker — usually for matches, since no-one would get a cheque for months, until they wanted to go into town.

That principle of 'Not on Sundays' for gambling did not apply to the men's quarters or to the contract gangs — twelve or twenty or even more in the big sheds for shearing, with a rouseabout, a wool sorter and their own cook. The rouseabout might be twelve or fourteen, and this his first time away from an outback farm where a large family did all the stock work and the shearing as well. The bunks would be double-tiered around three sides of the match-lined room, eighteen or twenty feet square, with a huge open fire in the end wall, often festooned with men's clothing, drying out after rain or washing.

The youngest would be in the top bunks, and heaven help the twelve-year-old who, clambering down at midnight, put his foot on an old shearer's face. Probably amongst the group would be a kind of stand-in father for the young boy, a protector if things got too rough — old Mick, the shearer 'daddy'.

At this time no-one would have eyes for the roses the gardener was growing round the homestead, or the peonies. The bulbs he had flung into the corner of the paddock — snowdrops, jonquils, double and single narcissus, their blooms almost finished — would be over-run by the noisy lambs, yelling for their ewes in shelter overnight, in case of rain. Wet sheep would not be shorn, to care for animal, wool and shearer. Days might be spent in the whares while the gang waited for dry sheep, and the farmer counted the cost of food and prayed that there might be no cold snap after the rain, to kill the shorn animals. Sometimes a southerly would rip unheralded over the hills in November;

the shepherd, trying to move the last of the mob to good pasture and some sheltered corner, would be caught in a narrow gully, where the wind whistled through, lifting the horse's mane, and suddenly pelting rain into the faces of the unfed sheep. Neither man nor dogs could turn them back or move them on; half the mob would collapse where they stood, a huddle of bodies in which warmth might save one but smothering kill another.

It was a life that Christine came to know well.

Not many months after the boss and his wife returned from England, she was dancing in the village hall, decorated as always with fern and lycopodium, after her sister's wedding at the local church. Caroline, of all people, and her husband had been in part responsible.

Her brother-in-law, Brian, had been employed for a while at the southern end of the station. A personable young man, rather full of himself in Christine's eyes, he had met Helen and the romance blossomed. (Long forgotten was Third Officer Len Jones, who had not made his intentions clear to anyone but Helen's mother.)

There were no other married quarters at the station. Helen preferred to put distance between herself and her older sister; Brian

Smith was going back to the northern Hawkes Bay, where he had been working earlier. He had heard of a hill country farm in from Wairoa, near the limestone caves where stalactite and stalagmite met, in the Mangaone valley. Bankrupt, the owner had walked off, leaving the stock and station agents to find a manager — or a buyer who would also be mortgaged to the hilt.

Brian had a deposit of sorts, acceptable to the agents, for he would be working for them for years. It would be unlikely that he would ever have a decent equity in the property, let alone own it. The run cattle were wild runts, resulting from a succession of cross-breeding from scrub bulls. Where wool was not blackened from burnt-off manuka, it was pulled off by clumps of tauwhinu and matagouri (Wild Irishman) and pointed Spaniard, or it drifted about poor, weedy pasture, shed from milk fever. Ticks, lice, fleas — the bankrupt farmer could no longer get credit even for dip — infested the flocks. It was two or more years since they had been dipped. Lambing percentages were minimal — there was not a decent ram on the place.

Brian had been bluffed, it seemed.

Away up there at Tangitere, fourteen or so miles from Waikokopu, where the coastal steamer from Napier had set them ashore, the young couple made a home, across the stepping stones of a creek that ran dry in the summer and isolated them in winter. Neglected the homestead had been, as well as the stock.

Like her mother before her, Helen set to work; she had the loneliness of the bush pioneer to face, also. The nearest neighbour was six miles away, the nearest village and doctor twelve. Mail was delivered twice a week, if the rivers could be crossed; a wagonload of stores could be expected every three months.

A poorly bred house cow gave them blue milk and a very little butter. The churn had vanished, though it had never been paid for. Helen set her milk in large pans, covered with muslin, skimmed off what cream there was, and beat that by hand — butter was a change from mutton fat on the bread she baked in an unreliable oven. Firewood, too, was short anywhere near the homestead.

Sheep that were 'dog-tucker' on any other station supplied the staple item of diet, until the neighbour gave Helen some old fowls — one or two of them were still laying, the others were boiled until one could get teeth into the stringy flesh. The dogs occasionally forgot their manners while they ran down a rabbit — there were plenty of those. A Sunday afternoon walk with Helen and a .22 rifle supplied humans and dogs with rabbit stew and dog food respectively for two or three days. In winter, mud to the ankles kept the walks to a minimum, the steep hillsides running with water. In summer, despite every effort to patch holes in the gauze of the old meat-safe, the blowflies and the heat would mean the dogs were over-fed and the couple went short of protein.

25

Christine, marrying one of the many sons of a nearby 'gentleman farmer', was to lead a parallel life. Jim Dyer's father had come out with his older brother from England in the 1870s, with enough money to buy a sheep station. Like Christine's father, he had imagined that grass grew, sheep flourished, shearers shore them — there was an annual income. Years later, disappointed and disgusted with the requirements for successful farming, he sat reading in his armchair, while his sons from the age of twelve did what they could to keep the place going.

As he kept a firm hold on what return there was, the boys worked for their keep only. He begrudged every cent spent on the station — fences, stock, buildings. Everything was expected to produce without input; the ridiculous size of the paddocks eight or ten miles out, close to 200 acres each, encouraged the spread of second growth, until the major part of that area was covered in manuka and tauwhinu. Not even four boys could cope with that, without some expenditure on scrub-cutting by contract.

One by one they had themselves gone off to contract work — fencing, shearing, scrub-cutting, bullock droving — to keep themselves clothed and shod. An urgent request from his father had brought Jim back, to face an impossible task. His five sisters were still at home, doing the usual chores at the homestead, but looking down from a great height on those, like Christine and Helen, who did the same work for wages.

Christine was unaware of this reaction until she was married. Old Mr Dyer — he was only fifty, but he regarded himself as a patriarch — was anxious to make sure that Jim continued to run the farm, and approved of the marriage. The sisters, however, expected to get the services of a domestic servant free of charge.

It took only a week for the veneer of welcome for the new bride to collapse into sneers. The sisters read books while meals remained uncooked, butter was not made and the milk was left in the buckets from morning till evening milking. Then the cow was left to dry off.

The subsequent explosion from the old father, who came out of his book often enough to find tasks undone, produced, from one daughter, the remark: 'We left that to the servant.'

Jim happened to come in early enough to catch that. The girls were unlucky, for they indulged in no sarcasm while they knew he could hear. Easy-going generally, he would not have his young wife disparaged.

One of his brothers had offered to return to the station on a fair wage. He could live in the homestead, said Jim, and they could build a whare beyond the Neck, where the young couple could live and Jim could work the back paddocks, joining his brother for major tasks such as dipping and shearing. His father, faced with the alternative of losing Jim or building a whare, had to agree.

Jim was good with bullocks, though he was dismayed when his bullocky language was overheard by a neighbour's daughter, home from boarding-school. He hitched up the team to the sledge to haul rough-sawn planks, corrugated iron and framing over the hills six miles or so to the site he had selected, not far from a swift-running creek. He cut out the second growth to make a space for the sixteen foot by twelve foot whare. There should be two rooms, he told his father, who grumbled at the cost of the extra partition. One would hold a bed built into the corner, with wire-netting as the base.

An outer wall of the other room was taken up by an open fire, with boulders of greywacke to hold the saucepans and the camp oven.

Then Father Dyer decided that he could drive the bullocks — Jim was spending too much time on this building job. (Probably that remark came first from the sisters, along the lines of 'It's only for her!') Father would not be told that the horse track was unsuitable, indeed useless for a team and sledge. That paddock was named the 'Neck' because there the property was very narrow; the track wound down the papa cliffs at a steep gradient to cross the creek. Horses had to be led both up and down, creating anxious moments for new chums on the steep downhill path, when four hoofs slithered close behind the dismounted rider.

So Father wasted half a day driving the team to the edge of that descent, and then grudgingly admitting that his son was right. The detour through the neighbour's boundary fence and back, a few chains further on, took more time. On the uphill stretch beyond, the team started to lag, with their sledge load of odds and ends and two small windows.

Jim had always cracked the whip over his leaders, not on them. But his father, by accident or design, sent the lash curling onto the rump of the off-side bullock. His mate in the yoke, untouched, did not respond; the whipped beast rushed forward a little; the sledge slewed as the other leader did not move, and over the bank it went, windows shattering as it overturned.

Father unyoked the team, kicked anything unbroken into the gully with the rest of the debris, hauled the empty sledge onto the track, and walked home, leaving the team to be recovered by someone else. More windows were sent out from town; this time Jim drove the bullock-team.

Christine and Jim soon moved into their first home. In later years she often referred to that as the happiest time, although she had so much to contend with. Bricks in the fireplace would not have split, as the greywacke did, upsetting the great iron saucepan in which the linen was being boiled, and sending showers of ash everywhere. Father Dyer would not send to town for bricks — his daughters did not need bricks. (At the homestead was a copper and tubs.) Christine could go without.

The motherless lambs she fed would break into the garden she was trying to make; the calf — Jim had found a reasonable cow among the run cattle, and persuaded it to be milked — would chew the clothes on the rope that served as a clothes-line. (Wire was to be used only for fencing, said Father Dyer.) Christine milked that cow if Jim was in at the homestead for any of the yard or shed jobs; she tied the cow as usual to a tree trunk, and sat on an upturned box, with the milk bucket (a kerosene tin, well-scrubbed and rinsed) between her legs.

Walking into the homestead involved a trip through the centre of the Neck paddock, past the quagmire where sometimes sheep perished. For some unknown reason, run cattle did not go near it, but they would approach the track where Christine walked beside it very closely; they may have been only inquisitive, but the massive collection of oddly shaped horns and closing hoof beats was most alarming — cattle on one side, quagmire on the other. One day, as rain started to fall, Christine discovered, as she opened her umbrella, that the cattle fled. Thereafter, summer or winter, she carried that black umbrella with the hooked handle whenever she went into the homestead. After the first stampede, the cattle would return, but she had only to open the umbrella sharply to send them flying away. Her progress through that paddock was punctuated by umbrella exercises.

This wintry evening, she was waiting for

Jim. She felt somehow fearful in the waning light, while the murmuration of starlings flew to their roosts in the willows. In such weather, with thunder and rare forked lightning, she wished he would return early from the homestead. Although the kowhai was blooming, it was almost dark at five o'clock, with such a heavy sky and pelting rain.

What was that? A faint call? From the creek crossing?

There could be only one rider out there, at this hour. Sobbing, she slithered down the muddy track — he was trying to scramble out of the water, while the horse, on its back on a stony bank above the creek, was rolling in agony, legs viciously lashing out.

It was only then that Christine realised that, thank God, both man and horse were strangers. The creek was rising so quickly that Jim would not tackle this crossing — he would ride some miles out of his way, to the bullock track on Ruru, where the creek bed widened out into shallows. The upper bank must have caved in, for the horse to be lying injured on the second level, well above flood height.

The stranger seemed to have broken no limbs. His head was bleeding badly, but he managed to stagger back to the whare with Christine's support.

She tore a strip off a clean sheet to make a pad for the wound; then the iron kettle was balanced on the stones. The stranger awkwardly scrambled into clothes borrowed from Jim — his own swag, he thought vaguely, was somewhere in the creek.

He was anxious about his injured horse. Was there a rifle in the whare? Could Christine help him down the path again, to put Darkie out of his misery?

By now she had made a pot of tea, and her injured visitor seemed to be reviving.

'Yes, there's a twenty-two and a three-o-three. But I'm sure, if I do get you down to the creek, you won't be fit to get back again.'

'Can't leave Darkie to die — been a damn good horse,' he gasped. 'Just ridden down from Akitio.'

'I'm a fair shot with a twenty-two,' said Christine, 'but that's no good.'

He tried to get up from the rail-back chair — there were two in the whare.

'Must get there somehow,' he muttered. Shocked by his weakness, he added, 'Legs don't work too well.'

'My husband should be home soon,' she said. 'You'd better wait — '

A brilliant flash of lightning lit the room; the thunderclap rattled on the corrugated roof, it seemed, echoing from iron walls. Then came the rain and the hail. They could not hear one another in a gloom lit only by the leaping flames in the open fire. Water poured down the muddy track.

Where was Jim? Please come, she prayed, it will be dark soon.

The stranger was again muttering. 'Must shoot Darkie — must — broken back, I'd say.'

In a sudden silence as the rain stopped, they heard a screaming neigh of agony.

Christine went over to the rifle. Jim had shown her how to load it, impressing on her the need to load only when the target area was reached, and to keep the safety catch on.

'In the head, I suppose? Between the eyes?' she asked.

'Just a girl,' he said. 'You can't — '

'Well, you can't,' Christine answered, 'and someone must.'

Reluctantly she went out into the gathering darkness, mud slurping round her gumboots.

Hoofbeats — Jim — leading his horse from the other direction, the whare side of the creek.

'Christine,' he called, 'Christine — what's happened?' he asked, as he saw that she was carrying the rifle.

'Oh, Jim, thank goodness! There's a horse — dying, we think — on the ledge on the far side of the creek.'

'Which horse? There's none in the Neck — a cattle beast, more likely.'

'No — it's a stranger — he's hurt, and he can't walk — and he's worried about his horse,' she explained.

'Here,' Jim said, 'give me that rifle.' As he spoke he was unbuckling the girth strap, taking the saddle off his own horse. 'Lead Bloss up to the whare, turn her out in that paddock at the back — if I tie her, she'll jerk back when she hears the shot. She's used to them, but that's when I'm near at hand — one never knows — '

Christine turned the mare out, and returned to carry the saddle into the whare. As she did so, a shot rang out. The stranger, who had seemed asleep, sat up with a groan.

'You?' he said, puzzled. 'The shot — ?'

'My husband is home,' she explained. 'He'll be here soon.'

Jim appeared, with the stranger's swag, not far from where Darkie had plunged into the undermined bank.

Their casualty brightened up. 'Thanks, mate. No chance of saving him, I s'pose?'

'No — broken back,' replied Jim. 'How did it happen?'

'Don't know, exactly. Darkie's sure-footed — he stumbled. I went over his head in a hurry.'

'Just as well,' Jim said. 'If you hadn't got clear of the stirrup and he'd rolled on you — '

'Yeah.'

'The track runs beside a bank there. It might have collapsed with this kowhai flood.'

'Darkie'll block the creek. What can we do?' asked the stranger.

'There's another ledge below the bank where your horse is — the creek spreads out lower down, it never reaches the upper level. Later on I'll get the bullock team to drag the body onto the flat.'

Christine was adding more potatoes to the stew. 'He was saying that he came down from Akitio,' she told Jim.

'What? Crossed the Owahanga and the Mataikona?' Jim asked. 'I thought they'd be in flood.'

'Crossed the Owahanga at low tide,' the stranger answered.

'The Mataikona was well up — logs coming down — so I cut in to Te Mai, and they said I'd get through your station to the road.'

'So you would. You're not far out now,

six or seven miles. What about the Tinui river?' Jim enquired. 'You'd cross that on our country, just below Te Mai.'

'Darkie swam that one,' was the reply.

'Then the Whareama will be up — you might have to wait at the homestead.'

Christine called them to dinner. Her dinner-set, consisting of enamel plates, heaped with potatoes and mutton stew, was set out on the scrubbed table. Their visitor was grateful, but made very small inroads into the steaming plateful.

'Your swag's wet,' said Jim. 'I'll help you unpack it — you can dry your gear in front of the fire.'

'Don't know what I'd have done if the whare was empty. Thanks, I'm still a bit groggy.'

He staggered as he stood up. His gear had been wrapped in canvas; his clothes were only damp, and soon were spread over strings in front of the fire.

'They'll smell of smoke,' said Christine, 'but we get used to it.'

The stranger refused to lie down on the only bed. Jim piled some sacks in a corner, and their visitor lay there. He was shivering now, and grey in the face.

'I'll ride in as soon as it gets light,' Jim promised, piling more logs on the fire. 'I won't take it on in the dark with the creeks in flood.'

'I don't want any more accidents,' the stranger agreed.

In the morning he was no better, sometimes unconscious, momentarily almost delirious. Nothing could be done. Jim must ride in to the homestead for help, while Christine cared for the unconscious man.

When the long day was over — flooded creeks, telephone lines down, bullocks sullen and unco-operative — Jim arrived with the sledge and a spare horse.

'Here I am, dear — we'll have to ride back. I wouldn't be able to get the team over the creek on Ruru now — they'd need to swim at the ford.'

Then he saw her face, white and strained.

'What's the matter?' Jim asked. 'Is he worse?'

'He's — dead,' replied Christine. 'Hours ago — he stopped muttering and seemed to go to sleep. I watched him, but he was comfortable, so I didn't disturb him. Then he stirred, and groaned — and he was gone, just like that.'

Jim put his arm around her. 'I'm so sorry, my dear.'

★ ★ ★

After that incident, even when her little son was born, the whare was no longer such a happy place. Ten days before the baby was expected, Christine walked the miles into the homestead. Next day Jim drove her in the buggy the ten miles to the junction, to catch the coach. Thirty miles by coach into the township — three days wait in the home owned by the midwife.

'Mother and baby son well,' she reported on the party line to the house where Jim was staying, while he worked and waited for news.

When Christine returned by coach and buggy to the homestead, her husband carried the baby the rest of the way in a basket strapped in front of him on the saddle.

The supply of stones ran low as she boiled the napkins in an old oval enamel boiler, the leak in the base mended with metal washers. Time after time the stone would crack, the boiler slop over onto the fire, ashes shower up into the washing.

The little son was always into mischief; plum stones on a jam saucer were a favourite diet if Christine was out of sight, perhaps feeding the few hens she had. He would wander off, his puppy following him, and fail to answer his mother's call.

The day she spent three anxious hours

searching for him was the end of their life in the whare. She had called and called, she had looked in every favourite corner — the pup, too, was missing. At last, from the opposite bank of the creek, she saw him in a patch of bush. He was sitting happily above a deep pool, chubby legs hanging over an undermined bank, the puppy intently watching as he threw pebbles into the creek, both of them peering closely at each ever-widening circle.

As soon as they could manage it, Jim and Christine packed their belongings. Helen and Brian were on that sheep station in the north, and there was work in the district for a shepherd.

They would return, Jim told his father, if there was a dwelling for them near the road frontage of the property — a house with a coal range was Christine's one requirement.

26

Over the years Dick had become an expert with the axe and the cross-cut saw. He and his mother had at first rented a little cottage in Taihape while he found odd jobs. The Livery and Bait Stables found many for him; armed with a letter from the Dannevirke Postmaster, he would be a temporary postman; more often he would find work up at Bennett's sawmill. That was rare, though — the men there were married, with families, living in the mill-houses nearby, at the Siding.

His mother seemed determined that he should go into the milling world. In her young days in New Zealand, she had disliked the bush, she had told him. He could never understand why she wanted to go back. The money angle he could understand; sometimes she was very frail, anxious to be settled where she would not need to take in washing. Dick was unhappy when, at first, in Taihape she had plodded around the township, laundering and ironing for anyone unable or unwilling to do this work for herself.

Through the King Country, new mills were being opened — Turangarere, Hihitahi (translated as 'One ray of sunshine', a Maori told Dick, a very apt name), Murimotu, all the way north to Makotuku, Mansons Siding, Taringamotu, north again of Taumarunui. With the completion of the Main Trunk at Pokaka, rakes of timber wagons rattled north and south to the cities. Wherever there was clearing and laying bush tram-lines, Dick went, taking Mother with him; later, as he grew older, he joined in the felling and milling.

He had a real love for the trees and the timber, the growth and the grain: the grace of rimu and the fine markings in the boards, the towering totara where the wood-pigeons nested, the brilliant red flower of the rewarewa where the tuis feasted on the nectar; the whorls of brown in the sawn timber of the native honeysuckle, the reddish boards of the totara, the straight-grained but brittle matai, tawa, kamahi, kaikawaka, miro, even kahikatea in the low-lying areas.

In the more open country where the Hautapu river supplied trout meals, kowhai spilled its gold in the late spring; in the summer the air was sweet with the scent of lace-bark blossom.

Caroline would live in an unused shack

while her son was in the bush, or in a tent in the bitter frosts of the high country, rugged and thickly forested. Felling was often some miles from the mill; it was easier and quicker to live on the job than to walk in when the horses hauled the loads of logs along the bush tram-lines, and out again in the morning, before day had fully broken.

A bench hand after a short time in the bush, Dick soon found himself promoted to head bencher, with weekends free. From Hihitahi it was a long ride into town, but sometimes that trip was necessary. At other times a party of three or four would saddle up and ride to the cold desert of the Waimarino, hunting wild cattle or brumbies (wild horses). From mobs of the latter, once rounded up, they would select what appeared to be the best, after a wild chase across the plain. In the evenings after work, these horses would be broken in; later, they would fetch a reasonable price in town. The Livery and Bait Stables might want a mare, or a local farmer be interested in another hack. The best stallion Dick ever had was one he brought down from Waimarino to Turangarere.

The beef from wild cattle provided a change in the cookhouse, where the single men had their meals. Dick's horse was expert at dodging the enraged charge of a horned steer. Once the horse was too quick for the rider, who found himself on foot. For a moment the steer's attention was distracted, while it made up its mind whether to charge human or animal. Dick was up a tree that he later vowed he never could have climbed; but the lowest branch was bending as the steer charged the thin trunk.

The kanuka tossed and swayed until the branch, with a rending sound like torn cloth, split in two. Dick was grimly hanging on, just above those wicked horns, when his mates, with dogs and rifles, came to the rescue. As the steer took off, a shot rang out — that, said Dick, was the best beef they had ever eaten.

When snow blanketed the Kaimanawas, the deer started to come down. Snow on the Waimarino did not stop the hunters — venison made a pleasant change. Wild pigs abounded, to the detriment of the scattered farms at lambing time. After two dogs had been ripped by vicious tusks, the men were chary of those beasts. With plenty of good pig dogs, three or four to each man, good shots all, and keeping together, they would go after pork occasionally. If the dogs could bail up a sow, one of the men would rush in to catch a squealing piglet or two. But old boars were left alone, unless a three-o-three could despatch one from a distance. For poultry, wood-pigeons were plentiful, especially when the tawa berries were ripe. Paradise duck paraded along the Hautapu.

Fishing there, then, was a matter of deciding to have trout for tea. The browns and rainbows were plentiful, and easily played. A manuka pole and a piece of string, with a nice fat huhu grub bound to the hook, would give the angler a meal; but a proper trout fly was the best lure. Many were the arguments in the cookhouse at night over the respective merits of a Taihape Tickler, or Dick's favourite, a Red Tip Governor. Of course, if the ranger had gone into town, the huhu grub was always the most reliable bait. Whether sport or the meal was the aim of the exercise depended on the lure.

Rounding up brumbies and hunting cattle beasts under the shadow of the mountains was exciting, but there was nothing Dick enjoyed more than a quiet stroll along the Hautapu in the evening. Rod in hand, he would watch for the tell-tale swirl of a fish; the flick of the fly on the water, the screech of the reel as a fighting fish took the lure — this was a delight.

27

Across the Island, Ronald and Henry carried on, although there was less coach work. The earlier years of horse transport were vanishing; no longer did a pedestrian waving a red flag precede a motor vehicle. No more did the doctor drive at a fast pace round and round the Carlyle Street block in an Edwardian car, with a tiller instead of a steering wheel, while Henry shouted to Ronald, 'Look out, mate, here he comes again'. Since the good doctor's steering was somewhat erratic, those on the footpath rushed for the fences.

Henry was often away from the Gully, taking on contract work in the homesteads beyond the Tukituki. Ronald was making a reasonable living writing signs for shops and hotels, as well as lining the exterior panels of the coaches still in service and painting those coats of arms.

The bach was a cottage now; Henry could turn his hand to anything. Whatever he tackled had to be perfect — a fraction of an inch out of line would annoy him. He crafted the furniture that replaced the old fruit boxes.

The drawers in the press were dovetailed, doors swung sweetly, fitted neatly. The millhouses his brother Dick lived in would have made him very angry, with their ill-hung doors and draughty windows.

He remained the better cook of the two. His only dislike of outback stations was the poor meals sometimes served by cooks who didn't know how to boil a potato.

Beyond Waimarama, he found himself cooking, for a shearing gang. Wet weather had delayed the shearers, as they moved on from shed to shed. The owners had expected that busy time to be over when they arranged for Henry to paint the homestead. He would have a whare to himself, and join the shepherds and the station cook for meals in the kitchen.

However, the boss of the shearing gang had come across Henry on other stations.

'Join us at the cook-house,' he told Henry. 'This cussed weather gets on our nerves — you can't get on with your painting, either.' Their homes were too far away for any of them to risk leaving the station for a few days. The weather might clear, they would be shearing a day later. And they had no money in their pockets — they would get their cheques when the shed was cut out. Henry had completed those verandah walls that were protected from weather by the curved iron roof.

The gang shuffled cards in the cookhouse until the cook, a greasy, fat chap, swept them off the table.

'Can't you get out of my cookhouse, you lazy hounds?' he yelled.

Henry, rarely involved in arguments, said, 'It's the boss's cookhouse, isn't it? Or have you bought it?'

'Don't you talk to me, you paint-slopper, you're not one of the gang.'

The rouseabout and a younger man went out to lie down on their bunks. New to the gang, they expected a donnybrook; they had not realised that the cook was a coward as well as a bully. The bunkhouse was the only retreat if they wanted to avoid being involved.

The cookhouse with its long table and bench seats was also their recreation room. It did not matter, usually; in fine weather the clatter of the machines in the wool-shed would start just after dawn, and often, to cut out before the weather broke, work would continue till near dark.

That did not suit the cook; they would forget to tell him that they would not be up for dinner until an hour or so later than usual. The food would be burnt and blackened, or flung onto the table for flies to crawl over.

Not that it made much difference, Henry fumed. Good ingredients wasted — the boss wasn't mean with meat or vegetables.

'Cookie, what you got for dinner?' one of the older shearers called.

The cook, with clenched fists, stomped up to Henry. 'Now look what you done, you — . No-one growled till you started!'

'Is that so? You must be stone deaf!'

Henry was in the mood for an argument. He had met that cook before — when this gang had joined in with another in a massive shed, and a woman had taken over the cooking. This man had given in then; there was nothing more likely to make him panic than a wet dish-cloth in the hands of a determined woman.

As he approached, Henry stuck his chin out. 'Go on, hit me,' he said.

The boss of the gang looked on with a grin. If only that cursed cook would start a fight, they could all work off their frustrations. No-one would worry about a group taking to one man, not this time. He had a difficult job keeping his gang together with these apologies for meals. It was a good gang, too, he didn't want to lose any of them — except the cook. They were used to rough servings; but they hated this greasy half-roasted hogget, and the potatoes with the skin hanging from them, like the wool from an old ewe with milk fever. When they were shearing — competing for the honour of ringer — they put up with it, too tired to complain. When there was nothing to do but laze about, waiting for the weather to clear, the grumbles came thick and fast, minor grievances turned into major disasters. They had never let him down yet — but the day might come. For the sheep already shorn, they would be paid; and they were clean, quick shearers, rarely calling for tar. Even though the flush of the season was over, they would find sheds somewhere, or go down south for the later shearing, and the cocksfoot.

Cookie looked at Henry's chin, and the glint in his eye — then unclenched his fists. 'You make me sick, you Scandy runt!' he exclaimed.

'I might be a Scandy,' replied Henry, 'but the food in this cookhouse would make anyone sick!'

'I won't put up with this,' the cook said to the boss. 'I'll go — unless you stop this — talking to me like that. You can all starve.'

'You can catch the mail-car if you hurry,'

said the burly leader. One try to persuade the character to stay, and he would ride rough-shod over them all. 'We can go without grease and flies tonight — we haven't been working today.'

'Hurrah!' shouted one shearer. 'Can I pack your swag for you, Cookie?'

The cook drifted towards the kitchen end of the building, and began to throw tin plates into a box.

'No, you don't!' shouted the boss. 'None of that is yours — it's all my gear for the gang.'

The cook ignored him. He nodded to two brawny shearers — no words needed. They frog-marched the cook to the bunk-room, and stood by to make sure he didn't lay his thieving hands on any of their mates' belongings. Cookie would have travelled more quickly with the swift kick his guards planned to administer, until they noticed the station owner ride in towards the quarters.

'Bully for you, Henry!' was the chorus in the cook-house.

'I wanted to get rid of him,' said the boss. 'It's not only the food, he's been pinching stuff from the homestead this time. But you blokes won't take a turn at cooking when you're shearing,' he added.

One or two were already prowling in the kitchen.

'Look at the trouble you've caused,' he said to Henry. With a grin on his face, he continued, 'You'll have to be the cook, now.'

'Right. What's the pay?' Henry asked, to the boss's surprise.

In these cold hills, Henry could not start his work until later in the morning, when any dampness dried out, and it was useless painting after late afternoon. The gang would be quite happy. They knew only too well how long it might be before the registry sent another cook, and he might be worse — or the same man might come back again, making a deliberately sickening effort at the cooking. It had been known to happen.

With the painting Henry had been employed to do, and his wages as a cook, he was doing very well. If the house painting was delayed, the owners did not mind — it was a contract job, anyway. It was more important to keep the shearers happy and get the wool away.

Ronald and Henry had talked about buying a sailing dinghy. They went out occasionally with a friend, fishing, sailing, or perhaps shooting rabbits for the pot on the Watchman, that sheer island toward the western shore of the Lagoon. A damaged dinghy was for sale cheap, Henry found when he returned to the Gully. He could fix it with cringles, tar and paint. He would make a sail — they had bought an old Westermann sewing machine, useful for patching and mending torn clothes. Cordage — that should not cost too much at Robert Holt's.

The boat was painted as a labour of love by the two master painters.

They were often out on the Inner Harbour — freshly caught fish supplied the evening meals for the weekend. Often a friend or two would join them. The boat was a broad-beamed, clinker built sailing dinghy; too slow for any racing class, it would never capsize, however hard the wind blew or the passengers moved round, excited over the catch of large fish.

In mid-April, 1912, Henry and Ronald set off for a day's rabbit shooting on the Watchman. A sweet little breeze carried them up-harbour.

'If that freshens,' said Henry, 'we might need to put a reef in when we tack back.'

'It might swing further round,' Ronald replied. 'Bert says there's masses of rabbits — we won't stay very long.'

They anchored the dinghy in the lee of the island, wading ashore carefully with their rifles, ammunition and half-sacks for their trophies.

The masses of rabbits had disappeared. After a fruitless two hours, Henry suggested they should give up. The island was too small for them to separate; hunters kept together, otherwise one might move ahead of the other, and his movements in the undergrowth be mistaken for a rabbit.

'You go back to the boat, Henry,' said Ronald. 'I'd like one rabbit to take home — I'll try over by the cliff. You could take the dinghy out a bit. The tide must be falling, and she'll sit in the mud otherwise. She's mighty heavy to warp out of that.'

Henry had taken the dinghy further out to the tide mark when he heard the shot. Ronald had wasted no time walking over towards the cliffs. It should not be long before he returned — unless he was looking for another shot.

The wind was freshening, slapping wavelets against the ebbing tide. It would be a long slog home, if they did not set out soon. Once in a while, with a storm blowing up from the Westshore bay, they had spent the night, marooned. Quite pleasant in the summer, but a little cold in mid-April. This season the usual Indian summer had deserted the area. They would have to buck the tide in the narrows, too, if they left it too long.

After a while, Henry waded back to the shore. He would remind Ronald that another rabbit for the pot was not worth a stiff battle with wind and tide. It was possible that his brother had caught a foot in a rabbit-hole and broken an ankle — but he was usually very careful.

By now Henry was on the plateau, with the dividing fence ahead.

Half-caught, it seemed, in the fence wires was Ronald. Henry ran.

The twenty-two had fallen to the ground, an outflung hand, still, above it. How often had they reminded each other never to climb through a fence with a loaded rifle? Leave it unloaded — put it through first, if there was no-one else about, with the barrel pointing away from the hunter —

Never again. The bullet had been immediately fatal.

The Watchman was deserted. Should he sail back for help, and return? What help would avail now? He began half carrying, half dragging his brother's body towards the shore.

Afterwards he could not remember how he had managed to carry Ronald over the mud left slippery by the receding tide.

It was still on the ebb; the flow helped

a little as he tacked single-handed towards the narrows and the jetty. As he approached the pier, one of his mates sang out, 'Where's your for'ard hand, the lazy bloke? Not seasick, surely?'

The comment raised a laugh on the jetty. Ronald was the one who preferred rough weather. Henry could manage, but he did not enjoy heavy seas.

He did not answer. He ran his craft up the beach, keeping it bow on, and somehow dropping the mainsail with a clatter as the boom hit the transom. Clumsy seamanship, and his friends were about to say so. One glanced into the cockpit, awash now where the dinghy had shipped waves and spray, and tinged with red. Ronald's unnatural pose, his head almost in the water at the bottom of the boat, told them everything.

A shocked silence fell.

As one, they went to Henry's assistance. While a man ran for a stretcher — or an old door, it didn't matter now — another called the local policeman. Others cleaned out the dinghy, carried it well above the high tide mark and stowed the gear. Henry said nothing — there was nothing to say.

The Coroner's Court brought in its inevitable verdict of 'Death by Misadventure', with a rider to warn others of the danger of carrying a loaded rifle. Dick, receiving a telegram at the Hihitahi mill, had managed to ride a goods train into Taihape, where he caught the Auckland-Wellington express. It stopped at Palmerston North at 5 a.m., leaving him with a four-hour wait for the Napier train.

Henry had sent telegrams to the girls, with the sad news; two of them were certainly unable to make the journey from their outback homes in time for the funeral — they had young children too. About his sister Caroline he was not sure — she could have reached Masterton in time for the Wellington-Woodville Junction train, and her manager husband was more able to take days away from the station.

And William? Address unknown, as it was to remain for nearly twenty years. He would reappear when his grandfather's estate was to be shared, then disappear before matters were finalised. Fifty years later his whereabouts — or his grave — would remain a mystery.

28

The report of the coroner's inquest published in the Napier newspapers brought a visitor to the lonely house in the Gully. A young officer now, Ian had been the 'boy' on the *Zuleika*, surviving the wreck by sheer good fortune. Roald had told him about his family in Napier; the young man had been interested in the nephews and their bach in the Gully. If ever his ship berthed at Napier, Roald had told him, Ian must call on these brothers.

In the years between, another link was forged in the chain. He found himself on a ship where Len Jones was First Mate. Chatting about vessels each had sailed on, Ian mentioned the *Zuleika* and an officer who had befriended him. Len remembered the widow and her family, sailing from London to Napier; it was a further step in the conversation to talk about the pride and courage of the mother, and the attractive ways of the two younger girls.

Len told Ian he should not only visit the brothers, but enquire about mother and her daughters. The youngest would be well over twenty, he thought. Len rather regretted

267

losing touch with Helen, but he had made no real effort to contact her.

Now Ian's ship had berthed at Napier, sailing from Lyttelton. He had been considering a shore job — there was a young lady at Blenheim — but that port was hampered by the Wairau bar. She had cousins in Christchurch, the city of the Plains. Ian thought he would look for a berth on one of the many little vessels that traded round Banks Peninsula. He and his future wife could have a settled home.

That was just what Henry wanted to leave. Ronald's share could go to their mother — it would not be much, but it might save Richard having to stretch his wages. There was no sign of William; his share could be left in trust. Henry would not live in the Gully alone. He could move from homestead to homestead, finding odd jobs of painting and papering to keep him in pocket money. He would sell the boat, too; he could never face going out in it again.

Helen, away up at Ngatapa now, out of Gisborne, had suggested he come to visit his two little nephews there. Christine and her husband were not far away at Patutahi. Jim had taken up fencing contracts in this warmer district, where the puriri grew in abundance. The timber made excellent fence posts, saving the farmer expense. Under the contract, the farmer was to supply materials; Jim found himself helping to cut and saw the posts. Old Mr Dyer had not built that house he had promised. So Jim and his wife and son caught the train to Napier, then the coastal steamer to Gisborne, staying at first with Helen and her husband.

The young cousins were in to every kind of mischief in that shepherd's cottage. As soon as there was trouble, the two older boys would vanish, leaving Helen's younger son, slower on his feet, to face the consequences. His brother was a tease; tired after running after bigger boys all day, he would be nearly asleep over his tea. His brother would keep talking to him, until his curly head dropped onto his food. Then the other two would shriek with laughter.

Helen and Christine, always close friends, would discover after an incautious comment that Mother had been right — little pitchers did have big ears.

A swift tap on a fat little leg under the table, or even a glare, would sometimes stop the chatter before irreparable damage was done. A kindly but unusual neighbour came to Helen's back door one day, when the older boy was clinging to mother's skirt. After Helen had agreed to lend her the sugar she requested, a small voice piped up: 'She sorta laughs when she talks' — a swift nudge on the little seat and a long pause — 'like them chickens do.'

Christine in the kitchen had to bite her lip to stop laughing. Helen was made of sterner stuff — she managed to carry on the conversation until the woman left, clutching the sugar.

Then Helen and Christine could collapse together in laughter. They agreed it was not good for the boys. They would get right out of hand if they knew how much they amused their mothers.

Christine decided it would be better if they had separate homes. Besides, Jim was not very happy, living in Brian's home, although, of course, it was not their own house. If the fact that Christine was living with her sister ever reached that Wairarapa east coast station, Jim's family would be more antagonistic than ever. If she would live with her sister, they would say, why not with her husband's sisters?

Sister Caroline had not acknowledged the telegram advising her of her brother's death. Later she would pick a quarrel with Henry for not telling her the sad news.

Unable to spare more than a few days from the mill, Richard — he was still Richard to his brother, very punctilious with names — had tried to persuade Henry to go back to the King Country with him. There would be work there, and Mother would like to see her older son. She had always seemed closer to Ronald, possibly because he had borne her favourite brother's name. Henry felt he could not bear her blaming him for that death. Caroline could be very harsh sometimes, often failing to understand those who had inherited her withdrawn nature.

'Why not come down to Lyttelton with me?' Ian asked. 'We're far from a full ship, paying off at the next port. You could — er — offer to paint the skipper's cabin — or something like that.'

That was the beginning of a long friendship that lasted through the war years. Ian found a job as skipper on one of the little boats. For a few weeks Henry helped him with deliveries and stowage.

Everything the Peninsula farmer would want came by water. The skipper carried a notebook, jotting down what was wanted at each jetty; those orders he would collect from one or other of the Lyttelton grocers — Russells or Agars or Forbes. From the farms the little ships would take farm butter, eggs, cheese from the farmers' own cheese factory, wool. The wool was railed into

Christchurch, but all the rest was carried up to the individual farmer's grocery store, where it would be credited against his account. Potatoes, grass seed, particularly cocksfoot, wheat, oats, chaff, even some stock, the little ships of Banks Peninsula carried it all.

Though parts had been farmed since the 1840s, and Akaroa settled, too, the few roads were little more than tracks. The ships carried the traffic, goods and passengers. Purau, Port Levy where the ships tied up only at the Maori side — site of the pa — unless mail or goods were being carried for the 'white' side of the bay, or the farmer ran up a flag, advising in that way that he wanted produce or mail picked up.

All the way round — Holmes Bay, Pigeon Bay, Menzies Bay, Little Akaloa, Okains, Le Bons — usually bordered by steep cliffs — into Akaroa Harbour, with its more sheltered anchorages — Takamatua, Robinsons, Barry's Bay (at full tide), French Farm, Wainui. All waiting for mail, goods inwards, or produce outwards. On the open coast to the west were smaller inlets and even steeper cliffs, a rugged shoreline stretching to Birdlings Flat and the Kaitorete Spit that runs out to the south of Lake Ellesmere.

Ian could show Henry the nearer bays and the ships that serviced them: the *Devron*, with its picturesque sails, that was to finish up on Purau's original wharf on the eastern shore, the *Orewa*, the *John Anderson* and the *Purau*, which was on the harbour earlier than the others. The little *Matariki* spent her time on Lyttelton harbour, trading to Church and Charteris Bays and Quail Island.

The skipper was as busy off the water as on, with all the errands for his clients, often as much as one hundred loaves of bread per ship, from Norton's Bakery. His off-sider, the engineer, did the necessary stoking as well as playing his part as engineer.

The barter system round the Peninsula was not confined to goods. Sheds and dips were used by adjacent farmers in return for so many days' work on the owner's property.

In the late summer, after most of the Mainland sheep were shorn, the shearing gangs would move onto the Peninsula for the cocksfooting. Often there would be Australian gangs reliant on the little ships for transport and stores. The tall grass was reaped, piled onto canvas sheets, and then beaten vigorously with flails. The straw, piled beside the site, would provide Cook with handy compost. Into this the thick peel of the potatoes were thrown, and the following season the gang would have a good supply of clean well-grown potatoes, that had never needed mounding or weeding.

The sacks of seed were taken down to the next ship to call at the Bay; by water they would start their journey to the stock and station agents, and so to other farms and overseas.

In years to come, Henry would catch sight of cocksfoot seed in a shed, or in a homestead kitchen there would be a tin of Norton's Egg Preservative. He would be reminded again of Banks Peninsula, and the little ships.

29

Pleas from Jim's father took Christine and her family out of the Gisborne area and back to the Wairarapa.

Helen left Ngatapa at the same time. The young man who had been running Tangitere since they had left had been able to buy a farm of his own — would Brian please return on most advantageous terms, asked the stock and station agents? No-one else seemed prepared to run the place.

A similar difficulty had arisen at Riverside. The sons who had returned when Jim and Christine left the whare had now paid a minimal deposit on another farm. They had realised, as had Christine and Jim, that no life of their own was possible while Father Dyer and his daughters lived in the homestead. Improvements of any kind were frowned on — there was no money available, Mr Dyer would say, and he kept tight hold of the cheque book. He even resented paying for the cartage of wool; the boys could take it out, a few bales at a time, on a dray if they could not borrow a wagon, the twenty odd miles to Whakataki and Castlepoint. When the coastal steamer anchored off the beach, they could ride down to help load onto the lighters that took the bales out to the ship standing offshore.

His sons' time and labour meant nothing; they had to be fed, and as poorly as possible, so they had to fill in their time. If other jobs were neglected, he did not see them. No farmer he — scrub and tawhinu, broken down fences, Taranaki gates, dirty sheep — none of it mattered.

As he had imagined at the start of farming life, he firmly believed still that all that was necessary for an income was sheep of some sort and shearers. On second thoughts, he would not need to pay shearers — his sons could do the shearing (and the mustering, the draughting, the fleece-o's work, and the baling). It might take longer, but they could finish before Christmas. What if woolly sheep were cast and dying in the back paddocks? He did not see them.

He had contracted for the mail run, too. His daughters would drive the gig, if the weather, the road and the creeks were all in reasonable condition.

Would — er — Christine cook for one of her sisters-in-law, for the remaining four months of the contract?

That was the last thing Christine wanted

to do, but Jim could not look after 3,000 acres alone, trying to make much needed repairs, and take on the mail run as well. Nor could she, with a small child.

Her brother Dick was convalescing after a midnight trip into Taihape with a burst appendix. He would not be able to handle timber for some time. Would it be a good plan, she asked Jim, to suggest that her brother help them out? Their mother would stay on in the mill house; Gardiners were very decent owners, they knew, and had told Dick there would be a job on the bench when he was fit again.

Jim was very much in favour of the idea. Dick was delighted. After his usual two hour wait in Woodville, wet and windy, as it was every time Dick had to wait for a connection at that junction, he was pleased to be met at Masterton, and delighted to see his sister and his little nephew again.

The boy would give his uncle no rest, which worried Christine. After all, Dick was supposed to be convalescing after a serious operation; with the delay in getting to hospital, his ultimate recovery had been in doubt for a few days. His sister suggested that he should shut himself in his bedroom for an hour or two of peace. Dick loved his adoring nephew dearly, but the latter was too full of energy for a man not long out of hospital.

Presently the three-year-old asked his mother where his uncle was.

'I think perhaps he's gone up to the fowl-house,' his mother answered.

The little boy wandered round the homestead, shouting 'Nunk! Nunk!' The fowl-house was across one of the house paddocks, 200 yards or so away. No voice carried as far as that, apart from the occasional bark of the dogs. The kennels were not far from the fowl-house; anyone collecting eggs or feeding the hens would not hear a voice in the distance, so 'Nunk' could safely be assigned there.

Sadly, the boy wandered back to mother in the kitchen.

'Must be in the fowl-house,' he stated firmly.

Thereafter, when anyone could not be found, 'Must be in the fowl-house' was the answer.

Generally his uncle was his saviour. Caught in any mischief, he would rush to Dick. 'She's af'en me,' he would say.

Chopping wood, Dick would hide him in the woodshed until his mother had given up looking for him. It was not good for discipline, but her brother waited until

Christine had calmed down before he 'found' his nephew. He had been fingering the china knob on the lid of a large teapot — the fowls were still unfed, Christine realised, as she started to clear the breakfast table.

While she was away, the knob, the size of a marble, had been neatly broken off. It had vanished, possibly down her son's throat, which was her second reason for looking for him so quickly.

The plumstones of the whare days had given way to a variety of objects, most swallowed by accident. As the boy dangled a wire puzzle overhead one day, one piece fell free. — He had spent hours trying, without success, to undo it. — Straight into his mouth, and down his gullet it went, before he could yell with surprise.

Cuts and bruises — born on a Thursday, his mother used to say — but never broken bones. His courage was partly the cause; he would stalk up the hill at the back of the homestead, so far distant that his movements could not be identified. He went to sleep on the stable straw one day, not far from the hoofs of the only untrustworthy horse on the farm.

The night of dance in their own woolshed, he carried the kerosene lamp, left alight in the centre of the big, scrubbed kitchen table — it seated eight comfortably — to his bedroom. Putting the lamp on the floor beside his bed, he clambered in and went to sleep.

Dick, crossing the paddock to check that all was well, found the little boy's blanket, already sooty and beginning to smoulder, overhanging the lamp chimney.

Feeding the fowls became Christine's private nightmare. It was too wet and muddy to take a toddler; but that was the period when her son got into mischief. She came back to the homestead one morning to hear a little voice from the bathroom say, in amazement, 'Ooh! Ronnie p'ick himself.'

There he was, standing on a chair — he was barely walking, and had never dragged a chair along before — rubbing his cut cheek with his knuckle, his father's cut-throat razor firmly held, and the blade missing his ear by a hairbreadth with each rub. Blood everywhere, and a crescent scar for life.

When Dick had returned to the mill, fit and well again, Ronnie invented a boon companion who even had a different voice; often the conversation would bluff Christine into thinking that the nearest neighbour with a son, six miles away, had called.

That nearest neighbour, unfortunately, was sister Caroline. They were better apart, as they so often clashed. Childless herself for the first six years of marriage, Caroline was very free with instructions on child care to Christine, and exceedingly critical of the latter's efforts. Once Caroline's own son was at the toddler stage, his aunt had never seen a more undisciplined child. Out to the fowl-house, much closer to the manager's house than at Jim's place, to wipe the sleeping fowls off their perch, in a flutter of feathers and squawks: 'They're Wyandots, they're wild,' he would say, on later occasions; the tiny calf, only just accustomed to drinking from a bucket, was chased around the house until it collapsed.

Christine gave up her rare visits to her sister when she saw her nephew sitting on the floor with a chased silver teapot (a wedding gift from brother Richard) and a hammer. The child was crowing with glee — the blows had a lovely metalic ring, and the teapot dented so easily. Christine wondered if her sister had noticed what was going on, and drew her attention to the destruction.

'Oh, don't worry, it keeps him quiet,' said his mother.

Helen and Christine had thought their boys mischievous up at Ngatapa, but sheer vandalism was not part of their plans. Sometimes something was broken, like the teapot knob; but the spirit of enquiry and exploration could be sensed in every move.

Their own cousin would pull the tail feathers out of fowls until they were raw and bleeding; the cat had disappeared — the little boy liked stamping on it. Only the dogs were safe: one had bitten him when he had poked his finger in its eye, and Caroline had shouted at her husband to destroy it: 'It's vicious — my son wasn't hurting it!'

30

The war would interrupt all lives, some more than others. The mill owners told Dick that his mother could live in the mill house at Turangarere for as long as she wished. That left him free to enlist in the Rifle Brigade, although he was under age.

They trained in Tauherenikau in the Wairarapa, windy and wet. The first fatigue parties cleared the old riverbed boulders to make a parade ground. Hardy men, from the mills and farms mostly, this particular intake of riflemen was nevertheless the last to be route marched over the Rimutaka hill, rising to nearly 2000 feet from sea-level in a five mile climb, and down seven miles to the plateau; and on again up hill and down dale, the Kaitoke hill and the Mangaroa saddle, through the Upper Hutt township to the camp four miles south. In a hot, muggy November day, it was the route march of all time. The next party for Trentham travelled by train.

Dick's contingent reached Egypt just too late for the battle at Gallipoli. The last mail while he was in base camp there was from his youngest sister: she had a little daughter, she wrote, his first niece.

Foreign names and stories of battles filled the newspapers; after the Dardanelles, New Zealand's own particular interest, Ypres where the Germans first used gas in 1915, Loos, Vimy Ridge, Passchendaele, the Somme, Arras, Amiens — casualties, white feathers, the Russian Revolution — all mixed up now in the old lady's mind.

Dick spent his twenty-first birthday in the front line; then he was gassed, and after that shrapnel wounds in the shoulder sent him to hospital again in England. Later he talked of Sling Camp, and the difficulties English permanent staff sometimes faced with the independent Colonial riflemen.

Watching the first combat planes overhead, from an orchard near Bapaume, he heard a burgeoning Squadron Commander saying, 'I'd rather be up there than down here — I think I'll join the R.A.F.'

'You can have it for me,' Dick replied.

By 1919 he could write to Christine about Cologne and the Rhine.

Henry, too, was overseas. All round New Zealand, the boys were leaving for theatres of war. Down in the Wairarapa, Jim had been a member of the East Coast Mounted Rifles for some time — 'the blind half dozen' they called themselves. Jim was making enquiries of his brothers as to who could run the station while he was overseas. But a circular saw put an end to that plan — two fingers amputated to the second joint, the fourth finger with the top joint missing, as a chunk of knotted willow jammed on the saw bench. Hospital was still forty miles away, but by this time the Oakland had replaced the buggy and the coach. A neighbour drove Jim into town, while Christine, with a two-month-old baby daughter and six-year-old son, managed as best she could for four days.

To Jim's fury, his damaged fingers graded him out. He could still use a rifle as tellingly as ever; but the Army would not have him.

It was just as well. Farm help was increasingly difficult to get, and inferior in quality. The distance from town did not encourage applicants, either. With so many men away at the war, there were jobs to be had much nearer civilisation.

Jim carried on alone with the stock work involved in 3,000 acres, now nearly all grassed. Only the Rough Paddock needed a scrub-cutter — when one could be found. But a cowman gardener to milk the house cows, separate and churn, feed dogs and dig the vegetable garden down near the cow paddock was essential; generally, a married couple was required.

The married couples came — and went, with unfailing regularity. As sure as the man was an asset, the wife could not cook; if by chance the wife was a good cook, a rare occurrence, the husband hardly knew how to milk, or to tell the difference between weeds and seedlings.

Often Christine was thankful that her second pantry — all the preserving — was off the long passage between kitchen and dining-room. Stock buyers would stay the night; the first course would be passable — the cook could not altogether ruin good hogget — but the second, particularly in winter was scorned even by the fowls. After one look at a dissolving boiled pudding, she would go to her preserves, shelves of them, for the trees in the two orchards were laden with fruit each year. All of it was bottled, or made into jam — damsons, greengages, pears and apples. Neither apricot nor peach had been planted — probably the older generation had regarded those as exotics — but hazel nuts and walnuts grew in profusion.

After a trying month in which no dessert could be eaten if it came from the kitchen, Christine sent one particularly revolting squashy lump of suet dough back. Because the husband was an excellent handyman, she had put up with the self-entitled cook.

The latter, arms akimbo, faced her mistress in the kitchen.

'What do yer want?' she asked. 'I made yer a lovely gingerbread pudden, an' yer woulden ate it.'

That couple left the day the mailman called.

The advertisement said 'Plain Cooking'. Christine expected to do all the baking; but one woman arrived who would not make desserts at all. To her mind, puddings were not 'plain cooking'. The husband was not much use, either — so they left at the end of the month, after four weeks of suffering (and paying wages) for Jim and Christine.

The next couple dragged across the home paddock from the swingbridge that led to the road. The woman was very lame.

'I'm afraid this work will be too heavy for you,' said Christine, as she greeted them.

'Strong as a horse I am,' was the reply. 'I tried to kick a durn fowl with both feet.'

A run of near disasters seemed to overtake Jim and his wife. First, it was Jim's fingers. Then one night — uncannily still in that wind-swept homestead, too warm for the time of the year — they were restless. Jim did something they had never done — he took the sleeping toddler out of her bed and

287

tucked her in beside his wife.

Perhaps he had felt the first quiver, though he was always sure that he had felt nothing. He could not explain his action.

In a few minutes the homestead jolted and swayed. Down on the little daughter's pillow fell a large oak-framed picture. Next the medicine chest burst open — broken glass everywhere; yet their son, running in to his parents, walked through this sea of glass and medicine and did not cut his bare feet. Windows shattered, chimneys swayed and crumbled onto the iron roof.

In the morning a soot-blackened face appeared in the doorway.

'I dunno wot you'll say w'en yer know, but there's not a chimney standing, and not a drop of water in the tanks,' the current handyman explained. Yet he had tried to light the stove — with the chimney bricks tumbled about the garden.

True enough, the six tanks at the house had crashed off the stand, and collapsed as if they were paper. The eight tanks at the woolshed were also on the ground. The heavy Wolseley Lister shearing machine, with its small iron wheels, had trundled out of the lean-to engine shed, knocking down and running over the door. Twelve feet out into the sheepyard it had run, and ten feet back.

The tracks were there to prove it. The angle at which the land had tilted could be imagined.

Every bottle of fruit, jam, pickles and tomatoes was smashed on the floor of the second pantry. It was a foot or more deep in broken glass and ruined food. The kitchen pantry was in the same condition — every ingredient was mixed with every other; the flour and sugar bins had sloping wooden lids, but bottles had broken over them, ruining these staple items.

Many of the fences were down, especially near the homestead, the sheep and cattle boxed; it took Jim days to draft the stock again, when he had repaired the fences.

The swingbridge over the Whareama, the only access to the car and the road, was touching the muddy river. To cross, one had to slide down and climb up. Before, there had been only the usual slight sag in the centre. The strainer posts supporting it had not moved; somewhere along that coast the land had shifted in four or five feet. The bed of the stream was much narrower.

The third trouble struck shortly after all the damage done by the vicious earthquake had been repaired. Either pneumonia or the current Spanish influenza epidemic struck Jim down. Sheets dipped in carbolic hung over the doorway to the bedroom, and a nurse arrived to share the twenty-four hour vigil with Christine. His temperature soared to 104 degrees before the fever broke and Christine dared to hope he would recover.

Their son was now attending the local school, riding nine miles each way. The pony had a mind of its own, the boy used to say when he returned to the homestead about 8.30 a.m. It would swing round, take the bit between its teeth and gallop back, although its gait on the outward journey was a slow amble.

Spring had brought more than its usual share of bad weather, with cast ewes and motherless lambs — Christine was bottle-feeding four, and going the rounds of twelve reluctant adoptive ewes in small yards or tied to fences.

Wool suddenly dropped from 10 cents to 2 cents per pound. Selling farm mutton and home-made butter to the road gang forming the vehicle link to Alfredton was the only thing that kept the family in staples such as flour and sugar. Surely things could not get much worse.

31

The men were returning from overseas, Dick amongst them — another shocking voyage for him, with migraine from shrapnel, it seemed, or from the noise of constant bombardment, added to his former failure to find his sea-legs. He vowed then and there never to go out of sight of land again.

Landing in Wellington, he took the opportunity to visit his little sister, as he always called her. Photographs taken with the plate camera had reached him in hospital or base camp; he was eager to see the nephew who had followed him round all day, when he had taken on that mail run for a short time. On the Masterton station he suddenly bent to hug the little niece, but she hid behind mother's skirt.

Once the small girl had overcome her shyness, Dick had another devoted follower, and school holidays gave his nephew a chance to tag round after him again. Now, lying with a blinding attack of migraine in a darkened room, Dick would hear a light feminine voice singing 'Must be in the fowl-house, must be in the fowl-house.'

Of course Christine phoned Caroline on the party-line to let her know that their brother was with her for a few days.

'Have you got a new clock?' snapped Caroline, disregarding the good news about her brother.

'With wool at two cents?' Christine replied. 'You must be joking.'

A receiver was hung up violently somewhere on the line, and the ticking stopped.

'Hasn't Dorinda shifted that clock into another room yet?' asked Christine. 'It's your party-line she's on, isn't it?'

'I never mind who listens in to my conversation,' Caroline said, tartly. 'Did you want to borrow something to feed Richard?'

As if Christine would borrow from Caroline; she would go without if the only lender was this sister.

'No, I phoned to tell you Dick was here. Could you come up to visit us? He'll be going home in two days.'

'I'm busy,' she sneered. 'Not like some people who don't get much for their wool.'

Christine ignored that slur. 'Will I ask Dick to come to the phone and chat to you?'

'No — I've got fish to fry,' retorted Caroline, slamming down the receiver.

Dick went back to the Turangarere mill, where his mother greeted him as if he had been away only a few weeks instead of several years.

She had wanted for nothing; those working at the mill — too old or too young for overseas service — had seen to that. Mill slabs appeared in the woodshed. Someone from the felling wielded an axe on a wet day. Trout fillets had been given to the old lady with the comment, 'The family's tired of fish — it would have been a pity to give it to the cat.' Or it would be a rabbit, cleaned and skinned: 'Too many of the things around — we can't keep them down.'

Rarely did a group go up to the Waimarino; but if they did, a piece of venison or a few chops from a Captain Cooker would find their way to the house the pine trees were beginning to shelter.

The married men milked a few house cows, and there was always milk and butter to spare. The mill owner had suggested that Caroline put her groceries on his account, the amount to be deducted from Dick's wages when he came back. There were times when it seemed unlikely that he would get back, let alone be fit for mill work again. In any case, Ted intended that the bill be forgotten.

Proud and independent as ever, Caroline

would have none of what she called 'charity'. To Dick's amazement he found, on his return, that almost the whole of the allowance the Army had paid to her was intact — she had opened a bank account for him. She did not trust banks for herself; when they had lived in Napier, William had been anxious about the effect of the rumoured collapse of the Bank of New Zealand. Caroline had listened to his predictions of disaster — he had failed to explain, later, that the government of the day, had averted the panic.

For Caroline, sovereigns in an old tea-caddy were a guarantee of ready money. She had not been into Taihape since the day before her son left for his training at Tauherenikau.

Dick settled in again at the mill. That winter, when the autumn stock sales had brought excellent prices, Jim and Christine set off with their young family to visit the old lady, so far away, and to have a holiday in Rotorua. After his bout of influenza, Jim had gone there with farmer friends and Bernard, Caroline's husband. He wanted Christine, too, to see that surprising wonderland, with its bubbling mud and sparking geysers.

An easy drive, for those days, across the

northern Wairarapa, then through the one-width road cut out of the cliffs of the Manawatu Gorge — it was a long day to Palmerston North. Through Halcombe and over Vinegar Hill; just as well Jim had chains, for parts of the road were mud and slush, the sun never reaching them in winter. Beyond Taihape the road was worse; snow had fallen, to block it completely. The Chandler was left in a garage there, beside the Livery and Bait Stables where Dick had worked as a boy. They caught a train that stopped at the mill siding, then walked across the snowy fields, where the children first met their grandmother.

A few days later a train took them on to Waimarino, then by coach to the southern end of Lake Taupo to Tokaanu, and by launch to Taupo, twenty-two miles by water. By coach again to Rotorua, where they stayed, as Jim had earlier, at Waiwera Guest House, still owned and managed by Mr and Mrs Falloona, who had escaped from the volcanic destruction 'when Tamaohoi awoke,' over thirty years earlier.

The trip that the little girl was to remember most clearly was a launch trip on Lake Rotorua, to Mokoia Island, the guide telling them the legend of Hinemoa, and to Hamurana Springs, which they approached by boat from the lake.

Back in Taihape, even with chains Jim could not drive the car over the Erewhon route to Napier. They retraced their journey as far as Woodville, then set off through what had been the old Bush settlements — Dannevirke and Norsewood — to Napier.

Henry had not been heard of since before the war, and Christine did not know where he was. They made a point of visiting Ronald's grave in the cemetery on the hill; it was well cared for. Henry must be back in Hawkes Bay somewhere, Jim thought.

On to Wairoa — fourteen open fords that could benight the traveller, with rain in the hill country — and chains again, as they turned off beyond the village of Nuhaka, immediately before the climb up the Wharerata to Poverty Bay. That route was rarely used; cars and the big Aard service cars were more likely to get through the Tiniroto road, the inland route.

Helen, watching from the window, saw the Chandler crawling up the unmetalled road. Down to the creek she flew, in such a hurry to greet her sister and the children that she disregarded the stepping-stones. Her shoes and stockings were soaked when she hugged Christine.

The days spent there were happy on the

surface. But Brian had changed. Never of a very bright disposition, he had become morose and sulky. His wife's delight in her visitors seemed to irritate him more. In every possible way he belittled Helen.

She would ask him to kill, as there was only a leg of mutton left, a scrawny one at that. He would stump off to whistle up his dogs. If Jim went with him — he did not encourage his brother-in-law to ride round the farm with him, and he refused every offer of help — he would lean on the fence where he kept the killers. Then, after surveying old wethers which Jim would have killed for the dogs, months earlier, rather than waste pasture on them, Brian would say, 'Good fat hoggets, aren't they? It's a pity to kill them.'

When Helen brought the last joint to the table, Brian hacked it to pieces with a blunt carving knife. He put helpings that were much too large on his own and Jim's plates, only slightly less for the three boys. The carving dish was bare of meat, Christine and Helen still unserved.

'You'd better bring in that other joint,' he ordered. 'There's not enough meat here.'

Helen turned all colours. Her husband knew — who better than the one who did the killing and hanging? — that there was no other joint. Jim came to the rescue — he had far too much, he said, and he shared the stringy mutton with his wife and sister-in-law.

In spite of Brian's disapproval, Jim managed to take Helen and the boys to the Morere Springs, only about twelve miles away, for a picnic in the bush and a bathe in the warm pools. Brian and Helen had been at Tangitere for some years now, but Helen had never seen the Springs. Nor had she seen the stalactites and stalagmites in the Mangaone Valley, not as far from her home. It was over a year since she had been to Wairoa.

Before they left for the Wairarapa, aided and abetted by Jim, the sisters had decided to rent a beach cottage at Wellington in the summer holidays. Christine will send the train tickets up, said Jim, determined to pay for them himself, and over-riding any objections on Brian's part.

32

At home all was well. During the two or three weeks of June, while Jim was away, there was not much to do; a reliable young man had ridden round the stock, as the owner would have done, an old scrubcutter who had worked there in earlier years wanted to bach in the shearers' whare until the weather improved, when he was to work on contract, living in the whare in the Neck. He could turn his hand to anything for his keep; he had milked the house cow that had not dried off, while the calves attended to the others.

Christine made arrangements about renting a cottage at Muritai. After the lambing, she started filling cake and biscuit tins with baking for the shearers. The morning batch of scones would be made every day, but blocks of light fruit cake, pastry cases and biscuits for afternoon smoko were stored away.

A reasonably good cook coped with the breakfasts and dinners — only two shearers and a fleece-o this year. When Jim had mustered, brought the sheep in from the back of the station, and yarded, he had time to use the third hand-piece on the board. His 'man' — man-of-all-work, for he was not an experienced shepherd, yet — drove the shorn sheep back to their paddocks. On his way, he had the task of leaving supplies for the scrubcutter, who was out on a block in the Rough Paddock.

With the shearing just about cut out, Jim asked his employee one evening, 'How's Mick?'

'All right, I s'pose. He doesn't eat much, does he?'

'What do you mean?' demanded Jim.

'Last week's stores were still in his box — I had a job finding room for what I took out today,' was the reply.

Jim's face showed his consternation, and displeasure, if not contempt for his employee's stupidity. Surely the man could have ridden down to the whare, to see if the old scrubcutter was on his feet; you did not ignore signs of trouble where anyone lived alone. However, he turned to the shearers, sitting in front of the kitchen range — the evenings were still cool, although October was at an end.

'You carry on tomorrow,' he said. 'I'll have to ride out to the whare — Mick might have gashed himself with the slasher or the grubber. If he's out on the block, he might be anywhere in it — I don't like this at all.'

Jim was away at dawn. If all was well, Mick would have left the whare to work on the block only a little later. It was a glorious dawn, pearl pink, skylarks singing; the sheep looked well, none had been knocked back by cold winds after shearing, the lambs were in great condition. So far it had been a good year.

He checked his horse by the store-box; the direct track to the back paddocks detoured here from the old track to the whare in the Neck, and a man driving sheep or working them further out could leave Mick's stores as he rode past. Mick enjoyed the walk up the side-track in the evening, after he had finished for the day; he had cut manuka on the property off and on for twenty years. Both lots of stores were in the box — wouldn't you have expected that stupid fool to go down to the whare when he noticed the bread still in the box?

Jim rode on down to the whare where he had spent the first years of his married life. No answer to his calls. No smoke from the chimney. The door standing wide — the light rain of early last evening had dampened the floor — cold ashes of a dead fire. Had Mick gone walkabout? Once he had decided on a trip to the nearest pub in the middle of a contract — but he had called at the homestead on the way, to let Jim know. He was on contract — time did not matter. But he appreciated Jim's concern for a solitary man living and working out of touch, if there was an emergency.

Had Mick forgotten the door? Spilt water there before he went off to cut scrub this morning? No — that would not answer the query about the untouched stores — and that door had been open longer than that.

Jim looked round — Mick still had some supplies.

Funny, he had never trusted this East Coast weather; Jim had not known him leave for a day in the scrub without a sou'wester — and there were his tools, unless he had two slashers and two grubbers. That was unlikely; Mick had his favourite weapons, honed to razor sharp edges.

Jim was astride his horse again, trotting up the track to join the main path to the gate. In the Rough Paddock, further out, he could see where Mick had made inroads on the standing scrub; the area here of freshly cut manuka was about the limit of what Mick could have done since he moved out from the homestead. It was no use looking further up here — he could not have started

302

cutting from the far side of the block. That would have meant further for him to walk, too, from the whare.

Jim would have to ride back, and start up the path that led to the corner where Mick could climb over by the strainer post to the Rough Paddock — no gates for stock, but a short-cut for a man. Had the silly old chump slipped down a bank and broken a leg?

Hitching the reins over his arm he walked downstream to the Ruru boundary. The stranger's death was vivid in his mind. No sign of Mick. Back up to the whare, where he tied his horse to a railing.

Into the bush, then? Jim was puzzled; what would Mick be doing there? Setting a trap for a wood-pigeon? Unlikely — Mick liked to hear birds, and see them, not eat them. Would he be trying to snare a stoat? or a ferret?

Jim had walked up the creek; that was where their young son had sat with his pup on the undermined bank.

He lifted his eyes. Mick had decided life wasn't worth living. He must have rolled himself off that overhanging branch, letting the noose which he had looped round his neck do the rest.

Somehow Jim cut the old chap down — he had been there for days — and dragged him through the bush to the whare. His horse reared and snorted as he slung the body across the saddle. He would have trouble on the papa track up the Neck cliffs. He would have to walk down the old bullock track, leading the horse with its grisly burden.

Old Mick would have liked a grave in the bush and the back-country he had loved; but the police would have to come into this. Another death near this whare. Jim was not superstitious, but it was just as well he could not see into the future.

He avoided the homestead, making direct for the woolshed. If the shearers had not cut out yet, they would give him a hand. Then he would phone the Tinui policeman.

Years later Jim would come to wonder if there was some aura of desolation in the match-lining of the whare. It was pulled down when tractor roads were formed and the station divided into three farms. The match-lining refurbished one of the kitchens — and two more similar deaths occurred there.

Helen's arrival with her sons for Christmas was a great relief after the tragedy. In the old orchard were trees for the boys to climb, early apples that were ripe enough not to cause stomachaches, and the billiard table case that became a lift going up to

Gamble and Creeds, the Wellington tearoom that had been advertised in the 'Auckland Weekly News.'

They must really go there, Helen said.

After New Year, Jim piled children and sisters in the car, and put them on the train for Wellington. The Rimutaka incline they had heard about kept the boys darting from one side to the other of the slow-moving carriage. They heard the bell clang as the bogey wheels trundled over it in the tunnel, and shot out into sunlight on the downhill grade at the Summit crossing. Engines changed there, as they had at Cross Creek to hook up the Fell, Helen and Christine holding firmly to the three trouser belts, in case the boys clambered out of the carriage and were left behind.

Wellington — trams, cars — the cable car that shot up to the heights of Kelburn; views across the harbour that set the sisters asking 'Do you remember?', across Salamanca Road to the University.

But it was time to go down to the wharves, to catch the ferry over to Days Bay and Rona Bay. The children were quieter now, still saucer-eyed. It was the last sailing of the day they caught. On the edge of the wharf was a man loaded to the plimsoll with beer and whiskey — he reeked of both. He was singing 'Goodbye to the Dear Old Duchess.' Since that was the name of the ferry boat on which they were travelling, the song caused not a little concern.

Days Bay first, then Rona Bay, with dusk veiling the harbour entrance. A cab, horse-drawn, to Muritai — nearly dark now, but they found a clean, neat cottage, bunk-rooms in which the boys could enjoy themselves, a comfortable living-room and tiny kitchen. Stores were unpacked, and linen and night clothes. There was a note on the table, with advice and instructions. It concluded: 'Do not go outside after 9 p.m. on Tuesdays.'

This was Tuesday night. Was there a peculiar prowler on that night only? Helen and Christine made all sorts of odd suggestions to each other after they had put the children to bed.

'It's after nine, now' said Christine. 'We'll never know the answer — we might ask at the store.' (They had collected the key there, on their way from the boat.)

'We'll put the kettle on again,' remarked Helen, 'Isn't it splendid to boil a kettle as often as you like, without a husband growling at all the wood you're using?'

'Jim never does, Sis, so I'm lucky.'

As they sat down to a well-earned supper, they heard hoof-beats, a slow pace like a draught dragging a milk-cart. And then a clanking down the path.

The milkman filled the billies in the morning, they had been told. Besides, that sound was wrong.

Helen looked at Christine.

'He's gone round the back of the house — on that path.'

Christine began to laugh. 'Now we know,' she said, 'it will be clean and fresh for the morning.'

The days passed so swiftly; the sandhills were not fifty yards away, the boys could hide and slide there all day long. A beautifully sandy beach, covered with interesting shells, was ideal for the little girl. The shallows stretched out rather far for swimmers, but for children, especially at low tide, there was no danger of their going into deep water.

Next door was a younger boy who sometimes tagged after these older visitors to the area. At other times he would amuse himself by passing a very dead dogfish to the little girl through the gaps in the fence palings. Small hands passed the fish forward and back; then there would be squeals of laughter as it was hurled over the top of the fence, to be returned over and over. The young ones never tired of the game, but the three-year-old's clothes did 'stink of fish', as

Helen's older boy said, wrinkling his nose.

They caught crabs in the rock pools, and winkles; they dug for pipi in the sand, and pulled mussels from the rocks.

Across to Wellington on the ferry they travelled for a day's excursion — they realised that 'the dear old Duchess' was unlikely to sink. They gazed in shop windows, rode again on the cable car, and lunched at Gamble and Creeds — a highlight for all the children, perhaps especially the little girl whose aunt had 'pretended' so often with her.

The shining days were over when they caught the ferry and the train home. Helen and her children would go right through to Napier, where Brian might meet them; Christine and her family would leave the train at Masterton, where Jim would meet them. There was the difference in husbands.

They planned a similar holiday for the following year, in those last hours on the train.

But there was no 'next year' for one of the sisters.

33

Farm life worked through its seasons on that east coast station that Christine's mother would not visit — too far, she said, every time her daughter wrote. Lambing was over, shearing ahead.

Again the kowhai floods came, this time with a steady persistent rain, ten days of it; silt over the river flats, the house cows shifted from their paddock beside the tributary that was backing up as the Whareama filled, flowing bank to bank. Over the lower orchard, where the first homestead cabin had been built in the 'seventies, into the yards and under the woolshed — muddy water swirling.

Where the earthquake had shifted the bank in, the water rose higher in its narrow channel, until it carried away the replacement swingbridge.

Out in the back paddocks the Tinui river overflowed; the sheep and cattle on the other side had to take care of themselves. The Neck creek was impassable; even the homestead creek that usually trickled the water from a spring to the tank roared through the nights.

For ten days there could be no movement from the house or beyond the first paddocks. At last, the rain stopped and the sun began to dry out the silt-covered flats. After another two days, the river dropped sufficiently for Jim to be able to swim a horse across. Indeed, only on horseback would anyone be able to get out dry-shod until a new swing-bridge was built — the ruins of the last one lay downstream in a pile of driftwood.

Worse could happen, of course: there would come a flood that would sweep car and garage into a neighbour's sown paddock, through a flattened boundary fence. (The growth of willows in the lower reaches would be the cause — not a kowhai flood, but January rains.)

Jim had business in Masterton; he had intended to go in just as the rain started in earnest. Delaying for a day or two, hoping the rain would ease, he could still have crossed by the swing-bridge — it was not carried away until nearly a week later. By that time it was doubtful if he would be able to return, and even more doubtful if the Blairlogie stretch of road would be open — slippery greywacke there made minor slips a constant, and major slips frequent. He would not risk leaving his wife and family marooned at the homestead.

The rivers were dropping, slips being cleared. He left early, swimming his horse across the Whareama to the garage beside the road.

Christine seized the opportunity to complete the spring-cleaning, delayed by the weather. The blankets were on the clothes-lines when the phone gave the three short rings for the letter 'S' — their call sign. She had thought Jim might phone from town, to tell her that he had been able to drive through, and to ask if she had thought of any other messages.

But it was a telegram.

Helen had died, leaving a baby daughter eleven days old.

First to tell the children — their first experience of a death of someone affectionately close to them.

Then to telephone her other sister, Caroline — their place was on the town side of a loop of the river. Bernard would drive his sister and sister-in-law, at least to Masterton and the train, possibly even to Nuhaka, if Christine could get as far as Ruru.

How could she cross that river? The quiet horse, the one she would have trusted to take her across, was over the river, waiting by the motorshed for Jim's return in the late afternoon. She would have to walk into the back country — the smaller creeks would be low enough to wade, as they dropped quickly once the Whareama stopped backing up — and cross into the back of the neighbour's property where it adjoined Riverside. Then, she hoped, she could follow the bullock track from the back station's shepherd's whare at Morepork — ten or twelve miles scrambling up sodden hills and down slippery clay tracks, carrying a suitcase.

Caroline, on the phone, was most abrupt. 'Bernard doesn't drive at night,' she said. 'We can't wait for you. He wants to leave before lunch. You had better stay home with your children — my cook will look after my son.'

She knew that her younger sister had no help at this time — replacements and a later sudden drop in the price of fat stock at the sales had caused a lean patch until the wool cheque should come in.

Fortunately Bernard, who so rarely criticised his wife's abrupt remarks, was near the phone.

Christine heard him say, in the background, 'There's no hurry, Caroline.' As she made no effort to comfort Christine, he took the phone.

'Christine, Bernard here. Just tell me if you are starting out — we won't leave without you.'

'Thank you, Bernard. I'll come through as quickly as I can.'

'Look — take care. If you don't get here, I'll be going back to search for you. Anything could happen, and there'd be no-one here to know about it.'

'I'll hurry, I promise.'

'We're not expecting you for three or four hours, and we'll expect you to stop for something to eat, when you get here. G'bye and good luck!'

Now for messages to Jim in town. Christine tried several firms, to find that he had already called. Usually he left the car at a garage — no, Mr Dyer had not been there. After six messages, she was finding it so hard to say over and over, 'Please tell Mr Dyer that my sister in Nuhaka has died, and I am going up with my other sister and brother-in-law.'

She could not wait any longer. And the children? She was sure her son, now ten years old, would take care of his sister. If their father was not home before dark, at least there were no lamps to light. The Delco plant had been charged the day before; a flick of the switch solved any problem of growing darkness. The day was warm; no need to worry about keeping the range stoked up. She *must* go.

Two sad faces watched Mummy start across the flat and up the hill.

If she could cross the tributary lower down than the Morepork whare, she could save herself an hour or so. She had to be sure to stay above all the loops and bends of the Whareama — once it turned to cross under the road bridge near Ruru, she would be in the clear.

By five o'clock Jim reached home, surprised to find the children alone. Every message had missed him — he had been there earlier, or the message had been overlooked, or the assistant had not noticed him in the store.

He comforted his little daughter, and his son who had held the fort so competently. They could both help him when he started building the swingbridge tomorrow; then Mummy would be able to come home the usual way.

Meanwhile, Mummy was somewhere on the road to Napier. She had phoned her son from Ruru, to tell them she had reached their aunt's place safely.

Caroline grumbled most of the way about the delay in their journey. They could have been in Napier if they had not had to wait for Christine; now they would have to stay the night somewhere.

At last Bernard said, 'If Christine hadn't phoned, you wouldn't know your sister had died.'

That of course was what rankled. Why hadn't Brian sent *her* a telegram? She was the oldest of the girls — she should have been told.

Then she wondered if they should have bothered going to the funeral.

That was too much for Christine. 'It's the baby I'm worried about. I wonder — '

'What baby?' Caroline snapped.

'Didn't you know?' asked Christine. 'Helen had a baby daughter nearly two weeks ago.'

Complete silence followed.

Bernard did not want to tackle the tricky Wairoa road and its open fords in the dark. They stayed the night in Napier starting off the next morning at six o'clock.

Neighbours were looking after the baby until Helen's sisters could get through. It was clear that Brian had told them the baby would be cared for by one of them.

'Which one?' Caroline asked herself. She could not even wait until after the funeral before she was asking the same question of Brian.

The sad little procession went down to the Nuhaka cemetery. So much rain had fallen that the approach was too greasy for vehicles;

the coffin had to be carried up the slippery hillside track.

Back at Tangitere, Caroline said, 'We can go home now. Bernard's busy. I'll collect the baby's things.'

'I think we should stay another day or two, Caroline,' ventured her husband. 'You know I arranged to be away from the station for a week or ten days — the boss said not to hurry back, as long as we were back for shearing.'

'The sooner we get that baby to Ruru the better,' Caroline continued, ignoring her husband, and hoping no-one else had heard what he said.

'But the baby won't be going to Ruru,' interposed Brian. 'When my wife felt so very ill, she told me that Christine was to look after the baby if anything happened to her.'

'Christine!' snorted Caroline. 'She's got two of her own to look after. Besides, Jim's nearly bankrupt — the baby won't have a roof over her head.'

'I think we can safely leave that to Jim and Christine,' Brian said quietly.

'She doesn't know how to bring up children, anyway,' Caroline added.

Even in this sad time that comment was almost too much for Brian — he had seen some of the antics of his nephew, and Helen had told him more of them.

'You'd better give her to me,' Caroline repeated. 'After all, Bernard is your brother — you're not related to Jim, or to Christine, really. We are in a much better position than Christine. She'll be cooking for shearers soon, she won't have time to look after a baby.'

'First it's money, then it's relationships, and then it's time,' remarked Brian, sadly. 'We'll do what Helen wished, if Christine is willing. Are you, Christine?'

'Yes, if that was what Helen wanted,' Christine replied. 'I'd love to have her anyway — our daughter will love a baby, too.' Forgetting Bernard's dislike of night driving, that she had made so much of earlier, Caroline tried to order him to leave immediately.

'We're not wanted here — we'll go — we've been made a convenience of. Christine knew she was to have the baby.'

'Don't let's squabble over the wee mite,' pleaded Christine, 'I did not know. If you want her so much, and her father agrees, you take her.'

'It's not a matter of what any of us say,' said Brian. 'It's what Helen wanted. We can't alter that.'

'I want to leave now!' Caroline demanded.

317

'How does Christine get back with the baby?' asked Bernard.

'If she wants to stay, she can. But I'm going.'

'Not tonight, Caroline,' said Bernard, more firmly than anyone expected.

Caroline shut herself in the bedroom, refusing a meal, and saying how ill she felt. That the illness was jealousy, she neither realised nor accepted.

The boys, aged ten and twelve, were expected by Brian to be able to manage without a mother. However, he persuaded Christine to stay over for a few days, to help them over the bad time, and to give the baby a chance to settle down.

Caroline was so unpleasant that they were glad to see her driven off to the south by Bernard. That entailed a very difficult trip for Christine with the baby; it was impossible for Jim to drive further than Masterton, for the swing-bridge and the muster had to be completed before shearing — and the shearers were due, now.

The neighbour who had tended the baby until the sisters came through was driving down to Wairoa; they would put Christine and the baby on the service-car there. She would spend a night in Napier, then go through by train to Masterton. Jim would

318

meet her, whatever he was trying to do.

So Christine walked across the new swing-bridge with a shawl-wrapped bundle. Auntie Helen had died, but she had left a present for a little niece.

Those two grew as sisters for three years or so, the dark-haired daughter and the golden-haired blue-eyed niece.

Christine would watch, as first her daughter pushed the baby's pram. When the little one could walk, they would play together in the doll's house Jim had built in the orchard. Then mother would see her daughter bring a little chair, made from a kerosene case, out to the swing — her niece was too young to be on the swing alone — no, she was sitting on the chair, with her cousin on the swing. The chair was in the right position for the little one to give the swing an occasional push; but, because she was sitting down, the swing could not touch her or send her flying onto the ground.

When 'Goldilocks', as she was nicknamed, was three, the blow fell. Brian had a reliable housekeeper now, both boys had left home to work on other farms, he was lonely. To him it was as simple as that. Christine had looked after the baby (and made ends meet somehow, though her daughter went without while clothes were bought for the growing child).

Now Brian wanted his daughter, once the troubles of rearing a motherless child were over. And what sort of life would Goldilocks lead? One housekeeper after another in that isolated, draughty farmhouse; as she grew older, the housekeepers would disappear (unless Brian married one of them) and Goldilocks would be expected to look after the father who had done nothing for the first three years of her life — not even a birthday present, or a few dollars to buy shoes or other clothing.

It had to be. Brian from the first had refused to let Christine and Jim adopt their little niece.

To avoid upsetting the children too much, Christine spoke of a holiday with Uncle Brian. Perhaps when he saw the two little girls together, he would change his mind. But he would not see how close the girls had become. Insensitive himself, he did not understand that other people had feelings.

A day or two later, Jim drove Christine and their daughter down the winding road for the last time. Brian had made it quite clear that they had done their duty and would not need to meet their niece again. The baby's birth had also caused Christine to lose both her sisters, for Caroline now ignored her.

Their daughter was subdued as they set off in heavy rain, but she still expected Goldilocks to return after she had spent a holiday with her father.

34

Grannie was feeling old. The winters were colder, the firewood did not burn so brightly — Dick was away longer. His mother had not realised that the Turangarere forest was almost cut out. She did not notice that there were few people about the mill.

Because she had settled so firmly in this house, Ted did not mind her staying there. Nothing against it, except that Dick had to travel up the line every day — the mill at Murimotu was handling logs railed down from the southern slopes of Mount Ruapehu. Her son tried to avoid leaving Caroline alone in a deserted mill village. It would be much easier if he could shift her into town, and come down at weekends.

The mill owners had looked after her while he was overseas; but they couldn't carry on making allowances forever. It was getting harder and harder to get bush blocks near transport or mills. A few more years, and milling up here south of Waimarino would be uneconomic.

Helen's death had shocked Caroline. Older people died, and adventurous young men;

but this daughter of hers, with the baby girl she longed for, that was hard to take.

Dick found this another point in favour of a shift. If his mother was in Taihape, Christine might be able to visit her with the children. That persuaded Caroline, determined until then to stay where she was until she died, to accept the move when Dick bought a house in Carver Street, near the railway station that would provide his transport.

Wherever a leading bench hand was required, there he would go. He realised that his wartime injuries were with him for life. He was young, but he would have to give up the heavier work soon.

Up the line at one o'clock on Monday morning, down most weekends about the same time on Saturday mornings. That gave him a chance to do all the odd jobs about the house, and see that his mother was well supplied with firewood for the kitchen range which she sat beside, as she had in moments of rest throughout her New Zealand life.

The further north he went — Taringamotu, Ngakonui and Ongarue were the most distant from Taihape — the more Caroline's independence deserted her.

'Don't go,' she would say, and then 'Money — you want more money, so go, leave me — leave me for a month.'

Of course he had to work, as Caroline very well knew, to keep her as well as himself. The remark rankled. Who had made him leave the telegraph delivery job for the bush so long ago?

Yet when he suggested, thanks to improvements on Sir Richard Seddon's 1898 moves, that she was entitled to a widow's pension, she was furious. Dick began to understand whence some of the less admirable personality traits of his oldest brother and sister might have descended.

'If you're too mean to keep your poor old mother,' Caroline exclaimed, 'I can take in washing again.'

'No, that isn't the point,' Dick tried to explain. 'You are entitled to a pension. It would give you a little more money than I can.'

'Accept charity?' she demanded. 'Never. If my son doesn't know his duty, he can leave me alone!'

Was she confused? Or would she never admit that her son had bought the house, paid the rates and insurance, kept the painting and repairs up to the minute? To her, Richard — still Richard, after these years of hearing him called Dick by everyone else — was still a boy, to do as he was told without question.

Once he was beyond Taumarunui, he

sometimes stayed the weekend in single quarters. There was good hunting for the pot on this western side of the Hauhungaroa Range: deer were plentiful, rabbits in the tussock and a wild cattle beast or two provided good sport, along with wild pig. The hunting was much more to Dick's taste than two midnight to dawn train trips.

One winter he managed to persuade his mother to stay in a carefully vetted rest home in Auckland. Taihape was not much warmer than Turangarere, when the old lady would not bother with a fire. The trips south in winter were difficult, too; once a fortnight was too often. A fortnightly visit to Auckland took longer, but he could sleep on the train without fear of over-running the station.

A crowd from the mill joined forces to go up to the Ellerslie Races, Dick with them. He could visit his mother, too.

When the train pulled in to Te Kuiti station, there was the usual blind rush for those chunky stale sandwiches and lukewarm tea. Dick's mate, a rotund and jolly red-faced man, was tapped on the shoulder.

'Want some cold tea, mate? Half a dollar a bottle.'

They surely did want some 'cold tea' in a bottle. It had been hot at the mill that day; somehow they had not made time for the usual trip to the bar.

Joe was quietly beckoned outside the station, where a crowd from the train was buying as fast as the bottles could be handed over.

'Wait till the train pulls out before you start drinking,' warned the seller. 'The cops are on the station, and this is a dry area.'

Because the government in its wisdom had decided that the Maori should no longer be exposed to the evils of the Pakeha liking for grog, the area was without a licensed hotel.

Joe and Dick returned to the train with their booty, branded clearly enough with the usual Speights label — plenty to share with the rest of the group. Tops were lifted with a most satisfactory 'pop', and the hardened drinkers took a long swallow. Dick, with his bottle half-way to his lips, watched their faces in dismay.

'Ugh! Cold tea, he said, did he, Dick? Wait till I catch the swine!'

Genuine cold tea it was. The bottles, opened or unopened, all sailed swiftly out the carriage window.

Caroline, when Dick visited her at the home, was complaining bitterly. She didn't like the food, they would open windows, they expected her to take a walk along those streets where the motor-cars rushed about, she couldn't sleep for the traffic noises.

That was the story on Saturday. Dick visited her again on Sunday morning, then returned to his hotel for lunch, staying there until it was nearly time to leave for the southbound train.

The desk porter called him to the phone. It was the Rest Home: was his mother there?

'No, of course not,' Dick replied. 'I said goodbye to her this morning.'

'She is not in the Home — we thought you might have seen her.'

'I'll walk up towards the Home,' said Dick, 'but she can't be far away. How long has she been missing?'

'We don't quite know. She went to her room for her usual rest after lunch. When it came to afternoon tea time, we called her, to find she had gone out. Don't worry,' Matron added, 'I know you have to get back on the train. Your mother will be walking round the block — perhaps someone has invited her in.'

Dick was not over-anxious, but he strolled to within sight of the Home, in case the old lady had decided to see him at the hotel — no sign of her, and just enough time to catch the train.

The platform was fairly crowded. Dick joined two other bushmen; they had been at Ellerslie on Saturday, and were discussing the form of the favourite. For a moment Dick thought he saw his mother on the platform. The crowd hid her — it must have been a chance resemblance.

Just as the warning to stand clear was given, he saw the same figure carefully helped up the carriage steps by an obliging young porter.

It couldn't be — ! It wasn't — ! By joves, it was his mother! What had the old lady in mind now? (And he had paid the Rest Home yesterday, two weeks in advance. And he would have to send them a telegram —).

He made his way to the third-class non-smoker. There she was, very pleased with herself, 'just like the cat that has swallowed the canary', he muttered under his breath.

Caroline greeted him as if nothing unusual had taken place.

'There you are, Richard boy, you won't need to come to Auckland to see me, now.'

'But, Mother, the matron at the home is looking for you — '

'Serve her right,' his mother replied. 'She starved me and wasted your money.'

He had to return to his own carriage, to explain to his mates that he would have to lose a day's pay while he took his mother home. She would say she could look after

328

herself — but the place had been closed up ever since he had taken her up to Auckland. He could not return to Ongarue that night — the expresses crossed at Taihape.

When they reached their destination in the early hours, Caroline was glad of Richard's company. Her independence had carried her this far. But the walk down the dark street — she had no money left for the horse-drawn cab she would have favoured — that would have been beyond her. (Any cab driver would have taken her home; all Taihape knew 'Dick's old lady', and had been told he would settle up for anything she wanted.)

Dick was still working at the mill there when the Auckland-Wellington express ran into a land-slide half a mile beyond Ongarue. The engine-driver saw the three ton boulder on the line, when the expresss emerged from a sharp bend through embankments, just a few feet from the slip. Twenty-eight were injured, seventeen killed; no comparison with the numbers lost in disasters at sea, or in the Tarawera eruption.

But people had felt that in trains they could always travel in safety; later years were to show that even greater disasters than this at Ongarue could take place on the rails. The gusts that had flung the wrecked Wairarapa train into the gully at Siberia forty years earlier had been disregarded, or had made little impact in the north. Wellington was reached by ship, then. The Wairarapa, if it had any meaning at all, referred to the Seventy Mile Bush.

To Caroline, disaster at Ongarue meant Dick and the sawmill. Rumours flew. It took a firm and kindly neighbour to explain that the express had been involved, half a mile south of Ongarue. As Mother grew older, her superstitions grew with her, those old sagas of Norway and her childhood freshening in her memory. There had been three deaths in the young generation, young to her; her brother Roald did not survive the third wreck.

When Dick came home the weekend after the Ongarue disaster, she said, 'You come home, Richard, you're too far away.'

He was surprised, but he agreed with her. The mill was running out of timber, too; they wanted him to go into the bush again, clearing and felling. Not enough logs were coming out — he could be bush foreman.

But there would be no sense in riding down miles from a bush camp to catch that train to Taihape; he had to go into Taumaranui for a timetable stop.

The Railways were wanting gangers and plate-layers — Permanent Way staff — in the Mangaweka stretch. He was not to know that men were constantly being replaced on the length of line between Taihape and Ohingaiti; there were seven tunnels and five bridges and viaducts on the Taihape to Mangaweka link. Through to Ohingaiti was just as demanding — all in all, the worst stretch of line in the country.

Dick did not mind. He was close enough to Taihape to go up from his railway hut at Mangaweka whenever two free days came his way. No more was he tied to weekends, when he could do little business. The varying days suited Caroline, too. On a weekday he could escort her to the shops, a change from staying always within four walls. Sit in the garden she would not — that was idleness.

Work in the garden was beyond her. Her son Richard grew the vegetables; if he did not gather them for her, she would go without. They were his vegetables, not hers. Of flowers she had no appreciation. Never admitting it, she was colour-blind now; she found reading beyond her. But she refused to get spectacles. She could see, or feel, to cook and clean; that was all that was needed. Occasionally, if a snapshot of the grandchildren was enclosed in a letter, Dick would be able to persuade his mother to use a magnifying glass.

Spectacles, no! Perhaps she looked back over the years to the dark glasses, the granny spectacles of those days, worn by her husband. So many little foibles appeared that seemed to relate to the very early days. Into the bush for Richard — and out again, just as she had done. Determined to stay in one place — if possible. Independent and proud, yet clinging humbly sometimes to her youngest son.

Caroline often wondered if Richard was now her only son — it was years since any of the family had heard of Henry, and further back still to any recollection of William.

* * *

The monotony of life was varied by visits from Christine and Jim and their two children. It was always school holidays when they arrived. Last time the old lady had been sorry not to see her grandson — he was working in the South Island. This granddaughter was growing up, too, but she still enjoyed sleeping on a stretcher in the front room, feeling the vibration of the trains as they thundered through the night.

On the line the maintenance gang found Marton Junction's most frightening habit was to send Specials through without warning.

As these Specials were only locomotive and tender, with or without a guardsvan, the gradients did not slow them down — the locomotive could roar into a tunnel, blocking out the daylight before the men on the jigger heard its approach.

Several of these tunnels are curved; one opens straight onto a viaduct, two hundred feet or so above the gully. More than one jigger went over the side while the man who had been riding it clambered hurriedly below the rails, clinging to a girder as the train thundered above him.

In the tunnels, where often the gang was working against the clock between time-tabled express and goods trains, the jigger could be flung at an angle against the tunnel wall. The men would flatten themselves against it; sometimes there would be a ditch in which the crouching workers could feel the lift of air over their scalps as the footboards cleared them by an inch or two.

Mangaweka was not a scheduled stop for the Wellington to Auckland journey. Sometimes there would be a crossing, when the goods train would be too long for the next loop south. Or the passenger train might have been delayed further down the line. The subsequent confusion of rolling stock could be averted by Train Control clearing the Goods for the next crossing.

Delays to passenger trains were — sometimes — man made. If the tablet was not squarely in the frame of the station, the arm on the locomotive would send it flying instead of hooking it on. That was one way to stop a through train when one of the Permanent Way staff — or his 'Missis' — wanted to board.

These little games sometimes rebounded. Dick was sound asleep in the whare one winter night when a thumping knock woke him.

The stationmaster was at the door. 'Get dressed in a hurry, Dick, you're wanted.'

Theirs not to reason why. A sudden call-out like this was an emergency usually related to slips on the line or accidents. He would find out when he walked over to the station. Bitter cold and frosty — steam from his breath clear in the moonlight.

The express was champing away on the main line, windows lighted except where the drawn blinds hid the sleeping-cars, heads peering out to find the cause of this unusual halt.

The tablet had been lost in the darkness beyond the station. The train crew and the stationmaster had hunted for it for twenty minutes unavailingly, before Dick had been called out. He was to act as tablet for the rest of the night, until the original tablet was found. Through the early hours of the morning and on into broad daylight Dick, with the white armband as the mark of the tablet, travelled up and down that line on the footplates. The express to Taihape was the first trip — then back with the Auckland to Wellington express. Up with Goods, back with Goods, up again with the Limited, south with the down Limited, and then Goods trains to and from Taihape till well after daylight, always in the locomotive, where the tablet should have been. About ten o'clock the missing tablet was found.

What a night! As they were short-staffed, he went on to the job — next week he would get two days' extra leave instead of overtime pay — with a splitting headache, legacy from the war.

A Special thundered down onto the viaduct. Jigger over the side. (Otherwise the locomotive would be derailed, engine driver and fireman plunging to their deaths seven hundred feet below, and the cheerful guard, too. That was where the road wound under the viaduct — there could be cars or horsedrawn vehicles involved, as well. The viaduct would be damaged, probably.)

Dick had no time to think that out. Over

with the jigger, over with himself. No time to reach the safety zone in the centre, or to work off the viaduct.

There were fine people on that stretch of line, all friendly; Dick was the sort of person with whom most were friends.

Presently Dick's term of Hades was up. Where would he like to go? Cliff Road, near Marton? or Hatuma, in Hawkes Bay? Those were vacancies on a flat and easy section of line.

Cliff Road was an almost forgotten siding on the main line a few miles north of Marton Junction — a junction because there the west coast line to New Plymouth veered away from the Main Trunk. Where Dick lived in his railway hut, the wind swept across the wheat fields of the Rangitikei plains, disturbing the chortling magpies in the bluegum trees.

Here was civilised farming, with no chance of hunting deer or wild pigs. Not too far away, however, was the Rangitikei river where, with the right lure, Dick could always land a reasonable trout.

It was a quiet life, needed after the strenuous years on the Taihape to Ohingaiti section. He found that his length of service there was a record. When men are exhausted, foolish accidents happen. Had it not been such a busy line, life would have been easier. The greasy country meant a constant watch. When land is water-logged, even a minor vibration will start a slide. No-one could say that those locomotives caused only a minor vibration.

Caroline, lying awake, would hear the mournful whistle as trains left for the south, and the puffing roar of locomotives hauling the wagons up, bound for the north.

The only disadvantage with Cliff Road was that Dick felt he was too far away from his mother. She was getting more remote, more withdrawn. Her son's company once in three weeks was not enough. Only once had she gone down to Christine's — that was after the family had moved into town, to send the children to school.

35

Christine's son had managed that eighteen miles a day on a pony, but neither Jim nor his wife expected their daughter to start off on that trek. Boarding school would have been required for their son's secondary education; the cheapest and most reasonable way out of the dilemma was to buy a house in town. Jim would continue to run the station, so there would be no manager's wages to be found. He would come into town for week-ends or when farm work permitted.

They had been some years in town when visitors called — a strange woman, and brother Henry. Christine could not remember when she had last seen him, but he had changed very little. After he had introduced his wife Mary, he explained that they were going south on their honeymoon.

They had thought they might see Caroline, Christine's sister, now living just out of Masterton. Christine, delighted at meeting Henry again, and happy with his new wife, telephoned her sister for the first time since both had moved to town. Perhaps Caroline and Bernard would like to come to tea?

Caroline, whose husband was now managing a property about twelve miles west of the town, as always with the family was abrupt and unwelcoming. She didn't want Henry and his wife sponging on her. Asked if she would like Henry to speak to her on the phone, she slammed the receiver down, with the expected comment about 'having fish to fry'.

Although Caroline had a wee son of her own, now, as well as the older boy, she had never forgiven Christine for 'taking Helen's baby from her'.

Christine, naturally, did not repeat Caroline's excuse. To herself, she found time to wonder why her sister always had fish if relatives arrived unexpectedly — one had to rely on the fish shop or the weekly van in this inland town. To the visitors Christine said, rather weakly, she felt, that her sister was very busy.

Mary was taken aback by this reception.

Henry laughed. 'Caroline hasn't changed, has she, Christine?' he asked.

'I haven't been able to see her for some time,' replied his sister.

'Don't you bother with her — Mary thought I should try to get in touch with all the family again.'

'If I had sisters and a brother, and nieces and nephews,' said Mary, 'I wouldn't leave them without even a letter for twelve years.'

'Never was much of a hand at writing letters,' he explained. 'Why did you leave the station, Christine?'

'The children's schooling,' she replied. 'How did you find us here?'

'When we looked up the telephone directory for the number for the station, we saw the town entry with the same initials. I didn't want Henry to waste time — he puts things off,' said Mary. 'He does feel guilty about not letting you know he was back in Hawkes Bay.'

'I stayed in England for a while after the war,' Henry explained. 'You knew I'd been over there?'

'We heard you had joined up,' answered Christine.

'That would be our mother who told you, I suppose?'

'Oh no, she didn't know about it,' she replied. 'I thought perhaps you said nothing rather than worry her with Dick at the front, too.'

'When did he go away?' asked Henry. 'With timber in demand for wartime purposes, I thought he'd have stayed — he'd be too young to go with the first lot, anyway.'

'Age didn't seem to matter,' said Christine. 'He spent his twentieth birthday in base camp in Egypt, and his twenty-first in the front line.'

'He must have gone over about the time I did, then,' Henry commented. 'How old is Richard now? I don't remember anybody's age. But let's get back to our mother's not knowing I'd enlisted. Had they left the mill?'

'No, mother stayed on at Turangarere during the war — the mill people kept an eye on her.'

'That's where I wrote,' he said. 'The letter couldn't have been delivered. She didn't answer it — come to think of it, I suppose I expected Richard to reply.'

'Henry told me about your older brother,' interjected Mary, 'and how cross your mother was about that death.'

'But she didn't go through to the funeral, did she, Henry?' Christine enquired.

'No — but she wrote. How she wrote! You know — I should be ashamed of myself for not taking care of my little brother, if I couldn't look after the family better than that, the family could do without me, all that sort of thing. The letter ended by stating that I 'was no son of hers' ' —

'Oh, Henry, I am sorry!' exclaimed Christine.

'It's years ago,' Mary said. 'But you'll understand, Christine, why he just dropped out of the family.'

'Of course, but why not write to your sisters when you went away, if you wrote to our mother?' Christine asked.

'I never thought of the letter going astray, and I thought Mother would tell you all. Letters I don't write if I can avoid them. How did you hear?'

'Dick wrote. He was on Salisbury Plain, I think it was on a — what did they call it? — a bombing course. New types of hand grenades and so on. One of the permanent staff commented on the unusual surname — a man of that name had been there on the previous course.'

'Now we say 'Small world', don't we?' laughed Mary.

'Are mother and Dick still at the mill?' Henry asked.

'No, Dick's left milling. He 'copped a Blighty', as he puts it — twice, really, one gas, the other shrapnel. He was only just back in the field when they went up to Cologne. He came back to the mills, but had to give up the timber work a while ago. Where have you been, Henry?'

'Australia, mainly. I told you I stayed in England for some time — then I got as far as Perth. Lovely place, that.

'That's where he met a New Zealander,' said Mary, 'I'd been with the Red Cross — I stayed there in Perth with an aunt, and decided to find a job somewhere in Western Australia. Henry went up country on contract then, and I didn't see him again for two or three years.'

'Where do your parents live?' Christine asked.

'I was brought up on the West Coast. My father managed a little coal-mine there. Then he got a better chance, out of Huntly — Glen Afton or Rotowaro or Renown, he moved about there. By that time I was working in Auckland Hospital.'

'Have you been to see them since you came back from Australia?' enquired Christine. 'Or are you taking Henry up with you?'

'I stayed across the Tasman for too long,' she replied, sadly. 'They were killed in that Ongarue disaster — they'd saved up for the trip of a lifetime, and were going to sail across to Sydney, and then to Perth. I was living in a little flat on my own, then.'

'I'm so sorry,' said Christine.

'Well, time has gone on,' commented Mary. 'But there seemed no point in coming back then. I've no brothers and sisters — only cousins on the West Coast.'

'That's why Mary insists that we see my relatives,' Henry explained. 'We're going up to Taihape after we've crossed the Strait to Nelson. One of Mary's cousins lives there.'

'Christine, we tried to find your other sister near Wairoa. Have they gone to another farm?' asked Mary.

'Helen died — over four years ago.'

'An accident on the farm?'

'No,' answered Christine. 'She didn't recover after her daughter was born.'

'Another little niece for us,' said Mary, warm-heartedly. 'Where is she?'

'It's a sad story, really. We looked after her for three years or so — she was a sister for my own girl — then her father wanted her back, and felt it would be better if we kept out of the way.'

'How heartless!' Mary exclaimed.

'Yes — but she was his daughter. I can see that the girls might have been upset by constant meetings and partings,' Christine pointed out.

'Nothing to stop us from getting in touch,' said Henry. 'Where do they live? And where are the boys?'

'Brian sent the boys out to other farms as soon as he could.'

'I guess he couldn't get on with them,' said Henry shrewdly. 'I always wondered why

344

Helen didn't find someone better.'

'Then they left Nuhaka,' Christine continued. 'A birthday parcel for our little niece was returned, marked 'Gone — no address.' I don't know where Brian is, now.'

'Well — never thought much of Brian,' Henry replied.

Christine looked across at Mary. Henry had married the right one, she would not let him crawl back into his shell again.

They set off by train for Wellington and the Nelson ferry. After their return to Napier, although the little cottage they had bought at Port Ahuriri was small, they hoped Jim and Christine would bring the children to stay.

36

Dick was anxious about his mother. She was lonely, yet she would not visit her daughter — after that crash at Ongarue, she trusted trains no more than she trusted motor-cars. As for these new-fangled aeroplanes — Moncrieff and Hood had failed to cross the Tasman, Kingsford Smith had succeeded — Caroline's reaction was predictable: 'If God wanted you to be up in the air, he would have given you wings.'

Dick could not help thinking of the lady twenty years before who had said to her husband, when they were sitting in the gig with the shafts broken and the mustang down the road, 'Now George, you've got one of those carts without horses, and I hope you're happy!'

Caroline would not leave Taihape for the winter; perhaps she thought she might find herself in a Rest Home again. She pointed out that she had lived in Turangarere, and that was colder — then her memory would betray her a little, and she would wonder if it was warmer at Nuhaka and Waikokopu where Helen lived. Earlier years, however, were very clear to her. She harked back to the Forty Mile Bush often. Just try to tell her or her son that it was the 'Thirty Mile Bush' where she had lived with the Greiners. Old as she was, she would argue most forcefully on that point — she had lived there. Caroline would take umbrage, too, at references to Havelock North: it was Havelock when she lived there.

Dannevirke would be as cold as Taihape, Dick thought — would mother go back to Hawkes Bay?

He applied for a transfer to Hatuma — that vacancy had occurred again. It involved an easy section of the line between Waipukurau and Takapau — a straightforward run with none of the problems associated with the Mangaweka stretch. Oversight of the yards was included; he was told that this step, with a watching brief, would lead to an appointment somewhere as stationmaster.

Told a house would be available at Hatuma, Dick arrived to find that he was expected to board with the other Railways employee, married, with a family.

Mother could not be left alone in the King Country, that was certain. And since Dick was likely to find himself at Paki Paki or some such out of the way station further north, it was no use settling Mother in

Waipukurau, a few miles north of Hatuma. He used his Pass to go up to Napier, where he hoped Mother would consent to live, and bought a little cottage there.

Expecting a good deal of antagonism, he was surprised to find, when he returned with a few days' leave, that she was already packing.

'Where you take me now, Richard?' she asked, seeming younger again.

Whether someone had talked to her about the dangers of the Permanent Way work in the vicinity of Taihape, he did not know. Whoever had coaxed the old lady into preparing for a shift, he was unlikely to find out — Mother would not tell him, for she liked to keep her secrets. He felt grateful; he was not up to a personal battle with his mother.

However, this secret came out as he was completing the packing and tidying up. In the chest of drawers was a letter from Christine. She had always kept in touch — they were the closest of friends. Sometimes she wrote to Cliff Road, at other times to Carver Street, addressing the letter then to her mother as well as her brother.

When he read it, he realised why the old lady was pleased about going back to Napier. Henry, a confirmed bachelor, had married.

The bride had written, too, from Nelson, wishing they lived closer, so that she could see her husband's mother more often. They would come up to Taihape to see her, after their visit to the West Coast ended.

Looking at the date, Dick realised that they would arrive the day before he planned to vacate the house. Dates meant nothing to his mother. She would move when Dick decided, once she had agreed to go. Even days of the week meant little — ever since he had been able to come home sometimes during the week, instead of only at weekends, she had been confused.

Two days before the tenant was to move in came the news of the Inangahua earthquake. A mountainous ridge across the Murchison area had split in two, the northern half falling right across the Matariki valley. The upper storey of one home there was carried quarter of a mile by the moving debris which had buried the ground floor. Fortunately this part of the valley was home to few people.

In the Buller Gorge the uplift of four feet or so had wrecked the road. Chimneys were down in Inangahua; along the fault line the North Island felt the tremor, although there was little damage there.

At first there was little news from Nelson. Dick began to wonder where his brother and sister-in-law might be. Christine had written that Mary's cousin lived somewhere inland from Nelson — none of the family had thought to ask her the cousin's surname. Dick and his mother would have to wait. Perhaps they would come off tomorrow's train, having been nowhere within the earthquake zone. Unless . . . Dick took himself to task. He was getting just as superstitious as his mother.

'Presentiment be damned!' he said to himself. 'Get on with your work.'

The latter was not quite the phrase Jim used, as he was driving his wife and one of his sisters down to the village that day. At the last moment, as his sister was placing her foot on the step, she drew back.

'I don't think I'll go,' she said, 'I've got a presentiment that something's going to happen.'

'Presentiment be damned,' retorted Jim, already half an hour later than he had intended. 'Get in the buggy!'

Her presentiment was not far out. The horse jibbed on the other side of the ford, where the bank was fairly steep; the buggy sat in the middle of the stream, while Jim, with a crack of the whip, tried to drive a stubborn horse. In the end, with his sister screaming, 'Let me stay! Let me stay!' he had to climb out of the buggy into the creek. Although for most of its length it was shallow in summer, there were deeper holes gouged out in floods by tree-trunks.

Into one of these Jim stepped.

No-one went to the village that day.

Dick was planning to meet the train when the boy brought a telegram. To Caroline telegrams were always bad news. She had seen from the window the boy's arrival — Dick would have to tell her the news.

Poor old soul. She had lost her husband, a son and a daughter — as far as contact went, another son and daughter were missing. The other son had just been found, rather his wife had found him for the family. Was Dick to be the only son, now?

The telegram, Dick saw relief, was signed 'Henry'. Surely Mary had worded it. Henry would have apologised for their non-arrival, and left his mother and brother to assume that he and his wife were uninjured.

'Regret unable to visit you. Both safe. Delayed by quake at Murchison.'

Dick packed the gear he had left out for the visitors, and took his mother out for a meal before they caught that train in the cold darkness — snowing, as it had been when they first arrived in Taihape.

Tunnels to Utiku, viaducts and tunnels to Mangaweka where the tablet was picked up firmly by the locomotive arm this time, viaducts and tunnels to Ohingaiti on the plateau above the Rangitikei river — fast running now, over the bare fields where the wheat would be golden in late summer, beyond Cliff Road to Marton Junction. Nothing to be seen in the wind-swept darkness but the blurring lights of townships. Over the Rangitikei at Kakariki by the road and rail bridge to pull in at Palmerston North, at 5 a.m., with a bitter wind blowing from the Ruahines.

There was a cheerful fire in the waiting-room, to keep them warm for two hours, when they caught the little two carriage connection that trundled through the Manawatu Gorge to Woodville Junction. His mother was standing up to the long journey very well, interested in these places she had not seen for so long.

Another wait at Woodville — nearly three hours, with the station so far from the shops that passengers transferring did not find it worthwhile to walk up to the township. It was not so bad for men on their own — the pub was only down the road, and the local policeman made a point of being absent until the Napier train had pulled out.

Only seventeen miles to Dannevirke. What

was mother thinking about? Not what she saw, that was certain. She had not been back to the area since they had moved to Taihape so long ago. Of course the changes then, from her first sight of the Thirty Mile — Forty Mile? — Bush would have been noticeable. However, her thoughts then would have been over-ridden by sorrow at losing her husband, the demands of the sea voyage, and the need to earn a living for her son and herself. That return was after a gap of nearly thirty years; now the gap would be about five years less, not much difference in development times. What most amazed Caroline was the number of houses out towards Mangatera, where the coach road had plunged steeply down to the river.

Caroline looked in vain for signs of Norsewood. Dick explained that the line avoided the hills there; the train ran further to the east, through Makotuku and Ormondville to Takapau. Near Waipukurau he pointed out Hatuma, where he would be working. Dick had wondered if she would want to live in Waipukurau, but she seemed happy about settling in Napier.

It was good to know that Henry and Mary would be living there, too. Certainly they were on the far side of the town, while the cottage Dick had bought was near the southern approach. The old lady could retain her independence, and so could Mary. Dick was determined to ask no-one to marry him until he could afford the upkeep of two houses — his mother, a little difficult sometimes in her younger days, could now be very trying. Everything should be done as it was in her time; electric irons, jugs, heaters, lights, they were all ridiculous.

You lit a fire in the stove — Dick had quite a job finding a house where the Orion had not been replaced by gas or electricity — that boiled the kettle, heated the iron, and gave a little glow of firelight. If more light was wanted, the kerosene lamp should be lit.

Some people even had refrigerators for their meat. Caroline snorted in disgust; what was wrong with a meat-safe? As for keeping milk and butter cool, all that was needed was a brick in the wash-tub, and some butter muslin. Once the brick was thoroughly soaked, you put your jug and your dish on the brick, sitting in cold water, and draped them with the muslin so that it touched the water.

The days of the 'fast foods' from the local dairies were thirty years away. Just as well. The old lady would have treated her granddaughter to a two-hour lecture on the folly of buying anything ready-made.

Dick settled his mother at the cottage, and went down the line with an easy mind.

37

The following year was the most pleasant ever for Dick and his mother. He was making new friends, as he always did wherever he went, at Hatuma and the township a few miles away. There were trout in the Tukituki and the Makaretu that flowed into it across the flats from Hatuma. The section of line rarely caused trouble; there was a ganger at Ormondville near the only difficult terrain. Dick could catch the train at Waipukurau, to see his mother.

Mary called at least once a week — the old lady looked forward to her visits, and would be more talkative with her than with her own daughter.

For Jim and Christine it was a much easier trip, three or four hours straight-forward driving in the Willys Knight Six. The Chandler had been replaced a few years earlier by a Willys Knight Four Cylinder, salvaged from a steamer wrecked beyond Pencarrow in Fitzroy Bay; then had come another Willys Knight, both of them taking the family over those demanding roads to Taihape and even to Taupo.

356

With wool at a good price, Jim had bought the big saloon, after a trip to the races across the Tasman, when his wife admired it in a display, in a shop window on Lambton Quay.

Though that plan for another trip to the beach with Helen had been destroyed by her death, the family had spent many summer holidays in that cottage. The January of the year of the Murchison earthquake they had spent in their newly built beach house across the road. Their journeys took them increasingly over the winding Rimutakas to Lower Hutt and Eastbourne. The ferry boat — the *Cobar*, now — still ran, but it was by bus that most permanent residents travelled to work.

In the May school holidays, however, Jim drove his wife and daughter up to Napier, arranging a time when they could pick Dick up at Hatuma. It was evening when they reached the cottage in McGrath Street. Only the school boarders were about, to stare at a car different from most.

Jim wanted to take Christine and their daughter up to the Morere Hot Springs. His wife wanted to see her sister's grave — she was sure it would need tending, as it was so long since Brian had left the district. Outside, smoking their pipes in the cool evening, the sea breeze blowing across the gravel beaches of Hawkes Bay, Jim and Dick agreed that they didn't think Brian would have done any work in the cemetery even if he had been still on that farm.

'Supposing we take Mary and Henry with us?' Jim suggested to Christine. 'I don't know if Mary has seen the Springs at all — and she was mentioning rheumatics a while ago, in a letter.'

'That's a good idea,' Christine agreed. 'I doubt if you'll get Henry to go, but we could ask.'

To their surprise, Henry accepted the invitation. Perhaps he was not very eager, but Mary was delighted.

Dick had to return to work, and their mother, as they had expected, refused to go. She would have found the journey very trying.

To show Mary how Christine and the children had first visited Helen, at Tangitere, they took the winding hill road out to Waiko-kopu. There they could look across to the Mahia Peninsula, standing guard over the Bay. Going on to Opoutama and Mahia, where the bittern haunts the marshlands, Jim and Henry met a local Maori, who told them a great deal about the district. He had lived there all his life.

He pointed to a dinghy, making out to sea in choppy conditions. There was little freeboard as it was, and the new-found acquaintance would have weighed sixteen stone.

'They wanted me to show them where to put their crayfish pots,' he said, 'they're new chums. But not in that little boat for me, eh?'

He looked up at a pearly pink cloud floating in the late afternoon sky.

'I don't think I look quite right up there, floating on the cloud and playing the harp.' He lifted his arms in a slow motion wave of wings as Jim turned the car to drive on to Morere before dark.

Those Hot Springs beyond Nuhaka were set in the midst of tall native bush, at the foot of the Whareratas. In May, the paths were slippery, but the water in the bath-houses was more attractive than in the heat of summer.

After spending two days there, they left in the rain on the return journey. No need to worry about keeping the magneto dry when they crossed the fords, or putting a sack under the bonnet, as Jim had done the last time they drove down this road. But the greasy roads made for slow progress, and the fords were rising. They stopped for midday dinner at the Waikari hotel, down the coast from Putorino — a long low building where the service cars called, with its view of the hills and a glimpse of the sea.

The hillsides were slipping, leaving barely room for one-way traffic; the overcast sky brought poor light early. Henry and his wife were very quiet.

Jim was relieved when the car climbed the last hill with its view of Napier, fourteen miles distant. Slowly down to the last ford, to cross the Tangoio. Then there was a good road through to Petane and Napier. Jim relaxed, as Christine beside him smiled in relief.

Too soon the relief. Already five vehicles were stationary on the roadside, one of them the service-car. No chance of taking a car through that muddy surge that filled the gully. The concrete strip was invisible, and logs were sailing down the swift current.

Stranded, they wondered if they should return to Waikari. There would be no hope of returning to Wairoa — those fords inland would be impossible now. Three or four more cars pulled up; while Jim was considering a trying drive back in the failing light, Christine was thinking about a night in the car, rather crushed for the three in the back seat. A truck pulled up some distance back; the driver walked down the road, pausing to chat at each vehicle.

Jim asked if he had come through from Wairoa.

'Yes,' he answered, 'just in time, too — I'd be the last one through the ford below the Devil's Elbow. A car wouldn't have got through then — the water was up to the floorboards, and the current! — I felt the truck sliding a bit —'

That comment decided them — there was, really, no decision to make. Tutira, Guthrie's old place, was the nearest homestead. Any benighted traveller would be welcomed there — but it was on the Wairoa side of Arapaounui; the road along the shore of Lake Tutira would be awash, now.

Through the dark night, passengers and drivers huddled in their cars. Earlier, those cars nearest the river had backed up the road, away from the ever-rising stream; often a creek in summer, it was a turbulent river now. Slipping and sliding, except for the car with chains, they could reverse only a short distance, but it put them beyond the reach of the river. Once in a while a lonely driver would sound his horn, while the others would reply. Headlamps were switched on occasionally, but no-one would risk a flat battery — those who had torches were just as careful.

About two o'clock, Jim heard a vehicle start up, with a roar that echoed in the cliffs. Car lights appeared suddenly behind him; those in front switched on their lights, thinking perhaps that the river had dropped. If a slip up in the hills dammed the creek, there would be a short period in which they could cross. It would be taking a risk, for when the temporary dam was washed away, the water would roar down with redoubled force. The headlamps in front revealed a higher level than ever, and stronger current — tree-trunks were now swirling down, and a carcase or two.

The motor in the rear was switched off, and darkness closed in again.

An hour or two later there was a rumbling crash behind them. Torches flickered up and down the road as a few men went to investigate. One of them, panic-stricken, rushed back down the hill, shouting, 'The slip's coming down the road, everyone out of their cars — they'll be pushed into the river!'

Jim got out of his car.

'Shut up!' he said, 'you're only upsetting the women. Let's have a look at this!'

The man — small, elderly, obviously

362

unused to the common incidents of back-country roads — turned back. They met the others, talking quietly near the toe of the slip — it had fallen from thirty feet or so, blocking the road completely and spilling over into the gully below. The muddy slush was certainly oozing down the road — but the great bulk of boulders and clay, with its fossilised shells, was stationery. The overflow had pitched over the bank, breaking it away with the pressure.

The truck driver who had moved his vehicle down two hours earlier was very quiet.

'I'll take a ticket in Tatts when we get to Napier,' he told Jim.

'I'd have been under that if I hadn't felt a bit lonely a few hours ago.'

'Was that where you first pulled up?' asked Jim.

'Yes. I thought someone might come through in a hurry if the creek was dammed — they wouldn't have got past me, if I parked where I am now, lower down the road.'

Daylight dawned on a miserable and muddy scene. Those in open cars were damp and cold. Christine and her daughter, and Henry and Mary were all warm, but rather cramped. They were all hungry, too, though only the youngest admitted it.

About ten o'clock cars appeared on the Napier side of the river. They sent a line across downstream of the ford to a high bank where there was a useful tree, and rigged up a flying fox. The Napier volunteers, led by the Mayor, came across with hot soup, tea and sandwiches. As soon as the marooned passengers had been supplied, a slow evacuation began — one by one slowly across the turbulent river, hanging on to one rope and hauled across by another.

Driven back to Napier, the passengers and drivers found, if they were visitors, that accommodation had been arranged. Others were driven to their homes — when the Tangoio dropped, arrangements would be made to take the drivers back to collect their vehicles.

Three owners went out to inspect the river a day later — the ford was almost clear of water. A natural dam in the hills, as the truck-driver had suspected, was holding all that torrent back. But how long ago had the slip fallen? How long would it hold? Dare they risk it?

One thing they would not do was to take the other vehicle across. Shoes and socks off, they paddled through. As the level had dropped, logs and carcases had piled up on the upstream edge. They ran for their cars — the flying fox was still there, so they could get back. But there would be little warning when the dam broke — every man who knew that country thought the creek could be blocked in the steep gully not far from the road. They might have three minutes! The 'Tatts ticket' driver was with them.

Their own vehicles safely on the Napier side, they were about to wade across the ford again, to bring other cars out for those stranded in Napier. The truck driver was on the Wairoa bank when a thundering crash echoed over the valley. Sunshine, no lightning flash —

'Thunder, is it?' asked one.

'Not thunder. That's the dam busted,' shouted the truck driver as he ran to cross the ford.

'Quick, you blokes, you've got two minutes at the most,' he added.

They were up by the vehicles in seconds; the road there dipped sharply to the ford. Advised by the local carrier, they had driven each car to the top of the slope, high above even this fifty year flood level.

Down came the torrent — logs, boulders, carcases that had all built the dam in the first place. Any vehicle, even the truck would have been swept onward by this rushing barricade.

'You taking a second ticket in Tatts?' enquired the Napier man who had driven the others out.

'I think I've had my share of luck today,' the truck driver replied.

It was three days before they could rescue the rest of the cars.

38

Another year went quietly by. Dick thought it unlikely that the suggested promotion to stationmaster in some small out of the way place would ever come his way. Life had settled down. This even tenor was very pleasant. Perhaps, if his mother continued to be so tolerant, he could dare to think about marriage to that interesting woman friend. Would she consider sharing the house sometimes with his mother? Would it be fair to either of them to ask? In the quiet summer evenings, trout rod in his hand, he would wander along the river bank, considering the future more than he thought about fishing.

It seemed that he was settled at Hatuma; he no longer boarded with his off-sider, he had a railway hut to himself now. Could he suggest that he and his wife share it, going back to Napier when he was on leave? The powers that be would frown at first — those huts were for single men. But they would not build the house they had promised him — there were signs that all was not well with the country, and retrenchment in government spending was noticeable.

Dick could not afford to set up a second home. With a pride as fierce and a spirit as independent as his mother's, he had rejected all offers of financial help from Henry and Jim. Henry had a new wife, Jim had a family — that was that! Fearful of offending him, Jim and Henry dare not raise the issue again.

He stayed at Hatuma that week — he would go home to Napier at the end of the following Friday.

Caroline thought he had left a long time ago. Or was that William her son? Or William, her husband? All of them gone — years ago.

She would make a cup of tea; a little more wood and that dratted aluminium kettle would boil. Richard was a naughty boy to take the iron kettle to the bach in the Gully — or did Ronald take it? It was black-leaded till it shone, and the boys would let it rust. They said this kettle was not as heavy — what were they thinking about, she could manage anything, she always had. Those baskets of laundry in Dannevirke, they called it then — it was the Forty Mile Bush.

With the pottering step of the very old — how different from the stride that had taken her through the Havelock orchard — she put some kindling wood in the stove. Richard was quite a good boy, he always chopped the kindling and split the wood. It wasn't like the mill slabs, though — it didn't boil the kettle as quickly. Perhaps the kettle was the trouble — she would ask the boys to bring her iron kettle back.

The tea made in the big brown earthenware teapot — she wouldn't use the two-cup teapot, given to her by her granddaughter. That was a gift, to be set on the mantelshelf above the never-used front room fireplace.

Had she two granddaughters long ago, she wondered, as she sipped the black brew. And grandsons? There had been grandsons — was it three? Had they died in the War?

The basket-chair swayed sideways, the tea lurched in her cup — those gin-sodden charladies in the 'Duchess of Edinburgh', careless mothers who soothed their grubby babies with a dirty finger dipped into the square gin.

Thunder rumbled down the road — in this breathless sunshine? Maori war parties? or had Tamaohoi awoken again?

Her chair rocked uncontrollably — the school bell rang furiously, clanging, clattering. Bells — ship's bells on the *Hovding* — funeral peals — alarm bells. The church bells the night of Mafeking — the slow eighty-two peals for Queen Victoria, dead. And for the dead husband, too, but only a few slow tolls for him — no passing bells for those who die as cattle — had Richard told her that, long ago? Or had her granddaughter read it to her?

Another uncomfortable lurch — could Richard make the rockers stronger? — the crockery on the shelves rattled. Those lorries on the main road made the house shake — or was it a train? She hadn't heard the whistle for the level crossing behind the cottage.

The whole house swayed, then shook as if it was a rat in a terrier's mouth; the brick wall of the neighbouring house was leaning towards the window, then leaning away.

That was the *Hovding*. Presently the water would surge across the deck, and down the companionway. They should seal the hatches more tightly. The cabin was jolting from side to side, the bedboards wouldn't hold them in their bunks. Bells — more than ship's bells — the alarm for boat drill? or did they have to leave a sinking ship. Roald — the *Wairarapa* — that was where Christine lived — the *Zuleika* —

A thunder of falling bricks; the wall was tumbling. The walls of Jericho?

Caroline stumbled as crockery fell about her — stumbled to the front room, where the treasured little teapot was held by its spout on the edge of the mantel-shelf. Everything else was on the floor — the glass in the photographs broken, the oak-framed 'Stag at Bay' hurled down, smashed.

Across the road the bricks were collapsing in rubble, smoke shooting up into air thick with destruction. Beyond the crumbling school the fields were moving in waves, like wind across ripening wheat.

Swaying, the horizon changed in a great rolling curve. On the coast the Bluff poured its tons of rubble onto the road and the wharf sheds; the Nurses' Home collapsed. Over in Port Ahuriri the wool stores leaned over Henry's cottage, almost at the point of no return. Great fissures opened up in the roads, swallowing cars.

The bells tolled on in Caroline's head — Roald, William, Ronald, Helen. Son William and daughter Caroline, where were they? Missing and obstinate, both of them.

The sea was too rough — she could not stop the shaking and trembling, the floor was moving.

'Richard! Christine! Come home, come home!'

Bricks from the chimney bounding, tumbling on the corrugated iron, then the whole chimney collapsing with a roar, the gas pipe wrenched apart by the violent movement of the building. A great draught of air fanned the dying embers.

Before the wooden cottage blazed into the sky, the tired old heart had stopped beating.

THE END